Kylie is a long-time fan of erotic love stories and B-grade horror films. She demands a happy ending, and if blood and carnage occur along the way, so much the better. Based in Queensland, Australia with her two children and one wonderful husband, she reads, writes and never dithers around on the internet.

Skin

Kylie Scott

mom**entum**

First published by Momentum in 2013
This edition published in 2013 by Momentum
Pan Macmillan Australia Pty Ltd
1 Market Street, Sydney 2000

A CIP record for this book is available at the National Library of Australia
Skin

EPUB format: 9781743341988
Mobi format: 9781743341995

Cover design by Carrie Kabak
Edited by Sarah Fletcher
Proofread by Paula Grunseit

Macmillan Digital Australia: www.macmillandigital.com.au

To report a typographical error, please visit www.momentumbooks.com.au/contact/

Visit www.momentumbooks.com.au to read more about all our books and to buy books online.
You will also find features, author interviews and news of any author events.

For Hugh

CHAPTER ONE

In the end they took a vote on whether or not to trade Roslyn to the stranger at the gate. They even gave her a say, demonstrating that democracy was not dead, even if civilization had gone belly-up six months back, when the virus first struck.

All nine survivors had gathered on the school steps. No one would meet her eyes. The weak winter sun above them did little to combat the bitter wind. Roslyn's marrow was ice and her teeth chattered. She wanted to wrap her arms around herself, huddle down into the green school jacket she'd purloined from a student locker. But she didn't. Spine straight, shoulders back. Her father would have been proud.

She cleared her throat. They couldn't do this. She would explain why in a sensible and rational manner, using small words. "I know we're running low on food, but there's no reason we can't make a trip into town to look for supplies. If we just make a plan—"

"Let's get on with it," said Neil, former head of the Math department. Still pissed she had refused to put out. Never had she met such a pretentious, unattractive git. "Please raise your hand to vote 'yea'."

Her gaze skittered around the group.

Six people raised their hands.

Shit.

The world slid sideways and she locked her knees, breathing hard. Holy fucking hell, they were really going to do this. How could they? How could this have ever happened? The world made no sense.

But wait!

Directly across from her, Janie hesitated. The girl's elbow jerked back and her fingers folded. Hope blossomed warm and deep in Ros's gut.

Neil harrumphed and dealt Janie a stern look, brows drawn tight. It was the face reserved for particularly painful students and staff who dared cross his path. Janie caved. She reached for the sky, pale blonde hair flying in her pretty face. Her eyes were shiny-bright and she blinked furiously, trying not to cry. The damn teacher's pet.

Double shit.

No point blaming Janie. Not really. The stranger at the gate wanted a woman and Mrs Gardner, formerly of the Home Economics department, was well past sixty, with an arthritic hip. That left Roslyn or Janie, and Janie was young, a trainee admin officer. They'd found her on day two, huddled behind a filing cabinet, a bloody letter-opener clutched to her chest. Apparently, she'd driven it through the Principal's eye socket when the virus got the better of him. For months the girl had woken up screaming in the middle of the night.

Roslyn couldn't have sent her out there. But why the hell did that mean she had to go?

The answer: because the shelves in the school canteen were bare and the cowardly, lazy bastards wouldn't dare a trip into town. Nobody at the school had ventured beyond the stout stone walls of Lowood College, and none of them were planning on attempting it anytime soon.

Spineless, back-stabbing—

"Nay," Ian, the former groundskeeper, said forcefully and raised his hand high. Mrs Gardner did likewise. Roslyn's eyes fogged up.

Her own vote to the negative was a foregone conclusion.

The end tally stood at six for, three against.

She was outvoted.

Her empty stomach spiraled. The material of her pilfered gray school uniform clung wet beneath her arms.

They were going to trade her to the stranger to be used for God-knew-what perverted sexual purpose. She stood there slack-jawed at the horror of it. She wanted to wake up from this nightmare, safe in her own bed. Wanted all of it to have been a warped dream she told her girlfriends about after one too many glasses of wine at the pub.

God, how many times had she wished for her old life back?

The man waited at the gate, lounging against the side of his panel van. It was apparently loaded to the brim with goodies. Perhaps it would turn out to be a Trojan horse, packed full of ninjas. He'd drive it through the gates and *kapow*! Bad guys would attack in a flurry of action. Game over.

It would serve them right, betraying bastards.

Well, some of them.

Janie cried openly now, blubbering into a thick wad of tissues.

Someone stamped their feet and another coughed, bored or cold or a combination of both as Neil blabbered on. The wind howled around the grand old stone buildings and shook the leaves in the gum trees. Her insides felt hollow. They had actually done it.

Roslyn rubbed at her temples, willing her brain back online. Her hands shook with fear and frustration. What fuckery was this? The whole world had gone mad.

Meanwhile, Neil still droned on.

"He said you'd be treated decently." Neil studied his sturdy, brown shoes. The wanker.

Something inside her broke. Roslyn balled her fist and swung wild. Giving it everything she had left in her.

Neil's steel-rimmed glasses flew and blood fountained from his nose, splattering the concrete vibrant red. The color was stark and beautiful against the dull gray.

Janie screamed.

Mrs Gardner nodded.

Ian grinned.

Roslyn's hand throbbed but satisfaction slid through her. She'd never hit anyone before. She abhorred violence, normally. Though this ... wow, this was all good.

"Gaanhh!" Neil grabbed Janie's bundle of soggy tissues and stuffed them beneath his nose. He bared his teeth at Roslyn like an animal. An animal in a worn tweed jacket and mission brown slacks. When he spoke his voice was muffled, heavy. "Exactly what I've been saying! You're out of control. No group-mindedness."

Right. Time to go.

Roslyn shoved a hand into her pocket, reassuring herself that her reading glasses were there. There was nothing else she needed from the storeroom she'd called home. It was one of the few small, enclosed spaces with a lock on the inside—partly to keep out the infected and partly to keep out Neil. If group-mindedness involved sacrificing herself to him, forget it.

Huh, he was really bleeding.

She smiled, pleased on one count at least.

Roslyn turned and took her first slow steps toward the gate, nursing her hand to her chest. The pain proved to be a useful distraction from her rising fear.

The gates were old and ominous. They'd always reminded her vaguely of where the Addams Family lived.

What was left of the world outside?

Neil raged on behind her. Soon enough the cold wind carried his voice far, far away.

The man at the gates watched her progress with eagle eyes. Roslyn averted hers and studied the cracked asphalt driveway. Already weeds were growing through. Wouldn't take long for Mother Nature to reclaim what she'd lost.

Heroines in books always held their heads high, but it took her a while to find the courage. When she finally looked up, the man straightened, pushing off from the van. He was built solid in a way that did nothing for her nerves. Getting away from him might just be a bit of a problem.

No. She'd manage.

Never say die.

Behind him the town lay sprawled out, slumbering. No signs of life. It looked like the southern side of town had burned down. She remembered the sky had been full of smoke. This would be the first time she had stepped outside since the morning of Christmas Eve. She hadn't known where else to go and she hadn't been the only one. All roads heading west had been choked with cars as people tried to flee. The radio news reports had been full of crazy carnage and chaos. A lab somewhere in Asia had apparently cooked up the bug and accidentally released it. Within days it went global. No one could have prepared for this. Principal Barry had made the decision to lock the gates, sealing them in. No one had protested. At the time it seemed the only course of action. They hadn't known Principal Barry had already been bitten.

Her car still sat around back in the staff parking lot. It would be there for a long time to come.

"Is your hand alright?" he asked as she slipped through the gap in the gates. He had a deep, smooth voice, deceptively warm and friendly. Light brown hair fell over his forehead. He had dark eyes and a neatly trimmed beard.

What the hell did he want with her?

Bad question. She didn't really want to know.

Her chin rose but her knees knocked, shaking from more than the winter winds. "Worried you're getting faulty merchandise?"

He gave her a curious look, but said nothing.

Maybe he had been hoping for Janie.

Maybe he'd return her, demand a full refund. God knew she wasn't anybody's prize. Average height, average weight, average pretty much everything. But she was old enough to be comfortable in her own skin.

Maybe looks didn't even matter anymore.

What did he want, and why her? Was there no one else left out there?

The man's gaze drifted over her, in no rush at all, beginning with her red, home-cut hair. She resisted the urge to shove a hand through it, and attempt to calm the crazy. Screw him. She'd hacked the bulk of it off a few months back, mostly for practicality's sake. Making herself less attractive to Neil had been part of it, though not something worth admitting to. It hadn't succeeded, on account of Neil being a letch, but maybe it would work with this guy. She had to make a ridiculous picture, a grown woman with a shitty haircut wearing the remnants of a school uniform.

She rubbed the toe of her battered black sneaker against the drive. Shoes courtesy of the Lost and Found bin.

Maybe he really would call the whole thing off. Or maybe he'd turn around and demand Janie.

No. That wasn't something she could live with.

Roslyn braved a smile. His eyes widened, looking startled, if anything. It soon gave way to skeptical. Fair enough. Dewey decimal 791, Public Performance: she sucked at it.

Up close, the man was even more intimidating. A black AC/DC shirt drew tight across wide shoulders. The colors were faded, like he'd worn it a hundred times. He stood half a head taller than her, his body built lean but solid. He had to be about half a decade older than her twenty-eight. In no way did his face look boyish, despite the twinkle in his eye. The rifle strapped to his back spoke of serious things, its muzzle sticking up beside his head.

She would still get away. There had to be others out there. Rational people. Trustworthy.

Her knuckles throbbed, the back of her hand swelling and darkening. Any escape attempt involving punching him was right out. Sneaky would be her best bet.

"I'm fine," she said. "Let's go."

The man tipped his chin, turned toward the van and pushed back the side door. No ninjas, but lots of supplies: canned goods and blankets, a couple of guns, some knives, and one shiny aluminum baseball bat. Her hands itched to wrap around the smooth handle and exorcise some fear and frustration.

He reached inside for a backpack, threw it over a shoulder. His gaze returned to hers, assessing. The corner of his mouth rose and little lines deepened beside his eyes. Ah, she'd apparently amused him. Her scaredy-cat shaking hadn't stopped. She clearly wasn't kidding anybody with her evil eye.

"I'm not going to hurt you," he said.

And for once, Roslyn didn't say the first thing to come to mind. Something along the lines of his shoving a can of soup up his ass to keep his false words company. Nor did she start in on the hundreds of questions sitting on the tip of her tongue. Instead she sucked in a deep breath, let it out slowly, and lied to her new arch-enemy. "Alright."

"What's your name?"

"Roslyn Stewart. Yours?"

"Nick," he said. "There's a pickup we can use just down the hill. Let's get a move on. Sun goes down soon. The infected'll be coming out."

CHAPTER TWO

Nick watched the woman out the corner of his eye. She was pressed against the pickup's passenger-side door like she'd melded herself to the metal. Physically as far from him as she could get without actually leaving the vehicle. He'd put the child lock on, jammed the window shut. She wasn't going anywhere.

It had actually worked. He had her. Fucking amazing.

Roslyn.

The skirt of her gray school uniform had hitched up one side, caught on the seatbelt. She'd been too busy staring out the window, trying to ignore him, to notice. What a very nice slice of skin. Her thigh tempted him big-time. Shot his concentration to shit.

And he needed to focus on driving.

The old farm truck rocketed along the road leading out of town, flying past overgrown orchards and vineyards, swerving around debris and the occasional abandoned car. Using older model vehicles was best. Newer ones with their fancy electrics were a bitch to deal with.

Behind them, Bald Rock sat in the distance. No signs of life. No one followed.

So far.

He had been observing the school for the past two weeks, monitoring the nine inside. Scaling the stone wall had been simple. Taking her would have been just as easy, but this was better. She needed to know those supposed friends of hers weren't trustworthy. Needed to know she'd be better off with him.

Roslyn was definitely something with her choppy, auburn hair and pointy chin. In her mid-twenties, most likely. She had a pretty mouth like a doll's, only she wasn't tiny or delicate, she was just right. That school uniform ... fuck, he couldn't get his head around it. Filthy thoughts, the sort bound to reinforce the pissy looks she'd given him, kept bubbling up inside his brain. The things he wanted to do with her.

The things he would do with her. Just a question of when. He needed patience. Timing was everything.

A zombie stumbled out of a lone farmhouse as they drove past what would have once been a man. Blood or dirt or some gory mix of both caked its chest, arms and chin. Its mouth yawned wide, an arm rising in some macabre version of a wave as they cruised by. Only the hello had more to do with its desire to eat them than anything friendly.

Roslyn gasped and bolted upright in her seat, the whites of her eyes flashing.

"You haven't seen one before?" he asked.

"No."

"This is the first time you've been outside."

She nodded.

"Shit. You really have no idea how bad it's been, do you?"

No answer.

"They don't like sunlight, but they'll come out if they think they can get a meal. Noise always attracts them."

She gave him another questioning glance, then settled back into her seat, face pale and eyes wary.

She definitely didn't trust him. Sure as shit didn't believe him when he said he wouldn't hurt her. It made her smart. He would never hurt her, but anyone who trusted strangers these days was an idiot destined for a short life. He would provide for her. He'd prove himself to her.

But first, he had to get her home and stay put for a while. Make sure their back trail kept clear.

"Nearly there," he said.

She nervously licked her pink lips. "Where is 'there'?"

"You'll see." He offered a smile.

She didn't return it.

The pickup rattled along the gravel drive leading up to the Serenity Eco-Chalets. The property sat on the edge of town. Far enough out to avoid the bulk of the infected. It backed onto kilometers of bushland and farms. She'd be safer out here. He'd done his homework, prepared. Everything and anything she might need to keep her comfortable for the foreseeable future.

Roslyn's knuckles were white where she gripped the door handle, the injured hand still clutched against her chest. She'd almost dropped the guy back at the school. Who could blame her?

"What is this place?" she asked, looking all around, eyes full of curiosity.

"Eco-chalets, for the environmentally conscious weekender. Or it was." Nick drove the vehicle straight up to the back of the Wattle cabin. Home sweet home. He threw his door open and grabbed his rifle from the back, rounded the pickup to open the door for her. Some weird kind of nervous energy coursed through him. He just about jittered. "Come on in."

She gave him another tense attempt at a smile and climbed out, hands smoothing down her skirt. Her eyes darted everywhere, preparing. Not long now before she tried to make a run for it. He could practically smell it.

Damn it, there was no reason why this couldn't work, given a chance. He was a reasonable man with an offer to make. Besides, the world wasn't exactly normal anymore and she had been set to starve inside those school walls. Either that or risk a trip into town and possible infection from a bite.

No. Not happening.

This was right for her. He'd be right for her. Those bastards had been wrong, making him leave Blackstone all those months back. He wasn't one of the bad guys.

He'd been part of the remnants of a military group wandering the countryside after everything went to shit. When they'd stumbled across Blackstone, a walled township with nearly a hundred survivors, it had felt like a fucking miracle. But their psychopathic captain, Emmet, had wanted to rape the women and burn the place down. Kill anyone left over. Some of his ex-army pals had staged a coup and put a bullet in Emmet's brain, and thank God for that. Blackstone had accepted the men who'd topped Emmet, but the remaining three, including him, had been booted out of town. Threatened with death if they ever showed their faces again.

He couldn't blame the townspeople for not trusting Pete and Justin. They were slimy bastards full of plans for revenge. But exiling him? That he could blame the folk of Blackstone for just fine.

No one had been able to openly stand up to Emmet. He'd crucified men for less. But Nick would never have let the captain's plan come to fruition. Not a fucking chance.

No, he wasn't one of the bad guys.

Eventually, she'd understand. He'd spoil her. Comfort her. Make life as easy for her as he could. Give her whatever the hell she wanted. If she'd just give him a chance.

"This way," he said, ushering her toward the long wooden ramp leading up to the cabin.

"Mmhmm." Her nod looked spring-loaded, like a bobble-headed doll.

Shit. What was she going to try?

Her sneakers squeaked noisily as she stepped onto the wooden ramp, stopping at the edge of the meter and a half of platform he'd removed. Like a moat with a drawbridge, it effectively cut them off from attack—by infected, at least. Other survivors were another issue altogether.

"Clever." She sounded surprised.

He took it as a compliment.

She peered down at the ground a good three to four meters below. The cabin sat up on stilts at the edge of a rocky outlook, positioned to make the most of the view. Handy now for defense reasons, since infected couldn't climb. Nick knelt and carefully extended the thick wooden plank he kept handy for crossing the gap. She jumped at the *thump* of the wood falling into place.

With a smile he held out his hand to her. "Ladies first."

"Thank you." Her fingers were warm and damp, and they didn't remain in his for long. She gripped the banister nearest the plank with her other hand and carefully crossed with tiny geisha-type steps. Maybe she didn't like heights. It wouldn't hurt his cause. Yet another incentive for her to not tear off on her own anytime soon.

Everything would be fine once she got inside. Once she saw the effort he'd gone to on her behalf.

"You're doing great," he said.

She nodded.

The minute she cleared the end he strode across, throwing her a quick smile. He pulled the plank back from the gap and ushered her into the waiting cabin. A cold wind shook the trees. The skirt of her uniform fluttered above her knees, her bare legs ripe with gooseflesh.

"Let's get you inside and warmed up," he said.

She blinked and gave him a forced smile, staying a step ahead of the hand he would have put to the small of her back. Keeping herself out of his reach.

The sun had slowly begun to sink in the west. For the hour-long drive home he'd taken the most convoluted route possible, mostly to be safe but also to chew up some time. They were right on schedule.

Roslyn wandered inside, head turning this way and that, taking it all in. "It looks nice."

"I think we'll be comfortable here." His chest warmed at her faint praise. Back in the day the cabin would have been on the more expensive side of things. There was a spa bath in the bathroom off to the side and, more importantly, a composting toilet. The kitchen sported black granite benchtops and all the shiny mod-cons. Though they didn't much matter now with electricity long gone. "Have a look around. I want you to feel at home."

"Okay." Her fingers traced over the granite and she half-turned to face him, chin high and forehead creased. "How do you see this going down exactly, Nick?"

He crossed his arms, widened his stance, proudly checking out the room and all his handy work. "Well, it seems to me we can be of use to one another. You need ..."

He caught a flash of movement in the corner of his eye. A dark object—a bottle of wine with her pale fingers wrapped around the neck.

Nick threw himself aside. He was a second too late.

Bam! The bottle clipped the side of his skull, fell to the floor and shattered like a gunshot.

Pain swamped him. He couldn't see. Blood ran down his face, dripped in his eyes. The rich scent of red wine filled the air.

Roslyn scrambled. He heard the sound of her sudden panting and the crazed squeaking of her shoes. Her leg brushed against his as she threw herself past him, racing back down the corridor, heading for the door. Not happening. Adrenalin surged and pain took a back seat.

She didn't get far.

Nick clambered to his feet and pounced, taking her down. Mostly, he just collapsed on top of her, half-blinded by blood. They hit the floor in a tangle of limbs, his chest to her back. He took the bulk of his weight on one arm, but not all of it. Air shot from her lungs with a startled *oooff.*

The silence didn't last long.

Roslyn drew in a sharp breath, opened her mouth and screamed, long and loud. The piercing noise echoed through the building, escaping out the back door and through the wide open bi-fold doors at the front. It rose up and out into the open air, exposing their whereabouts to anything listening. The noise was a hundred times louder than the truck engine could ever hope to be. With feet kicking and body bucking beneath him, the woman went nuts.

"Don't!" Nick crawled up her, knees scuttling on the slippery, wine-splattered floor. His head throbbed bloody murder, forehead fit to explode. He slapped a hand over her mouth and held on. Her teeth chomped, trying to bite him. More muffled shrieks rose up.

"Stop it!" he hissed into her ear. Or he thought it was her ear. Still couldn't see for shit. Her hair clung to his face, wet with blood and wine. "Fuck, Roslyn. Stop."

She ignored him. Her hands scrabbled, trying to pull herself out from beneath him. Which was useless; he easily had her in body weight. Like a wild thing she rioted beneath him, totally enraged. And his hand, slippery with blood, slipped off her mouth.

Another shrill scream hit the air. So fucking loud that his ears rang. Though that might have been the head wound.

"Shit!" Nick clamped his hand back over her mouth. This wasn't working. Time for a new plan.

He pushed back, sitting up and taking her with him, one hand over her mouth and the other around her waist. What a bloody disaster. Her sneakers skidded against the slick floor as she kicked out, fighting for freedom. Keeping a hold on her was no easy thing. Nick wrestled her back down the corridor, past the kitchen and straight for the king-size bed with its wooden frame.

Because while he'd hoped for the best, he'd prepared for the worst.

It was how he'd been trained.

Roslyn wriggled and squirmed, but she wouldn't be going anywhere. Not now. They were both covered in blood because his forehead gushed like a stuck pig, but he was damn determined. He got her onto the mattress, laying her on her stomach with him on top, pressing her down. She went insane again beneath him. A renewed bust of energy from fear, no doubt.

The cuffs were attached to the headboard, ready and waiting.

Nick snaked his hand out from beneath her and straightened out one of her arms, gripping the wrist and fumbling the cool steel around it. An elbow almost connected with his face. She put up a hell of a fight, battling him every step of the way. First one limb and then the other he restrained with the cuffs.

The next part had to happen fast. She screamed right on cue when his hand dived into the bedside drawer. She kept right on screaming as he searched for the rubber ball gag.

"No!" Her head reared back, trying to evade it when it touched her lips. He shoved the black ball into her mouth and whipped the strap over her head.

Blessed silence descended. A quiet so sudden it startled. Apart from the thundering in his head and the grunts from behind the gag, of course.

Shit.

He rolled off her and crawled out of firing range to the other side of the mattress.

Her foot kicked out, catching his. Not far enough. Nick groaned and crawled to the edge of the bed, smearing the clean sheets some more with his bloody hands. Beneath him the mattress bounced with her ongoing attempts to attack him. Wine and blood were everywhere. Broken glass glinted on the floor.

Oh, no.

"Were you cut?" His gaze raked over her. Blood stained her shirt. Hard to tell, but it seemed the bulk of it was his. She didn't appear to be injured. He still bled profusely, though. Gingerly, he prodded at the wound on his forehead. She'd really done him some damage. What a fucking mess.

Roslyn made a noise. Might have been her attempt at a growl but the rubber ball garbled it. She'd rolled onto her side, arms stretched out above her head. Eyes possessed. A thin line of drool worked its way down her chin. Her uniform had crept up to her waist in all the excitement, exposing curvy legs and a pair of black boyleg briefs. He was almost too tired to appreciate them. Almost. But he wouldn't take anything she didn't offer.

Except her freedom, maybe. Yeah. Except that.

Bloody hell.

"Are you cut anywhere?" he asked again.

Her jaw worked as she tried to circumvent the gag. Eventually, she shook her head. Thank goodness for that.

"I'll pull your skirt back down for you if you promise not to kick me."

Her face went nuclear, bright red.

"Do you promise not to kick me?" he asked.

Another livid look, followed by a reluctant nod.

"Alright." Nick walked around the bed and matter-of-factly tugged the skirt back down into place. "There we go."

Shit, the look in her eyes. He'd had ex-girlfriends who hated him less.

What the hell had he been expecting? Of course she wasn't going to take this the right way. How many ways were there to take someone trying to buy you?

Shit. Fuck. Damn.

He wiped more blood from his brow. His hand returned covered in the stuff. There were blotches of dark red on Roslyn's skin and clothes, face and hair. Bloody wonderful. What a great start. Nick pinched the bridge of his nose. It didn't help. His head pounded, brain fit to explode. Still her beautiful blue eyes bored into him. Laser beams couldn't have been more effective.

"I'm a fucking idiot."

She nodded.

Emphatically.

CHAPTER THREE

Roslyn's jaw hurt and she needed to pee. Who knew how long it had been since he'd cuffed her to the bed and gagged her. But facts of nature being what they were, she might disgrace herself before much longer. Jane Eyre never had to put up with this sort of shit. Roslyn suddenly felt quite bad for poor old Bertha locked up in the attic.

She rattled the cuffs, banging the metal bands against the headboard. Also, she attempted to wipe her chin off on her arm since she was dribbling again. Screw the indignity. Her throat felt parched, her shoulders ached and she remained covered in his blood. It'd dried to a clump in her fringe. She could see a streak of it on the side of her nose. The coppery scent turned her stomach.

Sunlight had gradually faded, leaving the room bathed in a soft golden glow. It'd probably been hours. Or half an hour, at least.

Nick had put a rough bandage on his face, cleaned up the kitchen and then disappeared into what had to be the bathroom. It seemed to be the only private room in the whole open-plan cabin. Her prison consisted of a lot of wood, with pine on the ceiling, floor and walls. A window across the way had been boarded up with more of the stuff. There was a big lounge. An ornate patchwork blanket done in shades of blue and brown hung opposite. A shelf full of books, leather-bound classics by the look. She couldn't see much else. There was plenty of bed-and-breakfast and cabin-style accommodation in the area. The local wineries had brought tourists in droves. Wine and wilderness and all the fun stuff. She'd moved to the area a year back, seeking a tree change. And thank God she had. Apparently everyone in the cities was dead.

Still no sign of Nick. He hadn't come near her again, thankfully. But she definitely needed him now.

She banged the cuffs against the headboard once more, calling up some customer service. It made a satisfying din. So long as she didn't further damage her punching hand. She might need it.

Hopefully Neil still felt the pain, somewhere out there. What a warming thought for the beginning of another cold night.

Nick stuck his head out of the bathroom, face cleaned up. No sign of the bandage and the cut on his temple had been sealed somehow. It made for an impressively angry, puckered red line. She'd done got him good. It sliced through one dark eyebrow and up the side of his forehead, trailing off into his hairline.

That's what you got for trying to buy girls with canned goods. Devil. She'd shelve him at 235.

His bloodstained shirt was gone. In fact, he wore only a scowl and a faded pair of blue jeans. He wore them well. No wonder she hadn't been able to escape; the man didn't have an ounce of fat on him. It'd been a while since her last yoga class, what with the apocalypse and all. Exercise had never been her strong suit. This man, however, appeared the epitome of lean and mean. He had the same long, hard lines as a swimmer. It took some effort to peel her eyes away, despite her profound hatred.

"What?" he grouched.

Poor baby. If only she didn't have the stupid gag in her mouth she'd have given him what for.

Roslyn tried to communicate several things with her eyes. Firstly, that she still believed him to be a fucking idiot. But secondly, and most importantly, she needed to pee and get a drink of water.

He made no move toward her. His gaze remained hard, unyielding. The jut of his chin looked distinctly unimpressed.

She blinked and cocked her head. *Please.*

He scowled some more. Then he winced, fine lips wrinkling in pain. His face had to hurt. Her enemy moved closer, looking down on her with wary brown eyes.

"If I remove the ball gag, do you promise not to scream?" he asked.

She nodded.

His lips tightened. "Do you realize that by screaming you alert everything to our presence here? That you put us both in danger?"

Huh. Well, no. It hadn't occurred to her. Thwarting him and escaping had been the only things on her mind, and rightly so. Because if she stopped to think about it, there wasn't anyone out there to hear her and come running to her aid, was there? No. There had been absolutely no point in hollering her heart out. It had been sheer instinct. And his face seemed deadly serious, giving her pause. Had she put them in danger?

"You need to think before you go making a lot of noise again." Nick leant over and released something on the side of the gag. The pressure eased and he slipped the rubber ball from her mouth. Oh yes, what sweet relief.

Her jaw cracked as she slowly worked it back to normal. It ached. To think that some people did this for fun. Clearly, they were crazy. She'd stick with the vanilla sex and leave the kinky crap to the couples in her smuttier books, thank you very much. She swallowed hard and wet her lips, tried to shift up the bed. Partly to ease the tension in her shoulders and neck, but also because she hated having him that close.

"Thanks," she croaked.

"Let me get you a drink."

"Problem."

"Mm?"

"I need to visit the bathroom."

Nick reached for a bottle of water and unscrewed the lid, carefully filled a glass waiting on the bedside table. For ages it had sat there taunting her.

"I have a solution, he said. "But you're not going to like it."

She jerked back and the water splashed on her neck. Cold shivers skittered across her skin. "If it involves something disgusting like golden showers, then you're right."

The man stopped and stared. "You have a hell of an imagination."

"Says the guy who ball-gagged me."

"No. Of course it doesn't involve anything like that." With the glass of water in hand he sat on the edge of the bed beside her. There was nowhere for her to go. His spare hand reached out, to lift her head or something, and no, no, no. She panicked, rearing back again and hitting the bed-head. Which smarted.

"You wanted a drink," he said.

"I don't want you touching me."

Nick's gaze narrowed but he moved back a smidgeon. He took his sweet time before speaking. "Alright. My solution is to put a chain around your ankle attached to the bed. But it won't stop you from trying to attack me again. It still requires a level of trust. That's the problem."

"You want to leash me like a dog?" she gritted out.

He studied her, face blank.

"You were right. I don't like it, Nick."

He placed the glass of water on the bedside table and set his ankle on his knee, his big body hunched over. If it was to try and make him appear smaller, less harmful, it didn't work. The guy seemed no less dangerous, especially without a shirt on. The tattoos on his shoulders were old school, black and gray ink. Nicely done, if you liked such things. Normally, she really did, but not this time.

"Roslyn, what were you going to do if you got away from me?"

Good question. Her mouth stayed shut.

"That's what I thought," he said. "You can't go back to the school. Those idiots just about pissed themselves when I showed up. They'd hand you straight back to me. And even if I was willing to let you go, you know you can't trust them now. Don't you?"

Being cuffed, she couldn't stick her fingers in her ears and sing or something to block him out. But it didn't mean she had to listen to him. It was a nice, high ceiling—infinitely more appealing than him and his words.

"You wouldn't be able to survive out there on your own," he said. "Not for long."

"I could."

One dark brow rose in response and then he winced. She hated people who could do that with their eyebrow. Such an arrogant and unnecessary, supercilious thing. Actually, she just hated him. Him and his cool tattoos and practical words. What a grunting, heaving Neanderthal. And this was his cave.

Which made her the bitch being dragged back by her hair, didn't it?

"Do you even know how to shoot a gun?" he asked.

"Yes. My father taught me."

"Good."

"Still going to think that after I put a hole in you?"

The side of his mouth kicked up. "No, probably not. You actually trying to convince me to remove the cuffs, here? 'Cause it's not working."

Her bladder made its presence known once more, like a boulder residing below her belly. "Nick, I need to pee. Please."

"Mm."

"Are you into humiliation?"

"No. Humiliating you is not the goal." He looked so sincere, dark eyes serious and mouth set. She almost believed him.

"And yet, the ball gag," she said.

He shrugged. "I explained about the screaming."

"Maybe. And I'm just not supposed to ask why you had the gag in the first place, hmm?" She pushed the back of her head into the pillow, turned her gaze back to the ceiling where it belonged. Clenched her thighs tight and hoped she didn't wet herself.

Man, oh, man.

"Well?" he asked.

"Well, what, Nick? You're not exactly leaving me any options, are you?"

"You haven't left me any either, Roslyn." He bent and reached beneath the bed. The insidious sound of metal slithering, the clinking of chain, left her no doubt as to his intentions. "Remember that."

"Yeah, right." She gave a rough laugh. "You had the chain there the whole time."

He watched her, face bland, fingers fiddling with the padlock's small key. The other end of the chain had already been secured to a bed post, ready for use. Fuck him. "Of course I did. I just hoped I wouldn't have to use it."

Cold metal touched her skin and the chain was wrapped around her ankle. She gritted her teeth. It was all she could do to stop herself from kicking him. Violence raged inside her.

She was tethered.

CHAPTER FOUR

Roslyn had been a long time in the bathroom. Nick tried not to worry. Not like she could get into any trouble with the lock disabled and the window boarded up. Still, it'd been a half hour at least. He shoved a hand through his hair, careful to avoid the fresh wound. The pounding in his head continued despite the painkillers he'd popped.

Fucking idiot.

He busied himself with chores as evening set in, lighting candles and closing up the fancy bi-fold glass doors leading out onto the balcony. Those he had reinforced with slats of wood, front and back. It made them heavy and awkward, but the extra layer was necessary for security. Nothing would get past him. He'd keep her safe whether she wanted it or not.

Whether she wanted *him* or not.

The side windows were boarded up, the door locked and barricaded. He started a fire in the pot-belly stove to warm the place up.

What the hell could she be doing?

He drifted by the bathroom door again, about-turned and hovered, antsy. His knuckles rubbed at the palm of his hand and his foot tapped. Like every other part of the place, he'd stocked the bathroom with the sort of shit girls liked. Bottles and tubes. Creams and lotions. But seriously ... how long did it take? It wasn't like she'd give a fuck what he thought of her appearance.

The beauty of the eco-chalet was it had been good to go despite the meltdown. Composting toilet and plenty of water in the tanks located beside each of the buildings. Spare tanks of gas for the stove sat waiting in the shed. They could be happy here for a long time. Or at least, content. Stupidly, he'd hoped she'd appreciate all the effort he'd put into making a home for them. That had been the idea. The reality was a little different. A shitload more difficult.

He scowled at the door and his temple gave an agonizing throb.

Maybe he had a mild concussion. It wouldn't have surprised him. This beat the worst of his hangovers, easily. And after everything went to shit, he and some of his buddies had spent days loaded. Weeks. With all the booze at their disposal and plenty of pills to be popped, why not? But those days were gone.

Nothing would distract him from protecting and providing for Roslyn.

Nick gave in and knocked lightly on the bathroom door. "Ah, Ros? You alright? Need anything?"

From within came the sounds of water splashing and the shuffling of feet over wooden floorboards. There was also the occasional jingle of the chain running beneath the door, connecting her to the bed. At the expected signs of life something loosened inside of him, unwound. He breathed easier.

"I'll be out in a minute," she said, her voice sounding off. Flat.

Yeah, well. Who could blame her for being mad about the chain? Or the ball gag? Some sucking up was required.

"Are you hungry?" he asked.

The bathroom door opened. Her unhappy face appeared, eyes rimmed red. Damn it.

"Maybe," she said.

"You've been crying?"

"No," she snapped.

He blinked.

Her puffy face emerged further from the shadows, the evidence obvious. Bloody hell.

Maybe this wouldn't work after all. The world was so messed up and he'd been so sure. Given a chance, she might see the benefits of the situation. But what if she never did?

Fuck that.

No. She would. He could be charming. Numerous exes had said so. Still, his throat constricted, fingers clenching and releasing at his sides. He'd spent months on his own, trying to get his shit together and figure out what came next. Because after a while, surviving day-to-day didn't cut it. In fact it became fucking meaningless. Just going through the motions: breathing and eating and pissing and shitting for the sake of it. Living long past when he should have been dead with the rest of them.

He'd spied a few other groups of people during his months on his own. But only Roslyn had tempted him into giving people another go. To set his shithouse attitude aside and try being social.

Checking out the group at the school for safety's sake, he'd seen her grinning at something some old guy said. Something inside him had woken up. For the first time, he'd actually felt lonely. But he'd felt something else, too. Hope.

Then he'd spied her a time or two through the school library windows and hope had turned to need. He had always had this librarian fetish—embarrassing but true. And he had one Miss O'Connell with her sensible shoes and tight sweaters to thank for that. It had been an epiphany to his preteen mind each and every time she went up on tippy toes to retrieve a book off the top shelf. Good God, the woman had been stacked. When Roslyn had done the same, reaching high with reading glasses perched on the end of her nose, he'd been converted to the cause instantly. The cause being to seduce her as soon as bloody possible ... that, and keep her safe.

"There's a fire?" she asked, eyeing up the pot-belly stove.

"Yeah." He sucked in a deep breath. "Look, I know this is unusual. But I'm really not going to hurt you. You don't need to worry about that."

"I'm not. Despite the chain." She shook her leg, jiggling the metal links. It sounded almost merry.

"You're not?"

"No. I nearly brained you with a bottle of Pinot. If you were going to hurt me, you already would have." She sniffed. "Which doesn't mean that I trust you. Or that keeping me like a household pet is acceptable. You're still very much on my shit list. Holding someone hostage doesn't exactly endear you to them, Nick. You're wrong to do this. And if you're waiting for Stockholm syndrome to kick in, then you're going to be waiting a hell of a long time."

"Right." He pinched his lips with his thumb and forefinger, thought it over. She was right, in a way. But admitting it wouldn't get him anywhere. It would be best to sidetrack her for now. "I'm sorry I made you cry."

"It's not that," she sighed, held out her hand. A busted pair of reading glasses lay in her palm, one lens cracked in the corner, the frame badly bent. "They were in my pocket during my great escape."

"Let me see ..."

Another shrug and a snuffle, but she let him take them. "You said something about food?"

"Just a sec." One of the arms had broken off, but the bend in the central part of the frame could be dealt with easily enough. "Mind if I hold onto these?"

A third shrug as she wandered closer to the fire. He bet it had been bloody cold up in the old school.

He took a deep breath. "We need to come to some sort of agreement."

"Regarding?"

Nick sat on the edge of the bed, watching her. How best to come at it? She was smart. She'd gotten the drop on him. But still. All of the screaming had been her reacting without a single thought. That sort of behavior could get her killed. "Think you could climb a tree if you had to?"

"What?" Roslyn squinted at him over her shoulder. She looked better. Her blue eyes were clearer and some color had returned to her cheeks. The pretty mouth, however, remained an unhappy bow.

"You don't look like you've got a lot of upper body strength to me. If you had to climb a tree or a building to get yourself out of trouble, do you think you could?"

She held her hands out to the flames to warm them. "Oh, I see. We're back to talking me out of my ability to survive on my own."

He didn't bother to answer.

"You're army, aren't you?" Her voice was thick with distaste.

"Yeah, I was. What's that got to do with anything?"

"So was my father." She gave him a contemplative nod. "I'd manage alright, Nick. Trust me."

"Would you? How fast do you think you could move if you had to? How far could you run before you had to stop?"

"Infected aren't exactly swift."

"True. But if there's enough of them it doesn't matter." Nick set his elbows on his knees and clasped his hands together. "So, running and climbing are limited. You know how to hot-wire a car?"

"Must have missed that day of school," she mumbled. "I'd find one with the keys still in it. There're enough sitting around abandoned."

"And they've been sitting there for six months now," he said. "Not good for an engine to be idle so long. What are you going to do if it doesn't start? Do you know how to do anything past checking for oil and water?"

"I'll ride a bike if I have to. Hell, I'll skateboard."

He ignored her devil-may-care grin. "If you actually manage to kill me next time you attack me then you run the chance of dying here, Ros. Either in here, chained up, or out there from the infected."

"I'm really sure concern for my wellbeing will keep you awake at night."

"You have no idea."

Roslyn studied the skirt of her gray school uniform, her bruised knuckles. She was tough, but not tough enough. Not to go out there alone. Not even just to get back to the school.

"This isn't going to work, Nick," she said. "You're not going to convince me of a damn thing."

The woman made no sense. After everything she'd seen, the blinkers were still firmly in place.

"You really want to go back to that place and those people?" he asked. "After what they did to you?"

Her top lip curled in distaste. "After what you forced them to do to me."

"I didn't force them to do jack-shit. They chose to screw you over with their own free will."

"They're not all like that," she bit out.

He grunted, frustrated but trying to hide it. Probably unsuccessfully. "You like them enough to spend the rest of your life with them? Not that you'll live long with bastards like them at your back. Especially once you have to start going on raids into town for supplies. How do you think that'll work out, Ros?"

The line between her brow deepened and her shoulders squared. "I don't know, Nick. But it sure would be nice if the choice of how and where I spend the rest of my life were mine to make."

"Those days are gone. No one's got choices any longer. No one's where they want to be."

She flicked out her hand in obvious dismissal of the subject. "Food, Nick. I want food. Or are we bargaining for that too?"

He sighed long and loud, but only inside the confines of his own head, in private. To her he gave the most charming grin in his arsenal. The one that almost always got him what he wanted with women in the past.

Her eyes made like slits. "Well?"

"No, Ros. Of course not. Let me fix you some dinner."

***

Nick was sprawled out on the king-size mattress, eyes shut and body lax. Forget sleeping on the couch. She hadn't been happy. Not even after he'd sworn he'd keep his hands and every other part to himself. Roslyn lay as far from him as she could manage without falling off the bed. But give it time. She was awful close to the edge.

There were infected outside moaning and groaning. Her earlier carry-on had definitely been heard. Who knew how many had gathered? After six months there should have been less of them. They should have been dying off from starvation by now. But they weren't, or at least, not in any great numbers. The virus somehow kept them going. Maybe they were eating each other or cornering the local wild life. Who knew.

Roslyn lay dead still, her breathing soft and slow. Not asleep, though. Not even a little. He could feel the tension radiating off her.

Fuck. Tiredness owned him. But all he could do was lie there and wait for her to attempt whatever it was she had her heart set on attempting.

Waiting.

Maybe leaving the cuffs off her hadn't been the best move.

Unlikely he'd get any sleep tonight, either way. His head remained in agony. Lucky he wasn't particularly vain, given the scar he'd have.

There was a rustling noise, the muted clinking of links of metal chain as she gradually lowered her foot to the floor. Beneath him, the mattress shifted as her weight carefully, sneakily moved. He lifted an eyelid and watched her shadowy form rise off the bed in slow motion.

"Going somewhere?" he asked.

A startled squeak escaped her.

Nick leant over the edge of the bed and flicked on the battery-powered camp light he'd left on the floor. He held it high. His jaw ached from ongoing tension. It didn't compare to the misery of his forehead, but soon, his teeth would be ground down to nothing. "Well?"

She blinked rapid fire and raised a hand to shield her eyes from the light. "What?"

He snorted. "Like you weren't going for something to attack me with. Again. After you promised ..."

"Nick."

"How can I trust you?"

"You kidnapped me!"

"You made a promise!"

"Would you just—"

"Die?" He kept his voice low, calm. Or he tried to. "I doubt you're the killing kind, darling. I don't think you've got it in you. But forgive me if I don't give you a shot at it just the same."

"You'd be surprised at what I could do," she seethed. "But, you idiot, I wasn't going to attack you."

"Yeah, right." He thrust the lamp forward like it was a weapon. "Then what were you going to do? Huh?"

The moaning outside rose in volume, no doubt spurred on by their shouting. She gave the door a pained glance and her voice dropped to a hoarse whisper. "I wasn't going to attack you."

"You thought you could get the chain off without waking me? Seriously?"

"I wasn't doing that either," she said. "I don't know how to do things like pick locks and hot-wire cars, remember? I don't have MacGyver skills like you do."

"Then what were you doing?"

She crossed her arms over her chest, pumping up the perfect swell of her breasts. He tried not to let it distract him. The school uniform looked tatty and faded in the glare of the camp light. Outside the groaning went on and on.

She took her sweet time in answering. His molars would be a

distant ground-down memory by the time they were done. Never in his life had a woman yanked his chain with such ease. Which would have been funny in another time and place, given the chain on her ankle. Or not. Humor required him to be more then semiconscious and not suffering from a head wound.

When she wavered in and out of his vision he got a little concerned. He rested his head back on the pillow. Bloody hell, falling on his face wouldn't strengthen his position.

Her gaze settled on some point behind him. "I was going to sleep underneath the bed."

"What?"

The woman just looked at him, mouth a bitter line. Dark smudges sat beneath her eyes. He wasn't the only one in need of sleep.

"Roslyn. Why would you do that?"

She flung out her hands. "Why do you think?"

"You're safe here."

"Nowhere is safe," she said. "Sleeping on that bed, out in the open ... it feels too exposed. The storeroom I used to sleep in was very small. And locked."

"We're inside a locked building."

She just looked at him.

Nick sighed and slowly sat up, pushed off his blankets and scooted across the bed. When he swung his legs over the side of the mattress she danced back a step or two, almost tripping on the chain. Not like he wasn't dressed. He'd changed into a T-shirt and some sweatpants to sleep in. The odds were good if he'd left anything hanging out she would have tried to cut it off.

He set the light on the bedside table and gave her a small, tight smile as his head spun queasily. "Easy. We're just talking."

The nasty glance she gave him seemed pretty fucking unnecessary, really. Not like he wasn't proving himself willing to discuss things. Also, not like he could do much, what with the condition he was in. Though she didn't know that.

He cleared his throat, took a deep breath. "Do you really think I would bring you here without making sure you'd be safe?"

Her face lifted in a mocking grin. "Oh, I'm sorry. Is my fear of dying a horrible, bloody death bruising your ego?"

"Ros, be reasonable ..."

"I'm so glad this is all about you."

"Wait, okay? Let's just stop and think this through," he proposed, leaning his elbows on his knees. Propping his chin in his fingers stopped the world from sliding south. "You are very valuable to me."

The sides of her lips turned down in disgust. "Yeah, a van's worth of valuable. I saw."

He ignored her baiting, still hopeful they could get some sleep tonight. Please God, let them get some sleep tonight. "Be logical, Ros. You like logical, don't you? I will not let anything happen to you. I went to too much trouble to lose you now."

"Aah, the power of the pussy."

"Exactly," he agreed with a smirk. Which was a mistake. If the woman hit him now, he really might be down for the count. "Calm down. It's the truth. You have it. I want it."

"I hate you so much."

"Because I'm honest?" He sighed. "No, Roslyn. This should comfort you. You're pretty much worth more to me than my own life. You and your pretty pussy."

Shouldn't have said it. Couldn't help himself. Wasn't like she didn't hate him already.

It was a little surprising when she actually hissed at him, though. "I mightn't even be any good in bed. Have you thought of that?"

"I'm willing to take the risk." He grinned. "I'm also willing to teach you. I'm actually quite a good instructor when I put my mind to it. You'd be surprised."

Her jaw shifted restlessly like maybe he wasn't the only one wearing away teeth. "I desperately need you to go fuck yourself."

"Roslyn," he tutted, and the fury in her eyes exploded. She was a lot of fun all stirred up. Pity about the reason. Still, it pleased him to know he could get to her as much as she got to him.

A long, low growl came from outside and her shoulders jerked. He hated seeing her afraid, for reasons even greater than his ego. There'd been enough fear and death. By locking this bird in a golden cage, he'd save her from experiencing more. Perverted, but true.

"You're safe," he said in a softer tone.

"I'm here. I'm clearly not going anywhere. We don't need to be discussing this any longer. Why do you even care?"

"I don't want you sleeping beneath the bed."

Blue eyes stared back at him, unhappy.

He smothered a yawn, searched for something to put her at ease. With his brain pounding, he couldn't have set himself a harder task. He'd promised not to jump her no matter how much he wanted. The place was locked down. The evidence on that front was obvious. His headache left little room for thought. Didn't put off his dick, but then his dick had no sense. It had gotten him into trouble for most of his adult life.

"Why don't I go back to my side of the mattress and you come lie down?" he said.

She didn't move.

"Roslyn, I spent weeks making this place safe for us. Reinforcing every door and window. Testing them. Nothing is going to get you. Not in here."

One slender, bare foot rubbed at the hardwood floor. The cold hardwood floor. She had to be cooling off fast, out from under the blankets. He knew he was. It had been hours since he'd seen to the fire. Stanthorpe in the winter could chap your ass, and that put it mildly.

Nick gave her a long, steady look, making sure he had her full attention, before crawling back over to the far side of the bed. Retreating to gain ground in the long term. "Your turn."

No movement. Maybe she had already frozen.

"It would be good if we both got some sleep tonight," he said.

"You said you wouldn't force me into anything."

"That only applied to sex. Sleeping on a cold, uncomfortable floor is wide open to intervention. Try it and see." Fuck, he hoped she didn't.

All the little subtleties of her face amazed him. The slight curl of her lip and wrinkling of her nose to diss him just so. Dangerously close to cute. He looked forward to learning her, in more ways than one. But first up, they both needed their shut-eye.

Please, let the cuffs stay put away. There were dark marks around her wrist from her tugging on them earlier. Bruises. Not good. He suffered twinges of guilt every time he saw them. Not that she'd given him a choice.

"Please," he said, trying for humble, if not trustworthy.

"You'll stay on that side."

He held his little finger aloft. "Pinky promise."

She rolled her eyes, checked out the windows, the balcony doors. Each and every one he'd fortified. They were safe. He'd swear his life on it, and hers too. And he didn't take it lightly, being responsible for her. Despite what she might think.

She moved forward an inch. No more. "They can't get in?"

"No. They can't get in."

Her mouth opened then closed. "Alright."

Roslyn shuffled back to the bed with shoulders slumped and climbed beneath the blankets. The mattress shifted as she tossed and turned before finally settling on a position. With her back to him, as if it had ever been in any doubt. She flicked off the camp light and darkness descended. Outside the noises seemed to have calmed down. Maybe the bastards felt the cold. Who knew?

"Thank you," he said. Because there was no need not to be polite, not when he'd gotten what he wanted.

He closed his eyes and listened to her breathing. Roslyn was beside him, safe and sound. Unhappy, but that couldn't be helped. At least she wasn't attacking him. Tomorrow he'd make it up to her, win her over somehow.

His limbs felt like lead. He needed to wait till Roslyn fell asleep, but he doubted he could do it. So fucking tired. Sleep stole over him, fast gaining ground. He could only hope he didn't wake up dead.

CHAPTER FIVE

Sunlight was flooding the room when Roslyn woke. The big balcony bi-fold doors stood open to reveal nature in its entirety. Lots of glory right there. Birds were singing outside, there was plenty of blue sky and a light breeze blowing. She lay buried beneath a mound of blankets.

Nick was nowhere in sight.

Then she heard whistling. Not a bird. A six-foot-something male strode in the back door, arms loaded down with sticks of all shapes and sizes. Today he wore jeans and another T-shirt, along with a sporty pair of sneakers.

"Good morning," he said with a grin.

What the fuck did he have to be so happy about? Oh, right. He wasn't chained to a bed by a whistling lunatic.

The lunatic dumped the load of kindling in a basket by the pot-belly stove, turned and brushed off his hands. "Such a pretty face to be so grumpy."

"I'm not a morning person."

"Then you have no excuse. You've missed the morning. It's almost one in the afternoon."

"It is?" Roslyn sat up, rubbed her eyes and scowled at him some more.

"You must have needed the rest."

"Hmm."

"Coffee?"

She hedged, pushing back her blankets. At some stage he'd obviously piled them high to keep her warm. Accepting anything from him felt wrong, even after dinner last night, the heat of the fire and the comfort of the bed. She did not want to owe this man a single damn thing if she could help it.

"It's just coffee, Roslyn." He appeared highly amused, lips raised on one side, brown eyes bright. Bushy-tailed bastard. The war wound she'd given him was impressive. A black egg sat above his brow with a pink line neatly bisecting it. "Coffee comes free."

"Comforting to know you'll inform me when I'm trading for favors."

"Oh, you'll definitely know when we're trading for favors. Rest assured," said the smirky jerk. "Milk and sugar?"

"Yes. Please." She swung her legs down, bracing for the chill of the hardwood floor. There were socks on her feet: thick, woolen, distinctly foreign ones. "I didn't go to sleep with socks on."

"I didn't want you to get cold." Nick had his back to her as he lit the gas kitchen stove and put on the kettle. However, the stupid know it all look was clear when he turned to face her. "I hope you don't mind."

Of course she fucking minded. "You promised not to touch me."

"That was only with regard to sex," he said. "This was to keep your toes warm."

She stood up, wide awake now. Anger did that to a woman. "No, there was no such caveat in place. You promised not to touch me and you broke your word."

His brows reached high. "Caveat? What a big word before breakfast. Are you going to explain what it means to me?"

"It means you're an asshole."

"Ah." He nodded. "Would you like eggs? Only powdered, sorry. Porridge, perhaps? Or I have some fresh apples I found in an orchard not far from here. Chemical free, I promise. You look like the type to buy organic."

"Funny." And true. But he didn't need to know that. How childish would it be to tear off the socks and throw them at him? They were nice. Thick, brown hiking ones. Her toes were toasty warm. It quite possibly made the situation worse. The thought of his hands on her when she was unaware had sensation creeping down her spine, spider-style. "Don't touch me again without permission. At all. For any reason."

He didn't answer.

"Nick?"

He crossed his arms over his hard chest, muscles moving enticingly beneath his skin. "You know I'm not going to agree. Why upset yourself?"

"How mad were you at me last night when you thought I'd broken my word?"

"I promise I will never touch you with the intention of hurting you." He held his fist in the palm of his hand. "Unless you're a naughty girl. Then there will be repercussions. Guaranteed."

"You're threatening to hit me?"

"What?" His eyes flared wide with surprise and his hands dropped back to his sides. "No. Of course not."

"Right." She wished she could do the one-eyebrow-raise thing. It would call down just the right amount of skeptical upon his bullshit. "This is never going to work. Whatever you think is going to happen here, it's not. You might as well just take me back to the school."

The man set his big hands back on the kitchen bench. His long body looked fully at ease as he watched her with an amused smile. How many women had gone for his particular brand of crap before the plague? Been tempted by the floppy brown hair and square jaw? The absolute confidence he had in his own propaganda?

Plenty. Heaps. She'd bet on it.

There was a certain appeal to him, if you were desperate. But he wasn't half as charming as he thought he was. Not when she wore a fucking chain around her ankle.

Not one iota of doubt sat in his dark eyes. It was unsettling. Her hands felt clammy, stuffed beneath her armpits.

"You're going to have to take me back," she said. Because belief was half of being.

"I guess we'll see. Why don't I fix you breakfast while you wash up?" he suggested, moving toward the kitchen.

The power he had over her. She hated it. The infuriating lack of liberty, just like back at the school only worse.

Her chin wobbled and he gave her his calm little smile, obviously taking her silence as assent. The look alone made her want to brain him with something hard. Again. He was hard to pin down. There were so many different smiles. She should number them, index them, all the better to keep them in order. Study him and defeat him. But she honest to God didn't want to know him that well. The thought was repugnant. He'd bought her, for fuck's sake. Bought her and fed her and put socks on her cold feet. Piled blankets on her and kept her chained to a bed. Her pride lay in tatters. Her eyes became inexplicably hot, sandy.

She had to get out of this.

But he was always watching. Getting the drop on him again wouldn't be easy. And then she'd do what, hack off her foot? Who knew where he kept the key.

"Go on and wash up," he said impatiently. "We don't have to fight about everything."

She fled into the shadowy bathroom and shut the door. The door lock had been disabled, the window barricaded. A bucket of cold water sat on the benchtop. It chilled her hands and stung her face as she began to wash. The fingers of her punching hand throbbed. Icy drops slid down her neck and soaked into her stupid dress. A hard shiver wracked her spine.

The woman in the mirror stared back, slack-jawed and dazed, confused and not so confident.

"Fuck."

***

"Is that really necessary?" he asked.

"What?"

"Pacing back and forth." Nick sat at the table. His long fingers dealt ably with the various parts of a gun, then got busy cleaning and oiling. So far he'd sharpened three wicked-looking blades before moving onto things that went *bang!* He was an industrious thing, his hands constantly busy. "It's annoying."

"Is it?" Roslyn sat on the arm of the lounge and kicked the chain to and fro, noisily. It slithered across the floor, metal clinking. She added a little extra oomph to the movement just for fun. Nick looked less than impressed, his eyes all flashy and dangerous. Bad luck, buddy. Chalk up one small, pathetic victory to her team.

The trimmed beard covered a lot of territory, but his eyes said plenty. Mostly she'd avoided looking in them since he'd laid out brunch on the table. He'd sat down across from her and dug into the porridge and chopped apples laced with brown sugar. Of course he knew how to cook, as he'd demonstrated with dinner last night. How typical. She tried not to be impressed. Also, she tried not to relish the food. A hot break-fast, however, proved to be worlds away from a ration of stale crackers at the school. At least her captivity would be passed in relative comfort.

"Why don't you read a book?" he suggested, gesturing to the shelf of dusty classics above the bed.

"I don't have any reading glasses. My spares are back at the school in my handbag." For fun she wrapped the chain around her foot and bounced and jiggled it on the floor. "Why don't you take me back so I can fetch them?"

"I'm not really in the mood for a drive. Aren't you tired of wear-ing the uniform?"

She barked out a laugh. "I think I'll keep my dress on, thank you."

"There are fresh clothes in the cupboard." He carefully set down a piece of his pistol, steepled his fingers and rested his chin upon the point. "That's all I meant. For now."

"What sort of clothes?"

"So suspicious. Go see for yourself." The look on his face would have made anyone think twice. A gleam had returned to his eyes. He sat perfectly still, watching and waiting. Vipers probably sat that still when sizing up their prey.

The chain jangled as she kicked it aside and stood. "Alright."

She wandered over and threw open the double-door cupboard, embedded in the wall opposite the open-plan kitchen. It backed onto the bathroom, obvious due to the big white water heater sit-ting in one corner. But there was a wealth of things packed around it and a whole lot more filled the shelves. All selected with a woman in mind. There were sweaters and jackets, shoes and shirts, jeans and underwear. Lots of underwear, far more than one per-son could ever possibly require. A veritable bordelloful of the fluffy stuff lay before her.

She poked a finger at the clutter of lingerie. A colorful mess of ribbons and lace fell at her feet, busting free of the cupboard's crowded confines.

"You've been busy," she said, dryly. "Where did all this come from?"

"Town."

She picked up the topmost item of filmy, ivory-colored silken nothingness. Took her a moment to figure out what it was. "Tie-on panties. Nice, Nick. Very practical."

"There's a matching bra for that one, I think," he said, his voice directly behind her. So damn close his breath warmed the back of her neck.

"Shit!" Her spine almost shot straight out of her. "Don't sneak up on me."

"Sorry." He smiled. It wasn't the least bit sincere.

"Would you mind giving me some room?"

"Not at all." He took one step back. Not even a very big one. God knew his legs were long enough.

"Better?" he asked.

She didn't deign to reply.

Instead she rifled through the nearest stack of clothes, a selection of jeans. Beside sat some woolen vests and a couple of long-sleeve T-shirts. They looked like they'd fit. So did the shirts still wrapped in plastic packaging. And the neat stack of sensible boyleg knickers. Nice to know they weren't all see-through. Cotton appeared here and there. She rather liked certain girly things. But there would be no parading that particular predilection in front of him.

Never, ever, ever.

Pretty much everything in the cupboard looked like it'd fit her. A weird twinge tickled her scalp. Like her skin was on back to front.

It wasn't him. He hung back, for now. Leaning against the kitchen bench, face neutral and eyes beady, waiting on her reaction, no doubt.

A black pair of cargo pants in her size. A set of sturdy brown boots, a pair of sneakers, similar to his. Both were the right size. Even the bras were close, a C cup instead of her actual B. Huh, he'd been hoping.

"How did you know?" she asked. A stupid question. She already knew the answer.

"Hmm?"

"You've been watching me," she said.

A creepy smile lit his face. He didn't even bother to deny the accusation.

"God, Nick. That's awful."

He snorted and shook his head. "Did you really think I hadn't watched you?"

"Stalking. Let's call it what it is."

He shrugged. "If you like."

"You're not even ashamed." Her face felt brittle. Stupidly surprised that the man who'd chained her to his bed had been spying on her. Of all the small, insignificant indiscretions—except it wasn't really. Her privacy had been shat upon and she'd never even suspected. When the hell would she learn that the old rules did not apply? Life had been stripped back to the basics of food, water, shelter and sex.

And this guy, the one lounging in front of her, was as primitive as they came.

"I think we should talk some more about our deal," he said.

"We have no deal. I have a chain. But *we* have no deal." She picked up the dropped scanties and shoved them back into their crowded space. He didn't need any more improbable ideas floating around his deviant mind.

"Of course we have a deal. We're negotiating it right now." He pulled his hands out of his pockets and rubbed them together, all enthused. "There's no reason we can't behave like honest, mature adults about this."

"You're such a creep." She shut the cupboard doors and set her back against them. "Congratulations, my skin is actually crawling. You make Neil look viable."

"Who's Neil?"

She mumbled a few choice expletives and headed back to the bed, chain trailing behind her. "I can't believe you were spying on me."

"Hang on, do you mean the bastard who cornered you in the Science labs the other day?"

"You saw that too, huh? Why am I not surprised?"

"Yeah. I saw." Nick's face twisted in anger, his lips a livid line within the frame of his beard. She'd have backed up if she hadn't already been at the bed. "Do not compare me to him. I had him in my sights. I nearly shot the fucker. The way he was looking at you."

"Least he wasn't spying." But he didn't scare her enough, apparently. She never did know when to back down or shut up.

Dark eyes flashed. "He was working his way up to hurting you, Ros."

She scoffed. "Please. Neil's a wanker, but he's not a rapist."

"He wanted you. Badly," he said. "Had his mates given you a talking to? Told you to stop being so difficult? To take one for the team, maybe?"

She tried to keep her face clear but apparently it didn't work. Neil hadn't scared her, or not exactly. Going out of her way to avoid him had, however, become a priority over the past few months. And yes, one of Neil's flunkies had approached her about her reluctance to copulate with him. She'd sent the idiot running with a few choice words.

Nick's lip curled in distaste and the muscles in his arms flexed. Whoa. It left her in no doubt as to his willingness to spill Neil's blood. He'd do it without a second thought. Death was right there in his eyes, shockingly clear. "They had, hadn't they? The fuckers. Still convinced you were safe there, Ros? Your little school was turning into *Lord of the Flies.*"

"You've read it?" Probably wiser not to insult him, but the words flew out of her mouth before her brain kicked in.

"Yes." He gave her a humorless laugh. "Year ten. I have a good memory."

"I can handle Neil. I'm not afraid of him."

Nick's eyes bored into her, brooking no nonsense. She got the distinct impression he could see straight through her skin. Not a comfortable feeling. Being open to him in any way was anathema. "Don't lie to me, Ros. You can tell me it's none of my business, but don't lie to me." His voice dropped to a harsh whisper. "Alright?"

"How did you know I was lying?"

The man gave her a wide, toothy grin. Her need to know usually rubbed people the wrong way. Trust him to be amused.

His two front teeth had a slight gap between them and little lines radiated out from beside his eyes. He was closer to rugged than handsome, of Irish stock, perhaps, with his ruddy skin. Far too raw for any sort of elegance, but he seemed totally at home in his own body. A body she noticed far more than she should. The man had no moral compass whatsofuckingever. Important to keep such relevant facts in mind while she discreetly ogled him. Stupid hormones.

"You shouldn't have spied on me," she said.

"Let's agree to disagree."

"Why couldn't you just come and talk to me like a normal person? Why the grand Machiavellian scheme, huh?"

"You needed to know what those people were capable of."

"You keep saying that. It doesn't justify a damn thing." She just shook her head in disbelief. "Your mind is so warped."

He didn't reply.

"You're wrong."

"He would have hurt you, Ros. And the rest would have just made excuses," he said, his voice horribly calm. "I had to get you out of there."

"Oh, please. Do not try to convince me this is all some altruistic crusade on your part." Her hands curled into fists, making the bruises ache. "This, what you're doing here, it's all about you, Nick, and what you want. You are not my knight in shining armor. You're not saving me from shit."

He stared back at her in silence for a moment. "I nearly talked to you. A couple of times I almost did. But I'm not the best with words. Besides, it was better to show you. Now you've seen what your friends are like firsthand. Eventually, you'll have to accept it. You can't trust them."

Maybe she couldn't. But she sure as hell couldn't trust him either. "So why me? Why didn't you want Janie?"

He frowned then winced, lips pulled wide in pain. Tentative fingers massaged below and above his mighty wound. "Who? The little blonde?"

She nodded.

"Give me some credit. How old is she, seventeen? Eighteen?"

"About that."

"Not interested." He took a deep breath then clapped his hands together, startling her so bad that she jumped. "So, are you on any kind of birth control?"

"What?"

"You heard me. Are you?"

"No. And I have every sexually transmitted infection known to mankind. Things are awful messy downstairs."

"Excellent."

"I'm never touching you."

The bastard smiled the sort of smile that reeked of thinking with his prick. 176: Sexual Ethics. He had none.

"Ever."

He snapped his fingers and cocked his head. "What's the line about protesting too much?"

She snarled. Hopefully like a lion but more likely a cranky kitten. Childish and futile, but, damn it, what was she supposed to do? Frustration had her furious. She could have thrown herself on the floor, toddler-tantrum-style, with limbs flailing at the unfairness of the world.

Nick licked his lips and looked away for a moment. The smile never faltered. Much more of this and she'd begin to think she was a constant delight. "Pick out some clothes, Roslyn. I'll take the chain off long enough for you to get changed. Deal?"

"I don't want anything from you."

"Or I can dress you. Your choice. And you know the tie-on panties will be involved." He stalked a couple of steps closer and loomed. "Fight me on something else, Ros. You being cold or hungry isn't negotiable."

"You're such a great guy."

His expression altered oh so subtly. She could have sworn he flinched.

"Hurry up," he said.

With a futile huff she returned to the cupboard, grabbed the nearest pair of jeans, a T-shirt and the rest. Searched out the baggiest bloody sweater she could find. Not one of those tight pin-up–girl boob-enhancing babies. Forget it. This required layers and lots of them.

"Good girl," said the patronizing son of a bitch.

"I meant to ask. How's your head?"

The asshole just laughed.

CHAPTER SIX

"Do you always have this much trouble getting to sleep?"

Roslyn wriggled about on the bed, finally rolling onto her side, facing him. He couldn't see her in the darkness, but he knew. The noise of her shifting on the sheets and rustling the blankets sounded so loud in the quiet, along with the clinking of the chain.

"Can't say. I haven't been held hostage before," she said.

Whatever sultry, flowery scent she'd lathered on herself had him happily high. How nice it would be to lick her all over. Start with her cute, cold toes and work his way up. Leave no inch of her skin untasted.

"Smartass," he mumbled.

Their first full day together had been largely uneventful. No further head wounds, at least, which was something to be grateful for. They'd talked a little. Not a lot. Mostly she'd given him shit about the chain. Fair enough. It wasn't coming off, though. Not a goddamn chance in hell of its removal anytime soon, given her furtive looks at the door. Thankfully, his headache had evened out to a dull skull-splitting roar.

"They're still out there," she said, talking about the low, occasional moan coming from outside their back door.

"There're usually a couple about. I gave up killing them. More just come to take their place. Maybe they smell the smoke from the fire. I dunno."

"Mm." Her voice was soft, sleepy. So how come she hadn't fallen asleep already? Because no damn way could he let his guard down until he knew she was out for the count. Not if he could help it. He heard the clink of the chain again. A small disgruntled noise. Who knew what it was about, but he needed sleep desperately.

Then sheer fucking genius struck him blind. "You want the chain off?"

The noises stopped. "Yes."

"Alright." He sat up and flung back the bedding, clicked on the camp light sitting on the bedside table.

Roslyn blinked and scooted up, backing into the headboard. Her red hair stuck out like crazy. Bed hair, from his bed. A strange sort of satisfaction rolled through him.

"You mean it?" she asked.

"Of course." He rose and retrieved the key, stashed beneath the mattress. Unoriginal, but close by if needed.

She cautiously stuck her foot out as though she were half afraid he'd chop it off. For bed she'd changed into a pair of truly unattractive sweatpants and a gray sweater large enough to swallow her whole. It left everything to the imagination. He'd still take her over Junie—or whatever the hell her name had been—any day of the week.

Nick picked up the padlock and unlocked it, slipped it free of the links of chain. The long length of metal clattered to the floor and lay silent. Ros made a small noise and looked at him, mouth slightly open, holding perfectly still.

"Um, thank you," she said eventually.

"No problem."

The woman stared at him like he was suddenly a stranger. One she clearly didn't know how to take. Her eyes were wide but the little line was back, sitting between her brows. He'd baffled her. Confused would work fine. He could use that. She stretched her toes, rolled her ankle.

"Better?" he asked.

"Yes." With a tight nod she slipped back beneath the blankets. "Night."

"Night."

The cuffs were likewise stuffed beneath the mattress, waiting. Her arm lay atop the blanket, hand curled into a fist. He snapped one end around her left wrist before she knew what had happened. Locked the other around his own limb and they were a done deal. Her elbow jerked back and smacked into his arm. Her fist flew at him, the one she'd bruised bashing Neil. He caught it midflight before she could do herself any further damage.

"What are you doing!" she screeched.

"Noise, Roslyn."

"What are you doing?" She tugged hard on the sudden, unwelcome connection between them. Lips drawn back, enraged.

"You didn't think I'd just let you run loose?" He didn't smile, kept it matter-of-fact. "Ros, you did attack me. And I am holding you against your will."

"But—"

"Of course, we're going to have to sleep closer together." He slid across the bed, laying their joined hands down between them. Or his half of the pairing, at least. Hers wavered in the air, unsettled. "There we go. More comfortable?"

"No. I want the chain back."

"Too late."

Her jaw hung open and her eyes were bright with hate. He'd seen it often enough from her to know it. "No. Nick ..."

"Actually, I sleep on my side. Just a minute." He lay down on his side and wound his arm around her middle, pulling her toward him. From this close her flowery scent gave him a headspin. "You can lie on your back with my arm over you, or you can be on your side with my arm around you. What would you prefer?"

"Why are you doing this?"

"It's done, Ros. Move on."

Her eyes promised murder. A brutal death without a hint of re-morse.

"Well?" he asked.

Her lips screwed up like a cat's ass. With a growl she turned onto her side, presenting him with her back, because she always slept on her side too.

"Good choice." Nick moved in for the kill. He molded his body to her back, keeping his arm tight around her. Of course she squealed and scrambled to try to escape him, getting nowhere. "Easy. Take it easy, Ros."

She continued to fight, squirming and kicking back at him. He trapped her feet beneath his legs. Slid his other arm beneath her neck and held her against him with both arms. Without bring-ing his dick into it, they couldn't have been humanly closer. His beauty bucked, twisting and turning for a few moments more. Pointlessly. The back of her neck dampened with sweat.

Shoulders heaving, she panted for air. "You fucker, you promised! No touching in a sexual manner."

"I won't take it any further."

"How can I trust anything you say? You're a goddamn liar."

"This is your second night with me, Ros. It's time to move things on a little. We're sleeping together. Only sleeping. Nothing more."

"So you'll *move it on* until you're raping me?"

"No," he said. "Never."

Fingernails dug deep into his arms as she tried to work her way free, again getting nowhere. "I repeat. A fucking liar."

"Hush. Go to sleep."

"Nick ..." A pleading tone intruded on her anger. He already knew what she would say, or close enough to it. Either way, things were staying the way they were.

"It's done. Sleep."

She growled again, low in her throat. If there'd ever been a sexier noise, he hadn't heard it. He shifted his hips back from her ass to hide the tell-tale state of his dick. It involved loosening his grip on her a little, but not a lot. Her hair smelled nice and the back of her neck even better. Salty-sweet perfection, not helpful at all to the state of his libido. "Is that better?"

"Awesome, you asshole."

Silence held for a few minutes. He could almost hear the cogs and wheels turning in her head. Without a doubt, she was the noisiest thinker he'd ever met. Or maybe it was the grinding of her teeth again.

"Let it go," he advised.

"Inflicting yourself and some semblance of intimacy upon me will not engender any sort of bond between us, Nick."

"No?"

"No."

"Huh," he said. "You ever noticed how your words get bigger when you're feeling cornered?"

She apparently had nothing to say to that.

"Tell me about your father," he said. "You mentioned he was army?"

More silence.

"Go on."

She sighed. "He generally wasn't around. When he was, he was an asshole. A lot like you. So certain he was always right and everyone else could go to hell." The fingernails digging into his arm eased a little, becoming more like a cat's claws flexing. Testing, not teasing. "The only thing that mattered was what he wanted."

"Harsh."

"Truth." She shifted, her feet twisting beneath his. Nick drew back a little, giving her more space. Earning himself a begrudging, "Thank you."

"You're welcome."

"What about your family?" she asked. "I've told you my messy tale. Turnabout is fair play."

He cleared his throat. If anything would get his cock under control it was thinking about his family. "My father was a builder. My big brother became his apprentice. I had an uncle in the army. He was always travelling all over the place having adventures. He made it sound so great. So when I was old enough I enlisted."

"Did you like it?"

"Yeah. Mostly. I didn't see myself doing anything else." He smiled in the darkness. He'd been counting on her curiosity. "But I wasn't interested in settling down then. Priorities change."

"Do you know what happened to your family?" she asked, ignoring the settling-down comment. "When this all went down?"

He nudged a strand of her short red hair with his nose. The scent of honey swept through his system. "They died. I went back a few months ago to check. To see if ..."

Roslyn turned and looked over her shoulder, all the better to give him a pitying stare. "That was brave, going back."

"Hmm." His mother had been a good woman. Maybe even a great one. She didn't deserve that sort of ending.

"My father got bitten," she said. Her voice was cool, distant. The look in her eyes, not so much. "Mum called me on the mobile, managed to get through. Dad was locked in the bedroom. She'd taken a handful of sleeping pills, wanted to say goodbye. They had a place in the city. No chance of getting out. I can't say I really blame her."

"I'm sorry." Inadequate, but true.

"There was another woman in the school," she said. "After a couple of weeks, when it became clear help wasn't coming, she killed herself. Drank a bottle of bleach. The others were furious, but I didn't really blame her either."

He stared back at her. "The early days were hard on everyone. What did you do to get through?"

"I had my library. I just kept reading, lost myself in my books. Mostly it worked."

"I drank. Took pills." His honesty caught her by surprise—he could tell by the way she looked at him. But he wasn't going to lie. "I can barely remember January and Feb. Still can't forget the shit that came before, when the plague first hit, but those months straight after, they're pretty much gone."

She was quiet for a moment. "I noticed you didn't have a glass of wine with dinner. Figured you were staying on the ball in case I attempted another attack. Why did you stop?"

"I realized I wanted to live. Wasn't sure how I was going to do it, but just giving up ... I couldn't do it," he said. "So I dried out. Haven't touched anything in months. Even stopped smoking."

She opened her mouth, but didn't speak.

"What?" he asked.

"I can't be your reason for living, Nick. That won't work."

He didn't answer.

"Can you shift the cuff to the other hand?" Her face was calm, perfectly reasonable. "We'd both be able to sleep on our backs then, with a bit of room."

"No."

With lips slammed shut she turned away.

Behind him the camp light continued to glow. He'd have to sit up and drag her halfway across the bed to switch it off. Stuff it. It was a waste of resources, but he enjoyed watching her. The movement of her shoulder beneath the bulky-ass sweater as she breathed. The red of her hair, so dark in the low lighting. He tried to keep his arm light on her, perched on her hip, not pressing down all uncomfortable-like.

When was the last time he'd spooned with someone? Never. Spooning had never been a priority before.

"This isn't going to work," she whispered.

"We'll see," he whispered back to her. "Are you warm enough?"

She gave a little nod.

No point telling her to go to sleep. Expecting her to relax with him wrapped around her would be sheer stupidity. Her shoulders inched forward, or tried to. His arm didn't let her get far. Outside the moaning went on and on. You could pretend it was the wind if you tried. It didn't always work.

"So do you think," she asked, "if we'd actually met somewhere back in normal times, you'd have been interested in me?"

Nick stopped and thought it over—or at least pretended to. "Yes."

She muttered something along the lines of "fucking liar" beneath her breath. She was so cute sometimes.

"You're a smart, good-looking woman," he said. "I'd have been all over you."

"Bollocks. I bet you went for the mouth shut, legs open, easygoing lay nine times out of ten."

He tried not to laugh. "Of course I did. I'm male. But you grow up and your tastes mature."

"Oh, please. Admit I'm here because I'm the only uninfected female under fifty in the vicinity."

"You forget your friend Jeanie."

Roslyn's sock-covered foot kicked back, catching him in the shin. "Janie."

"No kicking." He threw a leg back over hers for good measure. "She's your friend. What does it matter if I get her name wrong? Said she didn't interest me."

No comment.

"Are you jealous?" he asked.

She snorted. "Of what? That you didn't kidnap someone else?"

He shifted a little closer and sniggered in her ear. "I'd take you as my hostage every time, Roslyn. Promise."

"Hate you," she said, sleep blurring the edges of her words.

"I know," he said soothingly. "I've got the scar to prove it."

CHAPTER SEVEN

Roslyn woke up alone in the bed again. Beyond the wide-open bi-fold doors the sun shone bright and birds were singing. Again. Also, an axe was swinging. Took her a while to place the noise, but that's what it had to be. Having grown up in the city, hearing axes swinging wasn't exactly the norm. She'd only moved to the country a year back when the job at the school had come up. It had probably saved her life.

The idea of a tree change had intrigued her, but it had been a career move. All part of her plan to work her way to the top and be the big boss librarian in an elite city school by thirty. Her precious life plan had been shot to shit.

The noise broke her out of her pity party.

Thunk. Thunk. Thunk.

It came from somewhere beyond the back door, presumably where Nick was. Next came whistling. Something by AC/DC, maybe? Nothing she recognized.

She rolled out of bed and headed for the bathroom, where she brushed her hair and washed her face and so on. The chain clinked cheerily behind her the whole way—he'd put it back on her as she slept.

God how she hated this. Him touching her, the chain, all of it.

The scent of him lingered, reminding her she'd woken up once or twice during the night and each time he'd been there, plastered to her back with an arm thrown over her. It made for quite the desensitizing program. The second time she woke, her cheek had been mooshed up against his bicep, skin damp with sweat. No need for so many blankets with him right there, invading her space and treating her like his teddy bear.

She didn't want to cuddle. Not with him.

On the kitchen bench her breakfast was laid out for her. All knives, fire pokers and anything else she might have thought to use as a weapon were absent, as per the usual. She should dig his heart out with a soup spoon. Nice and blunt and messy.

She slathered her still-warm floury roll thing in jam and ate it. Because of course he'd been baking. Proving himself to be an excellent provider wasn't going to convince her. No matter the buttery brilliance of the breakfast.

What to do with herself for the day? The shelf of dusty classics sat on the wall, taunting her. If only she had her glasses. Already she missed her books. A big fat copy of *War and Peace* sat staring back at her. It wasn't like she didn't have the time to read it again.

The back door stood open and her chain reached just far enough to let her stick her head through. He'd moved the pickup, likely to get it out of the way so he could bring firewood inside.

The industrious man stood beside a tree stump with axe in hand. No shirt on. Dirty marks stained the side of his blue jeans, as if he'd been wiping his hands there. He had just the right amount of chest hair and his sweaty body gleamed appealingly.

Even sunlight was against her.

The axe rose high above his head, the handle held tight in both hands. Muscles moved in his arms, his shoulders, flexing and shifting in an amazing manner beneath his skin. His face appeared the picture of concentration. Eyes focused entirely on his target.

And down it came. *Thunk.*

Two hunks of wood toppled to the ground. Nick pushed his brown hair back from his forehead, shoving his fingers through the sweat-dampened mess. The axe dangled from his hand as he breathed deep and stared off into the distance. He looked like an ad for testosterone.

He was unaware that he was being perved upon. Thankfully.

Everything inside her felt in flux. Something about the sight of him half naked stirred her up, stupidly. Her only defence was that it had been a bloody long time between dates. Her body warmed to the view, an all too willing traitor. She could actually feel her pussy flutter with interest. Shit. No. Not him. She needed to gird her loins. Close her eyes and picture him as another version of Neil. Or worse, Heathcliff. She'd never been a fan of that abusive bastard.

Nick's head lifted and his gaze snagged hers. "Morning."

"Hi."

His lips widened into a smile, a cautiously warm one. The wound on his forehead was a blue-gray mess and yet he attempted to be friends.

Or something.

The chain looped around her ankle sparkled silver in the sunlight, an all too pertinent reminder of her situation. She should retreat back into the cabin. But damn, she hated being in there. The walls were closing in on her. Even the chain felt tighter, like it was rubbing at her skin.

"I want to come outside," she called out.

"Alright." Nick leant the axe against the tree trunk. Six feet worth of capable male strode in her direction, up the walkway and across the gangplank.

Excitement at having the chain removed far outweighed her nerves about having him near. She shifted aside, ankle at the ready. Her heart beat double time. To get it off for more than five minutes' respite. Yes, yes, yes.

Another brief smile as he walked straight past her toward the bed. Not removing the chain from her foot. Not even a little. She'd foolishly fallen for his shit again. Disappointment drowned her.

A pistol butt stuck out of the back of his jeans. She should shoot him in the ass with it.

"You're going to tie me up outside?" Her voice sounded strangled. "Seriously?"

He looked up from where he was crouched at the end of the bed, busy undoing the padlock. "I don't feel like running after you when you attempt your next great escape. Sorry."

"But there are infected somewhere out there. It's not safe."

"I'll be right there the whole time, Roslyn. I won't leave you alone for a second."

Breakfast tossed and turned in her belly.

"No," she said. "Don't worry about it. I'll stay inside."

Nick let the chain slither through his fingers and fall onto the floor. He remained crouched by the end of the bed. "Ros."

"Really, it's fine. Forget about it."

He licked his lips and made a pained expression, brows drawn down. "Come on. You want a change of scenery, don't you?"

Would have been easy to throw out an insult, because God, yes, she wanted away from him. Didn't want to be looking at him another moment, him or his bare chest. Inside she felt small and cold and defeated. Her shoulders slumped. She hated it, but it was true. Not as if anything had really changed, though. The chain would remain and she was stupid. Hope sucked. To put it poetically, it was a motherfucking sucker punch. Not necessarily the words Austen would have chosen, but germane just the same.

"Look at me." He wandered toward her. Eyes narrowed and head angled as if in scrutiny. She could smell him and the scent was warm and rich and male. It scattered what remained of her wits.

"Roslyn, promise me you will not try anything."

Her mouth opened but nothing came out. She hadn't thought of escaping him. Instead she'd been all over the idea of blue sky and fresh air. And the chance to watch him at work. It was entirely possible she was the worst hostage ever.

"I'm serious, Ros. You stay where I put you and you do not pull any shit. Understood?"

She nodded furiously. "Yes."

"Do you see this?" He got right in her face, finger pointed straight at Exhibit A, the big gray lump and long crusted cut on his forehead. "This says I shouldn't trust you, loud and clear. Doesn't matter why you did it. You did it. To me. Didn't you?"

No denying the evidence. She nodded again, fingers twined tight. Bone-breakingly so. It lay on the tip of her tongue to say sorry. But it would be a lie. Deep down where it really counted it would be a big, fat whopper because he had deserved it, and eleven times out of ten she would do it all over again.

"Because it really fucking hurt, sweet," he said. A muscle in his jaw danced.

Another nod. She tried for contrite, really and truly tried with sad puppy eyes and everything, but she struggled to hold back an ecstatic grin at the idea of heading outside. Damn her lack of acting ability.

He scowled so hard that little wrinkles appeared beside his nose. "Okay. You break our deal, I'm going to take a belt to your ass. Hard. You will not sit for days." He dropped to his knees and dark eyes glared up at her. "Understood?"

A belt? Like hell. She'd kill him first. Kill him painfully, via the soup spoon.

"I understand," she said.

Rough hands got busy with the padlock and the chain fell free, clattering onto the hardwood floor. Her heart beat so fast as if it would explode out of her chest, like a bird taking flight. Free. She'd be free.

Warmth swelled inside of her. She could have clapped her hands for glee. Jumped around. Sung. Made clothes out of curtains or recited a sonnet. Nick would probably just look at her funny and slap the chain back on. So she kept it all inside, not wanting to spook him, delicate creature that he was.

"Come on." He stuck his hand out to her, face not particularly happy. Who cared? His eyelids were at half mast, dark eyes dangerously bright. There were lots of sidelong glances of the suspicious sort. So giggling was right out.

She clasped his warm, calloused hand and he led her out into the sunshine. Open air. Blue sky. Gum trees waved high above her in welcome. Her head spun with delight.

He set a cracking pace, leading her across the gravel parking lot. Sharp stones hurt her socked feet, but she ignored them. His hand tugged at hers, hurrying her along. Ah, the breeze on her face. She bit back a sigh of pure pleasure. They stopped a few meters out from the tree stump and he pointed at a patch of grass. "Sit. Please."

Due to the *please*, she sat cross-legged on the straggly bit of lawn. Once upon a time, the resort would have had nicely manicured native gardens, but they were reverting to wilderness now.

"Stay," he said.

With a parting, hard-faced look, Nick meandered back to the tree stump. She sat out of range of any flying wood chips while remaining firmly at the edge of his field of vision. Never did the man fully take his eyes off her. When she leant over to snag a dandelion his head snapped round at light speed.

"Just making wishes," she said cheerily, waving the dandelion in his general direction.

He grunted and set up a big chunk of wood. Raised the axe, then swung it.

Thunk.

The log split straight down the middle. It was kind of impress-ive. The poetry of all that lean, hard muscle being put to work made her want to fan her face. Much safer to concentrate on the view, what little of it there was from her vantage point behind the buildings. The nearest cabin sat about seven or eight meters away from theirs.

Not theirs. "Theirs" indicated some sort of coupledom.

"What's wrong?" he demanded.

"Nothing."

"You were frowning."

"I was thinking of you."

His chin rose, but he said naught. The man turned back to his wood chopping.

Maybe she should make a run for it. Now, while his back was turned. Where would she go? The driveway led straight back out to the road, but there wasn't much out there. He'd taken some sort of higgledy piggledy route to get them here, but the truth was, there was little out here. They were a good twenty minutes drive from town. Doubtless he could run pretty damn fast. Faster than her. She could hide in one of the nearby sheds and play cat and mouse with him. Hope to find a vehicle to get her the hell out. It was worth a try.

Thunk. Thunk.

She rubbed her socked foot against the ground, flattening some long blades of grass. No shoes. It could be a problem. Had he thought of her lack of footwear when he brought her out here? It would slow her down.

Roslyn took a deep breath.

Gravel crunched beneath Nick's boots as he paced toward her. The noise snapped her straight out of her daydreams. He hunkered down, much closer than he needed to be, as was his want. Again, the smell of him infected her. Highly unwelcome, clogging up her brain.

Sweat dripped from his brow and trailed down the side of his face. "You're thinking bad thoughts."

She tensed. "No, I'm not."

"What did I say about lying?"

"You're not a mind reader, Nick. Don't pretend. You're simply not that special."

"Ouch," he mumbled, shuffling closer. "I've decided what I want for letting you come outside without the chain on."

"What!"

"You know me, Roslyn. I don't do things for free." His smile was hard and his eyes intent. It was his bastard face. Long, thick, dirty fingers splayed out over his jean-clad thigh. "Aren't you going to ask me what I want?"

"No."

"Come on, you're curious about everything. Aren't you dying to know what's on my mind?"

"I don't need to be a mind reader to figure that one out."

He snorted. "Why don't I save you the trouble and tell you. I want a kiss."

Her eyebrows felt ready to part from her face. "NO."

"Yes." He stared at her, his jaw set. "Just one kiss. Pretty reasonable of me, really."

"I don't want to kiss you."

"A small, harmless peck on the lips."

"You'd have to force me, Nick," she sneered. "Now where would the fun be in that?"

He licked his lips and grinned, apparently pleased by her vehemence. Though it was unlikely he even knew the word. "I don't have to force you. I've seen the way you look at me."

"Like I think you're a sociopathic, misogynistic, kidnapping cretin?"

"Like I'm a man you're attracted to."

Like hell. "I prefer my version," she said.

"I'm sure you do. But you're still going to give me that kiss." And he looked awful damn sure of himself.

Fuck him. She bared her teeth. "You're insane. Better yet, you're projecting. Do you know what that is, or shall I explain it to you?"

"I think I can figure it out." The bastard actually winked at her.

"Bright boy. The summation of it is this: I do not want to kiss you."

"You mean you don't want to want to kiss me. There's a difference." The corners of his mouth curled upward. What she wouldn't give to wipe the smirk off his face with the flat of her hand. "Would you like me to explain what that is, sweet?" he asked.

She held in the snarl of rage. Just. Her hands clenched into tight fists. It made the bruises from decking Neil ache. "You're full of shit and I have no interest in touching you, kissing you or coming within fifty yards of you. Do you understand? Are those words little enough to penetrate your thick skull?"

"Oops. You said penetrate. You know what I'm thinking now?"

She blinked, stupefied.

"I want my kiss," he said.

"I want you dead."

He hung his head but his gaze stayed on her face. "Come on, Roslyn. Just one. Why are you putting up such a fight over one insignificant little kiss? Hmm?"

She covered her face with her hands, blocking all sight of him. Just a second to pull herself together, that was all she needed. Because lunging for his throat with her bare hands wouldn't end well. No matter how tempting.

"Sweetheart, we were all cozy and warm last night. Every time you woke up and saw I was there, you went straight back to sleep. Just like a baby, safe and sound in my arms."

She lowered her fingers to glower at him. "You didn't give me any choice."

"Mmm." Dark eyes narrowed and he gave her an assessing look. "You prefer it that way, don't you? Me making you do things?"

"No." Her hands fell away and she literally saw red, a sheet of it, swamping her vision. A hot blood-red veil covered her world. How dare he insinuate such shit about her. "Absolutely not."

"What do you think that means? That you like me being in charge?"

"I do not like you being in charge!" Birds fled from a tree nearby as her voice hit a pitch just short of shattering glass.

"Roslyn," he groaned. "Why don't you just give me the kiss?"

"I don't want to kiss you because you're holding me hostage, you idiot."

"But besides that?"

"You're a dickhead and an asshole and I hate you. You repulse me."

"Really? Do I?" He laughed in her face.

Murder was too good for him. Only torture would satisfy the sick shame and anger hiding inside her.

"Yes," she said. "You make me want to puke."

His hand rubbed at his mouth, half smothering a smile, and he made a noise of disbelief.

"You do! You're dirty and sweaty and you stink and—"

And then the bastard kissed her.

CHAPTER EIGHT

Roslyn did nothing for the longest time.

Nick pressed his lips against hers and waited. His hands cradled her head, holding her to him. He didn't try to take it deeper and didn't try for tongue.

Just kissed her, hard but chaste.

And wouldn't she be impressed he even knew that word.

He poured all his lust for her into it, trying to show her how much he wanted her. Fuck but her lips were soft. He opened his eyes to find her staring at him with the familiar look of shock and horror in her wide eyes. But she didn't move. She seemed to have frozen rock solid before him.

Reluctantly he stopped and pulled back, hands still in place. Silky strands of hair slipped between his fingers. He sat there on his haunches, staring at her closed mouth. Not getting distracted by the set of breasts heaving beneath her baggy sweater. Her upper lip was a perfect dusky pink cupid's bow. Was her pussy the same color? Her nipples?

Nick sat patiently, panting, waiting for her to do something. Shit, she didn't even seemed to be breathing and he was about ready to hyperventilate.

Suddenly her face twisted into something like grief, eyes hurt and confused. A strangled, angry noise escaped her and she shoved him hard with both hands. An action so fast and violent it sent him reeling back onto his ass. He should have been ready for it.

"Roslyn. Don't."

She sprang to her feet and was off, getting the hell away from him as fast as she could. Arms and legs pumping, she sprinted down the driveway. Gravel crunched beneath her socked feet.

Nick pushed to his feet and took off after her, a bare body-length or two behind. It didn't take much for him to catch her. For all her effort, she wasn't fast. He grabbed her up in a big bear hug from behind. The woman yowled like a wet cat. Her feet left the ground and her heels drummed against his shins. She wrestled and growled and he just held on tight as he could without hurting her.

"Stop it," he ordered.

Her kicking increased.

"Alright. Alright, I shouldn't have done that." Because a half-assed kiss wasn't worth all this drama, not when it hadn't even gotten him anywhere. But he had to push her, didn't he? Fair enough if she pushed back.

He couldn't resist the opportunity to grab for more. His idiot dick stirred in his pants, seconding the notion, loving the feel of her curvy ass writhing against him. She made him greedy and stupid, stupider even than normal. "Roslyn, ease up."

Her elbows jerked, trying to reach him and failing.

"Easy," he said. "I'm going to put you down."

She slowly slid down him until her feet returned to solid ground. Bits of grass and debris clung to her socked feet.

"There," he said. "Now calm down."

"Let me go," she huffed.

"Are you going to run?"

No answer.

"Are you?"

"No," she said in a low voice. Fury radiated off her. If sparks had flown from her fluffy red hair he wouldn't have been surprised.

"Okay." He loosened his grip, set her free.

Without another word she turned and strode back to the cabin. Her movements were tight, tense.

Shit. How much damage had his idiotic kiss done? "Roslyn, wait."

He followed her and she sped up, jogging up the ramp and crossing the plank in a few hasty steps. Head down and ass twitching angrily beneath the sweatpants. Into the cool, shadowy interior of the cabin she stomped, with him on her tail.

"Ros, let's talk."

She turned an abrupt corner and ducked into the bathroom. The door slammed shut and he heard a thud, as though she'd set her shoulder to it.

Nick took a deep breath, hands on his hips. Huh, that hadn't gone well. He hadn't given any real thought to the consequences of kissing her. There'd been no grand plan. But if he had, this result would have been pretty fucking obvious.

"Hey." He leant his shoulder against the wall beside the bathroom door, scratched a finger experimentally against the pine. "Ros?"

He didn't expect a reply.

She didn't disappoint.

"I'm not mad you tried to run." Even though she'd broken her word by doing so. There, he'd given. Now it was her turn.

Silence.

"Everything's okay," he lied.

More silence. He searched his mind for something to say. The memory of her lips still messed with his brain.

"Um, I was joking about the belt. I wouldn't really spank you."

Something thumped against the door on the other side. It sounded angry, a mad ramming of a shoulder or something. At least she was still alive and, hopefully, unhurt.

So it probably hadn't been the right thing for him to say.

In all honesty he'd been dead serious about the belt. Deep down he happened to be rather keen on the idea of striping her ass pink. He'd indulged in a bit of kinky fuckery in his time, but Roslyn made his imagination boil over. Her creamy skin marked by his hand as she lay bent over the arm of the couch.

All of her displayed, just for him.

And her pussy ... he'd love to gorge himself on her. Far too easily he could imagine the taste of her on his tongue.

His dick throbbed in his pants, completely out of control. Rather fucking painfully trapped behind his zipper, too. Bad timing, but not so surprising. He was a beast, an animal reeking of sweat and ready to pounce, rock hard and hurting. His hard-on gave Godzilla a run for its money. If he swung it about, Tokyo would be leveled.

Thank fuck she couldn't see.

No wonder he repulsed her. Though, when he thought about it, she didn't exactly act like he did most of the time.

Nick winced and adjusted himself before the zipper of his jeans did him damage.

He scratched at the door again. A plea from the randy dog locked outside in disgrace. Probably would have gotten off easier if he'd just pissed on the rug. He drew the line at whining and pleading. Or at least, at obvious pleading.

He could go in there after her. Force the door open and force a confrontation. What would it prove? She'd been behaving, and the minute she gave an inch he pushed for the full country mile. Because he was an idiot, clearly. An idiot who would do it all again in a heartbeat for the chance to get close enough to touch her.

Nick slid down the wall with a sigh. Hung his head and rubbed the back of his neck. Got himself comfortable.

It was going to be a long wait.

CHAPTER NINE

Roslyn didn't end up sleeping in the bath. She wanted to, but she didn't. There was every chance he'd storm in and she didn't have anything suitable for barricading the bathroom door. So she gave him the silent treatment instead. A brick wall couldn't have competed. Even when hunger gnawed at her guts, forcing her to leave her haven, her lips remained pressed tightly shut. Every time he tried to talk to her she turned her back.

Untrustworthy, manipulative, repugnant piece of shit that he was.

After the hundredth mumbled apology he'd slapped the chain back around her ankle with a long-suffering sigh and gone off to wash up.

Poor him, so fucking maligned.

Kissing her had crossed a line. The memory of his breath on her face and his mouth against hers kept twirling about inside her skull. She hated him. She did. Loathed his firm lips and reviled his steady hands. Abhorred the sound of his voice and detested the scent of him. Every piece of him repulsed her.

Despicable fucking man. The rant went on and on inside her head. She'd drive herself insane at this rate. When it came time for bed she lay down and hid her head under a pillow. Her very own cone of silence. In a surprisingly intelligent move, Nick slept on the couch. It still took her hours to get to sleep.

He'd disappeared again the next morning when she woke. Everything lay quiet. No footsteps or wood-chopping or anything. She and her chain were alone by the look of things. But he'd be close by. Of course he would.

Roslyn climbed out of bed, stretched, and wandered around. The back door was closed. She ambled over and turned the handle, the metal cool against her skin. He'd locked it. The big front bi-fold doors overlooking the cliff stood open, exposing a cloudy sky.

Where was he?

More of the floury rolls waited on the bench, neatly set out on a plate. A jar of raspberry jam sat beside it and one blunt-edged butter knife. The kind of knife that'd do no one any harm. Well, not without a hell of a lot of effort. He'd even left an elegantly folded napkin.

For the fun of it she checked the utensils drawer. There were spoons of all shapes and sizes: dessert, soup and tea. He apparently didn't even trust her with forks anymore, because they were gone. Afraid she'd do a Betty Blue and stab him in the arm, perhaps. Nothing but an egg-whisk and a plastic spatula inhabited the second drawer. Tea-towels sat neatly folded in the third and a stack of placemats in the fourth.

The chain was thick, but there had to be something that could damage it, something to lever apart the padlock. People usually kept tools under the kitchen sink.

When she looked there, she saw nothing but a dusty old cockroach bait and some dishwashing detergent.

Frustration beat at her chest, making her blood race. He'd be back soon. This was her chance. Time to get the hell away from him before kissing and cuddling turned into anything more persuasive.

She sucked in a sharp breath. *Invasive.* She'd meant invasive.

As if he could persuade her to do a damn thing. The cupboard with all the clothes, maybe there'd be something in there.

Hurry, hurry, hurry.

Her breathing sped. She threw open the big doors and started dumping shit onto the floor, clearing it all out. Behind her a bower of clothes and accessories grew. She had to climb up some shelves to check out the back of the top one properly. Her socks slipped, but she persevered. Up she went. Out it all came. Jackets and sweaters and scarves and hats hit the floor. He must have emptied out entire shops in town to outfit her. Did he really think collecting all this stuff was going to get him somewhere? His mind was warped.

Nothing.

Shit. There must be something.

She climbed down before she fell down.

He wasn't going to be happy with the state of the place. As if his happiness mattered.

Quickly, she searched the rest of the kitchen cupboards, pulling everything out, piling it up on the kitchen benches and generally going crazy. Double-checked the bathroom even though she knew its contents back to front, thanks to the time she'd spent cloistered in there the day before.

Under the bed.

In the bedside tables.

TV cabinet.

Coffee table.

She tore the cushions off the couch. Like a pair of bolt cutters might have accidentally slipped out of someone's pocket along with their spare change. Mostly she found lint and a long-forgotten tissue. A couple of dust bunnies hid underneath the couch. Nothing useful over by the fireplace, unless she could bang the padlock apart with a block of wood. Unlikely. By the back door there was a little cupboard for stowing shoes and crap. It only held a couple of empty, scrunched-up plastic bags and an ancient umbrella.

He obviously kept anything useful outside. Out of her reach.

Fucker.

But she wouldn't give up. Not a chance. This might be her only chance to get away from him. Who knew where he'd gone, or for how long. Somewhere in the cabin he had to have missed something and she would find it. She would.

CHAPTER TEN

The school gates stood open. The first sign something was up.

Nick parked the pickup beside the tall stone wall, out of anyone's immediate view but close enough for a quick getaway. Wind shook the trees and a dark bank of clouds sat on the horizon to the west. The storm would probably hit in the late afternoon.

He'd left Roslyn tucked up safe and sound in their bed, still ignoring him because of one closed-lip kiss. He winced and the stiff, sore flesh around his cut pounded in protest. Such a stupid kiss. If he'd dared to try pushing his tongue in she probably would have bitten it off.

Fucking ridiculous.

He needed to do some wooing. Fetching her stuff seemed the obvious answer. Or the only one he'd come up with, lying awake on the couch all damn night. For hours he'd stared at the ceiling. All of his other efforts had failed up to this point. He'd fed her and kept her warm, clothed her and enabled her to be clean and comfortable. The woman wanted for nothing. He'd listened to her and tried to get to know her. He'd chatted and joked with her, tried to charm her pants off and got no-fucking-where at all.

So like a good little errand boy he'd grabbed his pistol and his bowie knife, and headed out into the great unknown.

For her.

Not that she'd thank him.

Difficult damn woman. He missed her smiles. They'd been rare, only an occasional thing. Just enough to get him hooked on pleasing her and *bang* ... they were gone. All due to one crappy kiss. He'd done better at twelve, sneaking a smack on the lips with some girl in a cupboard at a party. Of course, the girl at the party had wanted him to kiss her. Big difference.

Bloody hell.

He'd planned to scale the wall, get in and out without anyone knowing, but the gate stood open. The only other time that had happened he'd been exchanging the van for Ros.

His back felt inexplicably cold and his hair stood on end. He'd learnt to trust his instincts a long time ago, at least when it came to danger. He'd been to Afghanistan with the army. He'd felt this feeling before. Last time it had been the moment of quiet before an I.E.D. blast tore a building in two. The building his team had been about to walk into. He'd been lucky to survive that one. Others hadn't.

Things were very fucking wrong here. He could taste it. Something fierce and bitter hung in the air.

Thank God she wasn't with him.

Nick headed for the main building, dashing from tree to tree. The old wooden front door stood open and some dead leaves had blown inside. It didn't feel like a set-up. These weren't the kind of people to lay traps. They were, however, the kind of bloody idiots to screw up and let the infected in somehow.

He should head for home. Pretend he'd never been there. It wasn't like Roslyn would ever know. But what if someone had survived?

The thought of playing hero turned his guts over. Too many times he'd seen heroes die grisly, thankless deaths. Doing the right thing rarely worked out well, but walking away ...

Fuck. Shit. Damn.

These people meant something to Roslyn and Roslyn meant something to him. He wasn't sure exactly what she meant, but ... yeah.

In he went. Not that she'd thank him.

He palmed his pistol. Every bloody hair on him had frozen up-right.

It was a big old building, riddled with corridors and classrooms. The place stood two stories high.

Roslyn had been hiding in a storage room beneath some stairs. He hadn't always watched from outside. He'd seen her tucking herself away in there when things got interesting. Like when the shithead with the glasses hassled her. Nick headed there first.

The long hallway was quiet as a tomb, shadowy and cold. He kept his footsteps soft but he still made noise. And the noise was like the clanging of a bell in the silence. A big-ass announcement to one and all that there was fresh meat in the building.

A bloody handprint graced a gray-white wall. Beneath was a swipe of dried blood. No body in sight.

A wide staircase led up to the second level, wooden steps worn down from who knew how many years in service. The door to Ros's sanctuary was closed. Further down the hallway a shoe stuck out of an open doorway. A shoe connected to a leg. Neither moved.

A chill slid down his spine.

He should have stolen another kiss. Rubbed his cold nose against her warm neck before leaving, and held her tight. Not making it home was out of the question. She needed him, whether she admitted it or not. He'd taped the key to her padlock to the back of the bedside table just in case. Eventually she'd find it, but hopefully not before he got back.

Nick opened the door to her old room. He grabbed his flashlight from his belt and flicked it on. It illuminated a nest of gym mats and a blanket. A stack of moldy old school sweaters she'd obviously used for warmth. Pile after pile of books. How she'd read in here, he did not know. There was no window. Empty steel shelving lined the walls. She must have thrown out the collection of cleaning products, but the place still reeked of bleach.

To the side of her bed was a handbag with some things strewn about nearby. The sort of girly shit you'd expect, along with another book. This one was a yellow spiral-bound notebook, well used. It appeared to be full of her handwriting. There'd be time to check it out later. He chucked everything into the black handbag and slung it over his shoulder, out of the way.

Ros didn't need anything else from this shit-tip.

He about-faced and headed back out into the hallway for a quick tour. A swift search for any survivors, then he'd be out of here.

Everything was still. Silent. Nick walked fast down the hall, checking out the body in the doorway first. Lots of blood. By the size of the corpse it had been a man, but not enough remained to tell more. His upper body had been well chewed on. Probably a day old at most, and it stank to high heaven. One arm had been torn off completely.

Damn it, he'd be seeing this mess in his head for weeks. The kids had been the worst, back when everything was first going to shit. But all of it sucked.

Bloody hell. Go.

He kept moving, trying to look everywhere at once. Ears pricked, on the alert. He heard nothing, but then ... moaning. The noise was low and noxious. Hard to tell where it came from. It seemed to bounce off the walls and echo up and down the stairwells. Nah. No way. He was out of there.

Nick turned and jogged toward the front door. He trotted past the empty science labs with their rows of desks and past her room beneath the staircase, not slowing down for anything. He'd kiss her feet and suck on her toes. Do whatever it took to get off her shit list. Anything but spend a heartbeat longer in this death trap looking for her crappy friends.

Wouldn't.

Couldn't.

And sure as fuck shouldn't.

Then he heard the scream. A high-pitched wail, coming from the floor above him. It sounded like a woman.

"No." He forced the word out through his teeth. "Fuck!"

He ran, headed straight up the stairs, hitting another seemingly endless hallway. The noise came again from his right. This time feverish bursts of screaming, again and again like a record stuck on repeat.

Three infected were battering at a door, throwing themselves full body against it. Inside the room the screamer sobbed and coughed and screamed some more. One of the infected was an older woman, its dress hanging off one shoulder, ripped open and bloody. The other two were men. One of them was the asshole Roslyn had decked the other day. Its nose sat crooked above a bloody, gaping wound of a mouth. Still wearing the steel-rimmed glasses. Its eyes were empty and its teeth snapped.

Bloody marks covered the white linoleum floor like something had been dragged. A body, reduced to no more than pulp, sat against an empty wooden rack meant for school bags, not the dead.

His body temperature dropped, despite the adrenalin. Or it felt like it did. They could only come at him one at a time in this corridor. Nothing was behind him or to either side. Nick concentrated on the three zombies ahead of him.

He readied his Glock as the first infected twigged that he was there, turned and came toward him. Stumbling steps across the bloody floor. It wore heavy work boots and overalls and looked to be an older male. Didn't matter. The thing was infected and he would put it down.

He raised the pistol nice and calm. Only four, five meters from the target. Small chance he could miss. The weapon became an extension of him. He knew how to do this.

Boom. Boom. Boom.

The pistol bucked in his hand. Three bullets punched holes in the thing's head, blowing out the back of its brains. Blood and bone fragments sprayed the two infected behind it. It dropped like the live, rotting sack of flesh and bones it was, dead for good this time. Inside the room the girl screamed louder, knocking a hole through the sound barrier. Hopefully her throat would give out soon. The nerve-rattling noise didn't help anyone.

Nick walked toward the two remaining zombies. Their faces were gnarled and warped with hunger, stained with fresh blood.

Moaning started up behind him, bouncing off the cold, gray walls. It sounded close, far too fucking close. Shit. The other end of the corridor had appeared clear, but he'd missed some.

His back was wide open and exposed. The two in front of him shambled forward, one tripping on the freshly dead body on the floor and going down. It crashed at his feet with a groan. Raw, bloody fingers clawed at his boot. He stepped aside, balanced himself and brought his foot down on the thing's head. It was an old woman, but it didn't matter. No one came back from the virus. He stomped it, smashing his boot down, once, twice, three times to crush the thing's skull. Brains spewed out across the floor amongst shards of white bone.

Behind him the moaning got louder. Another joined in. One started growling.

Eight. There had been eight left behind once he took Roslyn home. The girl screeching in the room beside him. The body downstairs, and the other corpse stinking like the bowels of hell by the bag rack to his right. The two at his feet, freshly dead. Leaving the three closing in on him.

The one Ros had punched lurched closer, navigating the bodies on the floor to get at him. It was the fucker with the steel-rimmed glasses.

Nick ignored the two coming at him down the hallway. They were still a couple of body-lengths out. Hands outstretched, reaching for him. Shit, the smell of them filled his head. Smelt like death dug up.

The girl behind all the screaming stumbled out into the hallway, face red and dripping snot. Blonde hair hung in straggly knots about her face and blood stained her dress.

Janie. Roslyn had called her Janie.

"Help me!" she begged, running toward him. He stood surrounded by infected and the idiot girl flew at him, slipping and sliding in the gore on the floor. She fell to her knees, her chin cracking on the hard floor. Blood gushed out.

Steel-rimmed Glasses turned back to the girl with a roar of pure relish. It all happened fast, one fuck-up after another. It was insane. One of the handles on Ros's handbag slid down his shoulder, restricting his movement. Hands down, it had to be his stupidest fucking idea ever to come after it. Like the woman would die without her lip balm or something. She was so getting a spanking for this, her fault or not. Her ass belonged to him.

Nick sucked in a breath through gritted teeth. Time to go home.

The gun was deafeningly loud. *Boom. Boom. Boom. Boom. Boom. Boom. Boom. Boom. Boom.*

The back of Steel-rimmed Glasses's head caved in, face exploding all over the floor. Never again would that thing bother Roslyn. Never.

Janie opened her bloodstained mouth and the sound that came out was mindless, barely human.

He aimed at the closest zombie staggering toward him. Its claw-like hand had gotten too close. No way did he want any of the infected's body fluids near him. Nick's boot landed in the thing's groin and it toppled back, almost taking its friend with it.

Boom. Boom. Boom.

Chest shots. Its insides flew apart, intestines and fuck knew what else exposed. His hand shook as he switched targets. Why? Where was the calm? This was nothing he hadn't done a hundred times since the plague had struck. He squeezed the trigger and nothing. Nada. Out of bullets.

"Fuck."

The last one had crept too close. Nick slid his knife from the sheath on his belt. Good God, its breath—hot and foul, disgustingly humid.

He held up the knife and the bright silver blade buried itself in the thing's throat, the zombie's own forward momentum doing it in. Blood bubbled up and the thing gurgled, hands groping, reaching for him, hungry still. Nick pulled the blade free and the infected fell at his feet. There was a pool of blood down there. You could almost swim in it. His pistol lay in the center of the mess. He couldn't even remember dropping it.

Janie waited on the floor, making a weird squeaking noise. His hand might have been shaking but she looked ready to fall apart, her shoulders jerking convulsively. Her face was a mess. Fuck, the sight of blood, the smell of it. It ran off the girl's split chin. They were drowning in the stuff. She stared at him as if he was every bit as scary as the zombies.

The whites of her eyes were huge.

"A-are they all dead?" she croaked.

Too tired to speak, he just nodded. He squatted and wiped his blade on the pants of the nearest dead infected. The one with its throat sliced open. Ros's handbag slid down his shoulder and he shoved its straps back up into place.

"Will you stay with me?" Janie asked. Her jittery fingers drew back the skirt of her dress, covered in dried blood. A big, messy wound covered the side of her thigh. A bite wound. Nick just stared. Nothing moved inside him. He felt hollow, all used up. This girl was dead. Living, breathing, talking, and yet already dead.

Fuck. If Roslyn had been here, if he hadn't taken her away, this could have been her. His head spun and the scene before him blurred for a moment. Not Roslyn, never her. Once he got home she wouldn't leave his sight ever again.

The girl's mouth opened and closed like a goldfish, eyes big and empty. "I ... I—ah ..."

"You're infected?" His voice sounded weird, like he'd packed his ears with cotton-wool.

Hard to tell if she nodded or the shakes moved her head for her. Poor kid.

Janie. That was her name.

Cold and empty spread through him till it swallowed him whole. "Yeah. I'll stay with you."

CHAPTER ELEVEN

Nick had left her, obviously.

Roslyn huddled deeper into the blanket, her throat scraped raw from crying. She sat in despair on the cold, hard floor beside the bed because she was a fucking idiot. Not so much him this time. Oh, no. It was all her.

She'd trashed the cabin. Stuff was spread everywhere. Her stomach rumbled, but she couldn't bring herself to eat. What would happen when she'd worked her way through the collection of canned food? And he'd left her stacks of drinking water, but eventually ...

The lone butter knife he'd left her trembled in her hand. Her breath misted before her face. She should close up the front patio doors. Get organized for the night. Use up some of the precious store of wood and kindling, break open the last box of matches. Her cheeks felt like parchment, stiff beneath the tracks of her tears.

Because she was an idiot, an idiot who would die slowly and horribly in this butt-ugly pine prison.

She choked on another sob.

Why had he given up so soon? Nick had seemed different, but in the end he'd left too.

Everything hurt, inside and out. The first few times she'd lost it she'd picked herself up and told herself not to be such a melo-dramatic cow. So she couldn't get away. So she'd tried everything short of amputating her foot. Didn't mean he'd abandoned her.

Then hours had passed. The sunlight had slid away, leaving her sitting in shadows. Her will to live was at an all-time low.

Why had he given up on her? She beat him in the head with a bottle of booze, and he came back for more. Freak out and reject one little kiss and he called it a day. It made no sense.

Fuck. Just ... fuck.

She listened for his voice, his heavy footsteps coming up the ramp. Strained to hear the rattling of the key in the lock and imagined the back door swinging open. His face would appear in the opening. Nick wasn't handsome, exactly. He had a high forehead, thin lips and a blade-straight nose. His ears were maybe a touch too big, now she came to think of it. His dark eyes were too bright, probably from thinking bad thoughts. He looked like trouble. He was tall and lean and hard as anything she'd ever come across. But he'd been soft to her in lots of ways. Being with him had become a clutter of memories in her head. She couldn't tell anymore if he'd behaved admirably towards her in the ways that mattered or not.

All she knew was that she didn't want to die and she didn't know what the hell to do about it. Even if she gnawed off her foot and got free of the chain, what then? The back door was locked. Every window had been barricaded. She could tie together some sheets and climb down the two- or three-story drop from the front veranda. Her and her one foot, because she'd had to cut off the other one to rid herself of the bloody chain. Guess she'd have to cauterize the stump, *Misery*-style. The book, not the movie.

Tears flowed freely down her face. Torrents. Rivers.

"Roslyn," a voice said. "What the fuck … where are you?"

Her vision was too blurred to see. The room appeared a mass of murky shadows.

"Ros!"

"Nick?" she hiccupped.

"Shit," he muttered and crouched before her, a big black-jeaned, black-shirted, black-clad figure of a man. The heel of his hand smoothed over her face, thumb gently wiping away her tears. "What happened?"

She just stared at him, dazed.

"Was there an infected?" he asked.

"No," she sniffed. Then she sniffled. Then she gave in and wiped her nose on the back of her hand.

With a scowl he grabbed her, hands beneath her arms, towing her out of the pile of blankets she'd bundled around herself. He dragged her onto his lap and held her close. A palm settled on one of her cheeks. His skin felt blessedly cool against her fevered face. "You feel hot."

She felt awful, truly, deeply awful. And it was all his fault.

"Aren't you going to talk to me?" he asked.

"No."

"No?"

She swallowed hard. It felt like shoving down broken glass. "No."

Nick held her tight and she sat there too tired and sore to care. There was no fight left in her. Not right now, anyway. Maybe later.

"I'm sorry I was away so long," he said.

He smelled good, as if he'd just washed. Tomorrow she'd hate him again, but right now she burrowed in and laid her cheek against his chest. Taking what comfort she could get wherever she could get it. His hand rubbed over her back and the side of his face rested against the top of her head.

"You really went through the place," he said. "I'll leave you a note next time. Okay?"

No. Jerk. She sniveled as quietly as she could.

"Come on, Ros. Talk to me. I can't stand it when you don't talk to me." His hand slipped beneath her chin and he tipped his head, studied what had to be her disaster of a face. "Please?"

Her bottom lip trembled. She hated it when that happened. She blinked furiously, fighting back the tears. Trying to win the battle. Instead she lost the war.

"You left me alone," she blubbered, breaking down for about the hundredth time. She shoved her face into his shirt. If she got snot on it so much the better—he deserved far, far worse.

Nick grunted and grabbed her flailing fist, pulled her tighter against him. "I'm sorry, sweetheart. So sorry."

His hand smoothed over her hair, stroking her. He let her cry herself out. He murmured stuff to her all the while. How sorry he was. How brave she was. How he didn't mind she'd trashed the place. He even hummed to her. Some folky-sounding song she didn't know.

"I hate you," she said eventually, because it needed saying. And she did hate him, with all her heart.

"I know." Funny, he didn't sound the least upset about it.

"I really do."

"Yes," said the patronizing, abandoning son of a bitch.

"Never hated anyone as much as I hate you." Roslyn pulled up his shirt and wiped her face clean on it. As clean as it could get without the benefit of soap and water. Nick made a noise of resignation or something and pulled the black T-shirt off over his head. He held it up to her face, covering her nose.

"Blow."

She did. Noisily. "My head hurts."

"I bet it does."

"It wasn't fair, leaving me here like this. What was it, some kind of emotional manipulation?"

"No." Lots of lines creased up his forehead. "Course not. I just needed to grab a few things in town."

"What if you hadn't come back?"

"I was always coming back," he said in no uncertain terms. His overconfident tone of voice peeved her no end.

"You might not have."

"Roslyn, trust me. I was always coming back. I *will* always come home."

"This isn't home." She sniffed again, so he selected a new piece of shirt and held it to her face. "No, I'm okay."

He sighed and set the shirt aside. She sat on his lap, snuggling against his bare skin. The man felt like a heater.

"Don't do it again." Her ear pressed against his chest where his heart thudded away. Very evenly. Strong. Maybe he wouldn't be dying anytime soon. Still, she couldn't risk it. Right now, her life depended on his.

"Ros ..."

"I mean it."

"I know you do," he said. "But I don't want to make you any promises I can't keep."

"Bullshit." She sat up, looking into his face. He was awfully close, his hand firm against her back. "You break your word to me all the time. You're always pushing for more. Trying to manipulate me ..."

His mouth opened and widened in a pained expression. "But ..."

"No. You owe me," she insisted, pressing the point. This couldn't happen again. It wouldn't.

His dark brows drew close.

"You do."

"I know," he said. He licked his lips, looked away. But his eyes darted back to her, assessing. "I hate seeing you upset."

"You left me chained to a bed thinking I was going to die here if I didn't cut off my foot. It happens, Nick."

The idiot lowered his face and set his forehead against hers. "So you've forgiven me for the kiss?"

She pulled back. "You see why I hate you? This is why."

"I'm not convinced you do. Deep down."

"Oh, I'm pretty damn sure I do."

"No. I think you just think you do. " He sighed and stared at her. "But deep down, I think you're afraid."

"Yes. I am afraid. Afraid you're going to die and leave *me* chained up to starve to death."

He rolled his eyes. "Ros, we're talking about feelings."

"Fear is a feeling."

"Other feelings."

"Like my headache because I've been crying for hours because you left me chained up and I thought I was going to die horribly?"

Nick's brows danced high. "Alright. Alright. I give in."

He gently began to remove her from his lap and place her back on the floor. Something horrible tore through her, scarily akin to panic. Her hands clutched at him in a white-knuckled grip. No fucking way could she let go.

"Where are you going?" she asked.

"Hey, easy." He covered her cold hands with his own, warm and strong. "I was just going to find you some aspirin. Somewhere in this mess. I'll be right back."

"Because you won't leave me alone again."

"Roslyn ..."

"Promise." She demanded. Pleaded. Whatever.

He set his hands on the floor and moved in close, much closer than before, going nose-to-nose with her. "Do you really hate me?"

Her poor, tired mind dithered. "It's beside the point."

"Honestly?"

"Nick, how can I feel differently when you've got me chained to the furniture?"

The man actually snarled. "Ignore the chain."

"I can't. It's around my ankle. Mine. Not yours, Nick."

"Do you hate me?"

She groaned and sighed and winced. Being cornered didn't suit her. "I don't know. Okay? I don't know." The tip of his nose brushed against hers and she half-heartedly swatted at him. "Stop it."

He sat back on his heels, his dark gaze steady on her. "I promise I won't leave you on your own again."

"This isn't like the other promises where you change your mind when it suits you, is it?"

He didn't even blink. "No."

"Really?"

"Yes."

"Oh." She sucked in a deep breath and felt good for the first time in a long time. Her lungs expanded gratefully as relief flowed through her. "Thank you."

He nodded. "I did leave a key hidden here. You would have found it eventually."

"You did?"

"Yes," he said. "You don't really hate me."

"How do you know?" she asked, genuinely curious. He sounded so sure of himself. That need to know was her one very real fault, or at least the main one. God, the trouble it had gotten her into, curiosity.

The side of his mouth slowly curled into an untrustworthy smile. He sat there on his haunches, bare-chested, just like the day before when he'd kissed her. She'd been so mad. Now she simply lacked the energy.

"Right there," he said. "That look."

"What look?"

The other side of his mouth rose until he was giving her a smile to level mountains. Or at the very least move them. Her heart did some awful fluttery thing she didn't appreciate. Probably a result of all the upset he'd caused her.

"The look you give me before you remember to be pissed at me." He leant forward and she resisted the urge to shuffle back. "You don't hate me, Roslyn. Not even a little."

"Do too."

"Nope." He shook his head. "You don't."

"That's what you think," she said, because she needed to say something and that was the best her absent brain could do.

With a wink the bastard rose to his feet. "I can't believe how you trashed the place."

"Mm," she said.

He bitched some more about the mess.

She ignored him.

Because he was wrong; she did hate him.

Mostly.

CHAPTER TWELVE

Nick wasn't usually the type to hang about in bed. Or at least, not without a damn good reason.

His good reason lay half across him, sound asleep. Roslyn was sprawled over him, her cheek on his chest. Their cuffed wrists sat on his stomach and he lay on his back, reading. The position made holding the notebook tricky, but he was determined. It seemed more of a diary than a notebook and it had been jam-packed full of Roslyn's thoughts on pretty much everything.

How she hated red wine, but loved gin. The names of the many romance books she'd read and what she thought of them, in excruciating detail. Her tiffs with her mum and worries about her job. Some concerns regarding the size of her ass and how her breasts didn't sit as high as they used to. Which wasn't right, because her tits and ass were perfect. Judging from what little he'd seen of them, of course. A closer look would help him reassure her.

Fuck, he wished. She would have to be asleep or hysterical to let him near her.

Ros snuffled on his chest. Her fingers flexed against his ribs, the short nails scraping over his skin grabbing his immediate attention. Hard not to be hard with a hot woman all over you, and this woman in particular, she felt just right. He stroked her crazy red hair, crooning nonsense to her for a moment. She seemed to like that. Her body relaxed against him, soft and sweet.

Despite the room being closed up, enough daylight peeked through here and there for him to read by. There were complaints about her father in the diary, a fair few of those. Seemed her dad had been quite the army man, moving them around, handing down orders. In truth, he sounded a bit of a jerk. No wonder she wasn't impressed with Nick's choice of career. Those days, however, were gone. But they had left him with the ability to protect and care for her. Ideally, it'd score him some points, but she wasn't that easy.

She had dated. A decent number of men's names came up in the diary, maybe even a few more than he felt comfortable with. Though if he was being a judgmental prick, he'd say she put more energy into the books she read. They certainly got more line space and fewer insults lobbed their way.

Seemed Roslyn was a very picky girl when it came down to it. Not so surprising.

Eyelashes fluttered over him, tickling him, as she stirred once more against his chest. Her mouth opened wide on a yawn, jaw cracking. The length of her body arched and went rigid as she stretched her back, the mounds of her breasts pushing into him. He'd be fucking delighted to set her straight with regard to her breasts. They were delicious and so was she. What were the odds of the sweater she was wearing magically disappearing? Probably low.

"Morning," he said.

After blinking several times, she looked up at him and scowled. She abandoned her position, rolling off him and onto her side. Her wrist tugged at the cuffs, dragging at him. He almost dropped her diary.

She gazed at him crankily, terse lines bracketing her mouth. "What ..."

Hard not to smile at her. She was so cute, all sleepy and ruffled. She frowned at his chest as if it had personally assaulted her. Like she hadn't smeared herself all over him in her sleep of her own free will. Well, maybe she'd had a little help. A warm woman could be hard to resist on a cold winter's night.

"Keep making that face and you're going to get wrinkles," he said.

Her eyes cut to his. "What did you do? Did you move me in my sleep?"

"No," he lied.

"Right." She snorted and tugged again on her end of the cuffs.

Then she saw the diary. *Her* diary. Eyes huge with horror, she grabbed for it. But he'd been expecting that. Quickly he passed it into his other hand and dangled it out over the side of the mattress, keeping it out of reach.

"What are you doing with that?" she screeched.

"Didn't I tell you? I went to pick up your stuff yesterday."

"Give it to me!" Roslyn lunged, attempting to clamber over him. He grabbed a fistful of her sweater with his cuffed hand, holding her back. Her other arm thrashed futilely about for the notebook. "Nick!"

His eardrums rang. "Noise."

"Give that to me," she hissed, hand waving. Obviously she'd given no thought at all to the way she was wriggling on top of him. His morning hard-on roared back to life. Reading her thoughts on other men had cooled him off, but this sort of stimulation he couldn't ignore.

"So, this Tim guy, he refused to go down on you?"

"Nick." His name was a short, sharp bark.

"Any heterosexual male who doesn't like eating pussy is a fucking idiot, don't you think?"

"Give it."

"I mean, honestly. What's not to like? Pussies are such fun."

"Nick." Her fingers clawed at his arms. There'd be marks later. He grinned and she growled.

"All hot and wet and juicy. And each one tastes different. And looks different."

He liked it when she growled. Maybe he liked it a little too much. His body seemed fine-tuned to her every reaction. His cock, of course, poked her in the hip and she had to notice, no matter how mad she was.

And yeah, she did notice. Her eyes narrowed, homing in on his face. As if it was his fault.

He just shrugged. "Look at yourself. You're all over me. It's confusing for my dick. We don't know what you want."

Her mouth fell open. "Are you actually talking about your dick in the first person?"

"You can give it a name if you like."

"'Inadequate'?" Her hand made a swipe for the book. "Oh, no. 'Piteous'."

"There's no need to be nasty."

"'Pathetic'," she crowed, well pleased with herself.

Such a smartass, was Roslyn.

Which was when he decided to play too.

Nick flicked his wrist and sent the diary skimming across the floor, safely out of the way. In one smooth move he flipped her off him and onto her back, straddling her in two seconds flat. Three at the most. Another second to slip a knee between her legs, and then he lay exactly where she didn't want him, not ever, according to the look on her face. Her lips parted and her eyes flashed fire, most definitely not friendly. Her hands shoved at his shoulders and her head turned from side to side, searching for an exit.

"Get off me," she said.

"I think we need to get something straight." He grabbed her wrists and drew them out of the way, nice and safe on the pillow above her head. The first press of his hard-on between her legs had her back flattening and butt shifting, desperate to get away. His hips pressed down, holding her in place.

"Stop it," she said.

"So Tim wouldn't go down on you and Brandon couldn't get you off, hmm?" He gave her a grim smile and rocked against her, rubbing against her pussy. Only the thin material of his sweatpants and the even thinner flannel of her pajama bottoms stood between them. "What did you expect, with a name like 'Brandon'?"

"Because 'Nick' is so manly."

He'd have laughed if his dick wasn't killing him. "Why do you think you never stayed with any of them for more than five minutes? What's your take on that?"

"I don't know what you're talking about. Get off me." Her hips shuffled sideward, or attempted to, but she wasn't escaping him. Next she dug in her heels and tried to push him off. All that did was open her legs up more to him. The sudden hike in her brows when she realized it was priceless. "Don't."

"Two, three dates and you lost interest."

"Or they did. Stop, damn it." Her hand flailed for the headboard but that wouldn't help her either. "Nick."

"You think they lost interest?"

"Generally that's what it means when people don't text you back or ask you out again."

"Why?"

She shut her eyes for a moment. When she opened them, she still wouldn't look at him. "I don't know. I guess I didn't know the right things to say."

"Hmm. Maybe. But none of them really did it for you, anyway." He stared at her pretty, screwed-up face, thinking it over. "Even Craig the footballer didn't turn you on, despite the hot body."

"Much like you, Nick," she sneered, all bravado. Pity he didn't believe it for a minute. He was getting to her. The nipples poking into his chest and the way her body had begun to vibrate beneath him confirmed it. "Get the fuck off me."

"That sounded like a challenge to me."

Panic filled her eyes. "No. No, it wasn't."

"Mm."

Back and forth he stroked her with the length of his hard cock. So good he could barely believe it. Molten heat poured through him. He wanted to close his eyes, savor the moment, but he didn't. Ros stared back at him in dawning horror, which seemed to be her go-to look with him. Never mind. He was determined to make her feel lots of other things. Good things, starting now.

"Those morons didn't know the first thing about pleasing you," he said. "They let you down, didn't they?"

The woman slammed her eyes shut, locking him out. It didn't matter. She couldn't shut out his voice.

"I won't disappoint you, Ros. I won't let you down."

Her breath hitched, loudly, followed fast by the clench of her jaw. His mind reeled, trying to take her in. Talk about sensory fucking overload. The feel of her soft breasts caught between them, cushioning his chest, and the tease of her hard nipples. No amount of material could hide them. She smelled so good. If she'd have let him, he'd have stripped her out of those ugly, bulky clothes and licked her from top to toe. Rubbed himself against her, skin to skin. Blood rushed to his throbbing cock, as if he wasn't hard enough. But skin to skin wasn't happening. Not yet.

Her voice tightened and her wrists tugged against his hold. "Nick." She licked her lips and her gaze roved again from side to side, looking for an out. "Wait. Listen to me."

"No. You're not talking me out of this."

Already he could have come. Heat licked up his spine and the sensation grew, deep in his gut. No. This was all about her, but the pressure and the friction were perfect. His balls inched higher and his blood surged hot. He pressed his knees into the mattress, working himself against her, watching her carefully to gauge her reaction. Neither too hard nor too gentle worked best. Could have sworn he could smell her sweet cunt, her arousal. Because she was aroused, there was no hiding it.

"You had polite sex with Craig, because you thought you should. Sounds bloody awful," he said. "I'll make you a promise here and now that we are never having polite sex. Over my dead body."

"You have to stop," she pleaded, body arching beneath him, writhing against the mattress. Because her body knew what her mind didn't want to admit. And he read her body perfectly.

God, he'd been watching her constantly for weeks now, learning her. Watching the way she touched herself, whether it was wrapping her arms around her chest or pushing back her hair. All the little expressions she made. She thought too much. Her diary confirmed it. Those other idiots she'd let touch her hadn't been able to get her in the moment. Hadn't really tried, or had lacked the patience. He wouldn't make the same mistake.

"You've been pretty stressed lately. I think you need this," he said, sounding far calmer than he felt. Her breathing sped up and he could see her pulse, beating hard in the side of her slender neck. That pulse point right there beneath the skin. Nothing could stop him from kissing her there, from pressing his lips lightly against it over and over. If anything had happened to her before he'd come along ... No, he couldn't afford to think like that. She was safe now and she'd stay safe. "I missed you yesterday. You have no idea how much."

Her teeth sunk deep into her lip.

"You can trust me with this, Roslyn. Turn off that clever mind of yours and let me get you there."

She shook her head furiously.

"Yes."

Her body bucked beneath him, still fighting. Soft curves pushed at him, struggling to get free. She was insane to think this wouldn't work between them. There was no hiding the flush working up her neck, the gasp when he nuzzled the sweet spot below her ear. He barely touched her and she lit up for him. Skin to skin, there'd be no end to what they could do.

"You feel so good. Even like this, with clothes between us," he murmured.

Elbows knocked against his arms as she fought him.

"I'm not letting go. Fight me all you want." He dragged his mouth over her jaw. With a gasp she jerked her head back, pressing it into the pillow, unintentionally presenting him with the sexiest ear in creation and more of the smooth sensitive skin of her neck beneath. He couldn't get enough of her. Having her stretched out beneath him was amazing. A heavy petting session with this woman outdid anything that he'd done before.

He made circular motions with his hips, studying her face to gauge her reaction. Fuck, she was pretty. Her jaw dropped and her knees clenched at his sides, holding onto him despite herself.

"There we go," he reassured her.

She made a small noise, a lot like a sob, and her chin wrinkled.

Shit, no. Tears was cheating. "Ros ..."

"Fine! You can turn me on." Shiny eyes stared back at him and two bright spots of color sat high on her cheeks. "You win. Happy now?"

It didn't exactly feel like a win.

He stopped dead and held still, breathing hard. His dick throbbed unhappily. "Is me making you feel good so terrible?"

She nodded tightly and stared at the front doors, forehead scrunched up. He wanted to smooth the soft skin with his fingers. Comfort her. Only one thing, however, would make her feel better.

Shit. Damn. Fuck.

Nick placed a kiss on her neck. He took a deep breath and let her go straight to his head. Who knew when she'd let him get this close again.

"Alright," he said. "I'll stop. Look at me, Roslyn."

She hesitated, but he waited. This was, after all, a waiting game. One he intended to win.

Eventually she turned back to him with a wary look. "What?"

This time, when he kissed her, he did it slowly with his eyes wide open. Carefully he angled his head and lowered his lips to hers. He stopped once they were touching. She stared back at him, not moving an inch, face frowning but not turning away. Not rejecting him. Yet. Who knew why? It didn't matter. He kissed her again and again, pressing his lips gently to hers and watching her all the while. It felt mildly religious or something. It felt important. He didn't rub his dick against her. Not even a little, despite his balls aching like bloody murder. He wasn't ruining this for anything.

She exhaled and her lips opened slightly. A tiny sigh escaped. Ideally he'd have her sighing in ecstasy, but this seemed closer to relief.

"What are you doing?" she whispered.

He kissed her again, just her bottom lip this time. Such a succulent bottom lip; he'd love to take a bite of her. The idea of biting had never occurred to him with other women, but Roslyn was special.

"I'm kissing you," he said.

"Oh." A frown flickered briefly across her face. At some stage she'd stopped scowling. Gradually her body relaxed beneath his. Hands no longer fought his hold. "I thought you were going to get off me."

"Soon," he agreed.

She gave him her curious face, her brows hunched in. "I'm not kissing you back."

"Yeah." He kissed her again. The side of her mouth, where top and bottom lip met. "I know."

"Are you trying to prove another point?"

"No." Lightly he brushed his lips over her cupid's bow. "I'm just kissing you."

"I don't trust you."

"Mm."

Restlessly her hips shifted against the bed, accidentally rubbing against him. His cock pulsed, jabbing at the top of his sweatpants, wanting out. Or, more accurately, wanting in. God help him. What a ridiculous situation. He choked back a laugh. Fact was, he could probably come just from kissing her. It would take longer. But it could be done.

"What was that?" she asked.

"I was laughing at myself."

The woman tucked her chin in, drawing back from his wandering mouth. "Why?"

"You know, I've met two-year-olds who ask fewer questions than you."

"You had kids?"

"No," he said. "I didn't have kids. Never been married, either."

She digested this information with a slow nod. No smartass comment was made.

"We could get married," he suggested with a smile.

"We are not getting married. Don't be stupid." Her scowl deepened. "Why were you laughing at yourself?"

"Well." He sighed and leant in, brushed his nose against hers. "I was thinking I could come just from kissing you. Wanna give it a go?"

"No." Her stomach rumbled loudly. "I'm hungry."

"I heard."

"Offering me your cock as a source of sustenance would be a bad idea." The top corner of her upper lip rose to expose her teeth, like he needed the hint.

"Guess it would." He grinned.

"Get off me, Nick."

"In a minute."

"Nick."

"Come on. Can't you kiss me just once?"

She swallowed and studied the ceiling above him. "No."

"Why not? One little kiss wouldn't kill you."

"Don't."

"Roslyn. Just one."

"Oh, for fuck's sake." Her face screwed up tight, eyes thunderous. "Really, we're back to this? And you say I'm immature."

She was right. It was a waste of time. Who was he kidding?

"I'm sorry," he said. "You're right."

She rolled her eyes.

"No problem," she said, voice bored. "I'm almost getting used to you sexually harassing me. Now, get off."

He shook his head and grinned some more with relish. This would be fun. "No, not for that ..."

CHAPTER THIRTEEN

"Yum," the asshole enthused, shoving another pikelet into his mouth. This one was loaded down with sugar and lemon juice, just how she liked them. Of course, he knew this because he'd been reading her diary, the abysmal shithead.

They were actually pretty good. The man could cook. But it would take a hell of a lot more than showing style with batter and toppings to make her smile.

Roslyn sat on the big lounge opposite him, concentrating on the stunning view out the front. Hectares of pristine bushland and beautiful mountains rising in the distance. An awesome view, much more calming than watching the asshole eat. Her fingers tightened around her lukewarm mug of coffee in one hand, her reading glasses in the other. Their return along with the rest of her handbag did little to abate her pissy mood.

"Ros, have some more."

"I'm fine. Thanks." She sat with her legs curled up beneath her and a hand discreetly covering the spot where her neck met her torso. Just above her collarbone.

"It's not that bad," the asshole said around a mouthful of food. His eyes lingered on her hand.

"Eat with your mouth shut, please."

The asshole grinned. With his mouth shut. That smile was pure pig—shelve him in 636.4—animal husbandry, swine. She'd tell him she hated him, but what was the point?

Nick downed the last of his coffee and licked his lips. "I've never bitten anyone before. It was kinda fun."

"I hate you."

"I wish I had a dollar for every time you've said that." He leant forward and got busy topping up another pikelet with honey. "Actually, I don't. What would be the point? Money's useless these days."

She said nothing. She had nothing to say.

"So, what do you want to do today?" he asked.

"With you? Nothing. How are they doing at the school?"

"Fine," he said.

"Did you talk to them?"

"No. Just snuck in and grabbed your stuff," he said.

"Did you see any of them, up at the school?"

"Ros, I was trying to avoid them."

"But you must have noticed if they were around. How were they going?"

"Same as usual," he said, his eyes all over the task to hand. No way could the surface area of the pikelet handle that amount of honey. What a disaster waiting to happen. "They were arguing about who ate the last tin of canned chicken or something. You need to eat more. Go on, have another."

He continued to stare at his well-laden pikelet. Honey dripped onto the side of his hand and he licked it up. Tongue lapping. Like a dog. Her belly did something odd. Because he revolted her. Not because there could be anything weirdly appealing about what he was doing with the sugary-sweet condiment coating his skin. The sure, strong swipes of his tongue were repugnant.

She shifted on the lounge, trying to get comfortable. No position worked. Her sex was still swollen and sensitive from earlier. Everything felt uncomfortable and in need of relief. Apart from a quick pee break, he didn't seem to be interested in letting her out of his sight. Bastard. Five minutes of privacy was all it would take and he knew it.

She repositioned her arms so the overly obvious points of her nipples were concealed from prying eyes. Even her breasts felt heavy, awkward. Why was he still licking his damn hand?

"You're staring," he mumbled.

"I think you missed a spot."

"I like sweet things." He winked.

"Ooh, good one."

He tipped his chin at her and the hand still sitting against her neck. "Why are you covering it up? I'm the only one here and I know all about it."

Jerk. Though he did have a point. Just the same, Roslyn rather pointedly scratched the side of her neck with her middle finger.

"Nice." He blew her a kiss over the top of his pikelet.

She crossed her arms over her chest, still aware of her boobs screaming *look at me!*, and sank down in the chair. Maybe the neck of her sweater would do some damage control, bite-wise. It looked like a Rottweiler had been at her. Nice red teeth marks imprinted in her neck, with a bruise blossoming beneath.

"I know about your perky nipples too," he said, smiling lecherously. "I thought we could read some more of your diary later."

Not likely. "Where is it?"

"Somewhere safe. I noticed you didn't write as much after the plague hit."

Gently, she massaged the tender spot on her neck, wishing she could erase it. It and him. "There wasn't much to say. Life sucked."

"There was a bit about that wanker bothering you."

She studied the view, quietly squirming inside. "That's none of your business. Do you have any concept of what a massive invasion of my privacy your reading my diary is?"

He puffed out his lips and blew hot air her way. "Yeah, I do. But if you were better at opening up and talking about yourself I wouldn't have to, would I? So really, it's all your own fault."

How badly did she want to beat him with a stick? Instead she crossed her legs and swung her foot, making the chain jiggle and sing. Because she knew it bugged him, and scowling got old after four days. Four. Long. Days.

Shit. He really would give her wrinkles.

He flicked her ankle a brief, irritated glance, thin lips flattening. "Communication is what relationships are built on."

"We don't have a relationship, Nick. We're not friends and we're sure as hell never going to be lovers. So I'd really appreciate it if you'd give me back my diary."

"Lovers?" He stuffed the last of his honey pikelet into his mouth and chewed with what would have been a contemplative expression on anyone else. On him, it was more aggravating shit-stirring then anything. "I was thinking we'd be more 'friends who fuck'. But 'lovers' does have a certain ring to it."

She bit her tongue to hold back the retort that sprang to her lips. Best not to encourage him, or contradict. He might take it as a challenge.

"I thought we could talk about your daddy issues," he announced.

God, but she hated him. "I don't have any daddy issues."

"Your diary says otherwise. Why don't I grab it, so we can read over the stuff I'm talking about?"

Her stomach roiled. Two years' worth of her most personal thoughts and feelings laid bare. All her hopes and dreams, along with the occasional rant. Well, maybe more than the occasional rant. Secret things she would have never said to another living soul. He would smash the sanctity of that outlet for shits and giggles. Every tendon in her body tightened, fingers clenching closed. "Nick, please. Don't."

"Hmm?" He busily licked his fingers clean.

"Please. Don't read my diary. Find some other way to mess with me. I can't ..."

The man sat forward in his seat, his sudden focus on her unnerving. "You can't what?"

How to say it? She felt drained. He wouldn't give her diary back. For all his little niceties, he wanted to fuck with her head as a way to get at her body. That much was obvious.

Nick stood and moved over to her side, sat down. "Talk to me."

She opened her mouth but for once the words deserted her. Her shoulders slumped dejectedly.

"Ros?" He waited, hovering.

"Nothing."

Silence reigned supreme for a moment.

He cleared his throat. "Why don't we get out of here for a while? Go for a jog?"

"A jog?" she asked, voice laced with disbelief.

"Yes. A slow one. Come on, I'll find you some sneakers. I think we could both use some fresh air."

***

Nick loped along like a dingo. By putting in a minute amount of effort he would have left her for dead, easily. Instead he jogged along beside her, looking far too fit in his cargo shorts and T-shirt. A cap sat on his head, the tops of his ears stained pink from the sun. Definitely descended from English or Irish stock. He had a long-limbed, athletic build. She was more of a robust peasant, herself.

Down the gravel driveway they went, heading toward the lonely stretch of road leading into the eco-lodge. It was nice to be outside. The scent of eucalyptus from the gums and some sweet nectar carried on the breeze. Not everything waited for spring to arrive. Warmth from the sun permeated her shirt. Sweat already dampened her back. Her cheeks felt like glowing braziers.

"I'll race you to that tree." He pointed to a big old jacaranda gracing the side of the road about twenty meters away.

"You'll win," she puffed.

"I'll give you a head start. Go." His hand drew back and then swung. Too late she realized his intention. The palm of his hand collided with her jean-clad ass in a flesh-shaking smack. Her left butt cheek howled bloody murder. "Go!"

"Ow!" She took off to elude his hand more than anything, throwing herself in the general direction of the tree. "Damn it. This is not a fair competition."

"Keep going."

She'd covered half the distance when he started after her. Attempting to run and look over her shoulder at the same time slowed her down, but keeping an eye on him had become second nature. Who knew what he'd get up to next?

A wide grin split his face, appearing alarmingly wolfish. His long legs ate up the distance with ease. Her heart raced faster than her feet could manage.

"I'm gonna catch you, Ros," he taunted, as though stating the obvious was clever. Fingers hooked into the back waistband of her jeans and tugged her to an abrupt halt. His arm snaked around her waist, steadying her before her forward momentum could put her face first in the dirt. "Got you. See that tree?"

She squirmed and pushed at his arm, out of habit more than anything else. He wasn't hurting her.

"The one we were racing to?" she asked.

"I'm a zombie and you have to climb that tree to get away from me."

"No. You're delusional, and I'm not climbing the tree."

His breath warmed the side of her neck. "If I catch you I get to bite you again. That's what infected do."

Teeth snapped beside her ear in warning and she recoiled with a grimace. "Get off me, Nick."

"Go. Climb. You said you'd be fine without me, so show me." He released her with an overly dramatic moan. "Grrr ..."

"Nick."

"Argh." He curled his top lip and snarled. "Hungry for girl flesh."

"Infected can't talk."

"I'm special. Climb."

"Oh, you're unique alright."

"Better move." His hand landed again on her rear with an almighty crack. It stung like nobody's business. Like he'd lit a fire in her bloody jeans.

"Ouch!" She rubbed at her aggrieved butt with both hands. "Stop doing that!"

"Climb. Or I'm biting."

She hated him so hard.

The tree stood a good three stories tall, a majestic old beauty. Come spring it would be ablaze with purple blooms. Today it was mostly bare. The fork of the tree's big branches sat about a meter off the ground, just high enough to be a problem. A suitable handhold branch stretched out a bit above her head. Ros wrapped her hand around it and tested. Good and solid. It should hold her weight.

"You'd be dead twice over by now," Nick said from behind her. "What's taking so long?"

"I'm getting there." She secured both hands around the trunk and raised a foot. Fitting it to the break in the branches was harder than it looked. Muscles in her legs stretched and strained. Her sneaker hovered high above the ground.

Nick sighed. "Have you even climbed a tree before?"

Probably, but damned if she could remember. The toe of her sneaker slid against the bark, seeking purchase and failing. "Crap."

"Grrrr."

"You're not helping."

He snorted. "I'm not here to help. I'm here to eat you. As unpolitely as possible."

"It's 'impolite', and shut up."

"Impolite. Sorry."

She flinched as a stream of air stirred the fine hairs on the back of her neck. "Stop it, Nick."

"Just tenderizing the meat."

She ignored him and focused solely on forcing her foot into the fork. Tendons strained and bones creaked. She could do this, yes she could. But a meter off the ground was pretty damn high when it had been so long between Pilates classes. Then ... yes, success! Her legs were not happy. Neither were her arms, as she pushed off the ground with her other foot in a bid to have it join the first. Sweaty hands slipped against the bark.

"Shit!"

Nicks grabbed her hips, stabilizing her as her foot flailed against the tree trunk. "Hang on. I've got you."

"This is stupid," she snarled, hanging from the tree like a defective ape.

"You're doing great." He laughed against her back, his chest shaking. Big hands cupped her butt, taking her weight off her poor aching arms. Hard to object to the manhandling when it was the only thing keeping her off the ground.

"I'll give you a push up," he said. "Okay?"

"No!"

"Calm down. You can do this."

"Wait." With his support she managed to wedge her other foot into the divide. Someone had lit her shoulders on fire. How did people do this shit? Why did they? Idiots.

"Ready?" he asked.

"Okay." And up she went. With his hands all over her ass, splayed out, steadying her. She wrapped her arms around one of the big branches and hung on for dear life. Rough bark scratched at her cheek. She clung on like a koala, but with less style.

Nick looked up at her from where he stood on the ground, hands on his hips and a broad grin on his face. Delighted with her again, apparently. She tried not to smile back. The corner of her mouth twitched in betrayal.

"There we go. I said you could do it. Move over," he said. "I'm coming up."

"What? Hang on."

Nick grabbed at her handhold branch with one big hand, propped the end of his foot beside her and swung himself up. That damn easy. "Hey," he said.

"Hi."

"Nice view," he said, staring into her eyes.

Unease slid through her. Their noses almost touched. He didn't have to be crowding her again. She looked at all the elsewhere over his shoulder. Anywhere but him was good. Her gray T-shirt clung to her in patches, nice and sweaty. Strands of hair stuck to the side of her face. Catching her breath took time. The idiot just kept staring. She leant back a little, but there wasn't anywhere to go and he just followed. Like it was a game, damn it.

"Stop it," she mumbled.

"Stop what?"

She probably smelled fantastically bad. He smelled like a man who'd been jogging. Clean male sweat and all that, the same as the other day when he'd been chopping wood. Her heart capered around inside her chest due to the physical exertion. Nick grabbed at another branch stretching out from the tree beside his head. The sleeve of his blue T-shirt rode up a little, stretching around his bicep.

"Wanna go higher?" he asked, looming over her.

"Um, no. This is good."

"Zombies could chew on your ankles at this height."

"Fortunately, you seem to have lost your appetite."

"Have I?" His eyes darkened perceptively, never once leaving her face. "Bet you can guess what I'm thinking right now."

"Yeah. I bet I can too." She gave a small, reluctant smile. "That one was a little too easy."

"Hmm."

The silence that followed was not comfortable.

Eventually he took a deep breath. "Right. Let's go find another tree to climb."

Shit. "Another?"

Effortlessly he jumped back down to earth, turned and held his hands up for her. "Yep. Best of three."

"And if you win?"

He smiled and eyed up her neck like it was a tenderloin he intended to baste with his tongue. "Come on."

CHAPTER FOURTEEN

"I hate you so hard."

"You know, in my head, every time you say that I substitute 'hate' for the word 'love'." Nick exhaled on a sigh and watched Roslyn limp toward the bed, chain trailing behind her. Apparently she'd pulled some muscles today. The woman was seriously out of shape. They needed to fix that. He was so used to working with other fit people it hadn't occurred to him how behind she was. What if something happened? "Lie down on your stomach and I'll rub you down."

"No."

"Yes." He rose from his seat at the table, forgetting about the last of the creamy salmon pasta he'd cooked for dinner. Not a bad effort for tinned ingredients, if he said so himself. He'd spent the time drying out from the drug and alcohol binge developing new hobbies. He'd actually found he enjoyed cooking. "Please come and lie down."

"You're only saying please to pacify me." Her forehead crinkled and she crawled onto the bed with achingly slow movements. Damn it, he shouldn't have pushed her so hard. She'd washed up and changed into comfortable clothes after they'd gotten back. Thank goodness she'd gotten it out of the way before her muscles seized up.

"Sure. If it makes you feel better." He had body oil in the bedside table. Just like he had sex toys and shit to tie her up with. Nice to know that this time the use would be for her pleasure. "Lie face down."

Roslyn gave the drawer of supplies a dirty look. "You're a pervert, by the way."

"Butt plugs have their place, darling." Nick sat on the bed beside her, unscrewed the cap on the oil then set it aside. "I can demonstrate on you if you like."

"Sod off."

"You've never played with one? Really?"

"You're a freak."

"Says the woman who can't admit to liking it when I take control."

She growled.

"Lie down," he said, placing gentle pressure on the middle of her back.

"We need to establish some ground rules."

"Sure. Pants off!" He tucked a finger either side of her black yoga pants and dragged them down her legs before she had a chance to fight him. Pale blue silk panties remained, cut to reveal a nice slice of her ass cheeks. Silk. He liked silk. Satisfaction hummed through him at the sight.

"Hey!" Her hand flailed at his thigh, landing a slap that was half-hearted at best.

"Hush. How did you think I was going to give you a rubdown? Relax."

She huffed and grumbled, but bad luck.

"Ros, if we don't work the kinks out it'll be worse tomorrow."

"It's your kinks that concern me."

He snorted. "Come on. Stop fussing."

"Fine. Just make it fast."

As if. He poured the almond oil into his hand, letting his skin warm it. "Fast is up there with polite. Bloody unlikely."

It would be nice to start with her thighs, but he knew it was best to work his way up to them. Safer. She lay still, tolerating him for now, though who knew how long her lack of resistance would last. Physical exhaustion was an old army trick for breaking down willful resistance. Get down and give me twenty, and all that. It worked just fine on Ros, too.

He smoothed his hands over one tense calf, working the line of muscle in long strokes with his fingers and thumbs. No chance of rushing; he just enjoyed the feel of her lovely soft skin beneath his hands. Tension eased out of her gradually as he made no obvious grab for her ass or anything. She relaxed against the mattress, body going lax as he worked over the bottom half of first one leg and then the other. The rounds of her ass cheeks were clear against the silk panties. He would have loved to have sunk his teeth into her there. He hadn't bitten her again, despite her epic loss to him regarding the tree climbing. Encouraging her was more important than getting his jollies.

For the time being, at least.

"Should have put a towel under me," she said, interrupting his filthy thoughts. "We're going to get the sheets dirty."

"Never mind." He wished. Dirty he could definitely do. Time to change the subject. "We'll just go for a walk tomorrow. Take it easy."

"We can go outside again?"

"Mmhmm."

His fingers slowly massaged her thighs, inching higher, but not too high. The palms of his hand slid over the sides of her legs and the sensitive area below her butt. Nice, long upward strokes to lull her into submission. That was the way to go. She almost didn't fight him when he went for the hem of her long-sleeve T-shirt. "Let's get this out of the way."

"Oh, you've done enough. Thanks."

"Roslyn, at the very least your arms need a rub. We have to get the sleeves out of the way. Don't want to get oil on them." There were already marks where his fingers were holding it, but she didn't need to know that. "Okay?"

She looked back at him, brows a straight line and face argumentative but tired. There were faint bruises under eyes and lines of tension around her mouth. Now was the time to strike.

"You've got a bra on. What's the big deal?" He gave her his most open, harmless, boyish face.

"Alright." She frowned some more but let him draw the shirt up and over her head, off her arms. Slowly, carefully, he revealed soft skin and magnificent fucking curves. Nick swallowed hard and licked his lips, kept the lust off his face in case she still watched him. Ros reminded him of a schoolmarm, one with a twelve-inch ruler ready to come down on his knuckles—or somewhere far worse.

"Relax," he said.

The notches of her spine intrigued him, the feel of that line of bumps beneath his fingers. He poured some more oil into his hands, all ready to get to work. It would be hard to reach everything from where he was.

"Hang on." Nick got to his knees and swung a leg over her, crouching above her thighs.

"What are you doing?"

"I can reach better from here." He leant over so she could see him and smiled blandly. "Relax."

Without waiting for a response he started in on her arms. The knots in her muscles were right there, sitting beneath the skin.

Ros sighed and rested her head on the mattress. "That feels good. Thanks."

"No worries."

"You're still not getting sex."

"What a surprise." He laughed.

The funny thing was ... she laughed too. A low little chuckle he'd never heard before. Her shoulders shook beneath his hands in time with the noise. What he'd give to really make her laugh, a big belly laugh that had her clutching her middle and tears leaking out of her eyes. How amazing would it be for her to be that happy and carefree, and for him to be the reason? A sort of selfish thought, but then again, sort of not.

He snorted. What about this set-up wasn't selfish?

"What?" she asked, trying to peer back at him.

His hands cupped her shoulders, just sitting there. Again, he angled himself so she could see him without killing her neck. "I don't think I've heard you laugh before."

"Oh." She gave him an awkward smile and laid her head back down.

"I like it."

She blinked several times, but made no reply.

Fair enough. He got back to massaging her shoulders, letting his fingers wander along her arms, all the way down to her hands. If she could see him stretched out above her, over her, measuring out her body with his own, she would have been very fucking uncomfortable. As it was, her breathing picked up its pace. He could smell the flowery shampoo she used in her hair, familiar enough to make him smile. Of course his dick twitched in his pants, but he ignored it. Being with Ros was a unique sort of torture. The feel of her beneath him sat front and center in his brain every minute, no escape. Best thing to do would be to think of something horrible, like the other day at the school. What would have happened if Roslyn had been there without him? Fear wiped the smile right off his face. Never, ever, ever would she be in that position. Nick rested his forehead against the back of her head for a moment, taking a second to calm himself. She was alive and fine and she'd stay that way.

"What are you doing now?" she asked in a small voice.

"Just thinking." He rubbed the pads of his fingers over her delicate knuckles, between them. "I'm glad it was you I found."

She didn't reply but he could feel the tension running through her, beneath him. Not what he'd intended. He sat back, giving her some breathing room, letting her have her space. His hands slicked over the surface of her skin, getting back to business. Back up her arms and over her shoulders, tracing out her ribs. Carefully avoiding the pale blue straps of her bra.

There was a mole to the right hand side of her spine, a third of the way down. He brushed a finger back and forth over it. "It's okay. You don't have to say anything."

"I don't know what to say." Her voice wavered, like the fact stunned her, or unnerved her.

"Tell me you hate me," he said, half joking.

He waited for the words, fully expecting them but not quite as hardened to them as he'd like to be. Those pretty lips parted and her ribcage moved beneath the palms of his hands as she took a deep breath. But then her lips sealed shut again.

"Ros?" He leant around to get a better look.

Her eyes were closed and her face relaxed. Really relaxed, more than he'd ever seen.

"It's okay," he said. "Go to sleep."

She gave an almost imperceptible nod and her breathing fell into a deep, steady rhythm and stayed that way. He'd really worn her out.

"You don't hate me. You trust me," he whispered, because it was true.

CHAPTER FIFTEEN

"I need a knife," Roslyn announced the next day.

She stood beside Nick, hands hanging by her sides and face serene, waiting calmly. Or hopefully it looked like she waited calmly. What a joke. Her insides had been a jumble all day, humming and buzzing, anxious about everything. She'd read *Gone with the Wind* for a while, paced for a while, then read while she paced for a while. Not even having her beloved spare reading glasses could help her mood. Scarlet schemed and it just pissed her off. Normally she adored that southern belle, but not today. The walls were pressing in again but there would be no walk outside as promised the night before. The constant drum of rain on the rooftop assured her of that.

"Why do you need a knife?" Nick crouched beside the fireplace, feeding it wood. He pottered along, one job after another, keeping himself busy. His industriousness peeved her, too. The dude couldn't sit still. Flickering flames cast weird shadows across his face. The hollows beneath his cheekbones made him appear positively evil.

Candles were scattered about the place. With everything shut up they'd be sitting in the dark without them. No need for socks or sweaters in the cozy, warm air. She'd been plodding around in jeans and T-shirt, feet bare. All the better for dragging them across the wooden floor, making the chain scrape and sing. Nick rewarded her with a flinch each and every time, like clockwork.

Fuck him. He deserved that and so much more.

With a flourish she brought forth the glossy red fruit. "I need a knife because I like to peel the skin off my apples."

"The skin's good for you."

She just looked at him and waited.

"Alright." He rose to his feet with a long-suffering sigh and looked down at her. Eyes boring into her like he could read her mind. He wished. He'd wisely refrained from any further recitations from her diary. Just as well; her insides were wound tight enough. From his back pocket he pulled a Swiss Army knife and extracted the shiny silver blade. "The rest are in the truck. Will this do?"

"That'll be great. Thank you."

But he didn't hand it over, just held it there. He appeared to be doing the rugged-man thing again, overdue for a shave. She'd shove him into 573.3—Prehistoric Man. A couple of days' growth lined his jaw and framed his mouth. His fringe flopped over his high forehead and he pushed it back with an impatient hand, not taking his eyes off her. "Why don't I do it for you? Don't want you to slip up and cut yourself."

"I won't. And I know how I like it done."

Dark eyes stared her down for a long moment. If he wanted to unnerve her he'd have to try harder. Familiarity had definitely kicked in. "Okay."

Without further ado she took the knife from his hands. Her fingers accidentally brushed against the palm of his hand and heat raced up her arm. She jerked back, almost dropping the knife. Best not to touch him. Safer. Distance was her friend. "Thanks."

He nodded.

Sadly, the furthest point of retreat remained the kitchen. She pulled out a chopping board in preparation for part two of the process. But first for part one. There was a ritual to this. One she'd always been rather particular about.

Nick's eyes were still on her. She could feel him attempting to mess with her mind. Trying to drive her batty seemed to be his life plan. Her shoulders rose and her spine curved, creating the illusion of privacy. He had no place in her thoughts.

Things had become weird, or weirder, since the massage last night. Or even further back to the turning her on bullshit from yesterday morning. Neither of them spoke much. Talk had become quick and to the point, efficient and minimal. But he watched her.

And while he'd always watched her, now there were subtle differences. Her traitorous body seemed over-aware of him. Nerve endings lived in a constant state of high alert. Ignoring him had become more taxing than usual. Being tuned into him sucked the life right out of her.

No more.

She about-faced and set her butt against the kitchen cabinet, began the slow and careful procedure of taking off the apple skin in one long strip. Round and round she went, sinking the sharp blade in just the right distance, her concentration absolute. She was a pro at this. It had been her trick at the school when she'd been rostered on to monitor lunch breaks. The kids loved it. Had loved it. There was something almost Zen about it.

She did her best to ignore him when he joined her, his stare set on her practised hands.

Not so fucking relaxing. Because she couldn't have a minute's peace, could she?

Sure enough, the atrocious testosterone-laden scent of him clogged up her nose. Damn it. He stood far closer than necessary, but she could block it out. Hold her breath so his smell couldn't reach her and concentrate on the task.

But he radiated heat. The back of her hand warmed, the one carefully wielding the knife while her left tended to the apple. Round and round she turned the fruit, keeping the depth and width as consistent as possible. It was so much damn harder to do with him scrutinizing and distracting that she went much slower than normal. She could feel her face scrunching up in concentration. The tip of her tongue sat firmly between her teeth.

Good, this was good. Already, she felt more like she had herself back under control.

A nice slow exhale followed by a robust inhale, that's the way. She hunched over further, focusing, trying to block him out. No problem. She'd done this a thousand times, a million. He meant nothing to her. He was a nonentity. Then he shifted slightly. He moved his weight from one foot to the other.

Her hand slipped, slicing through the apple's skin, and the length of red peel tumbled to the floor.

"Fuck, no." Inconceivable. That hadn't happened in years.

"Never mind," he said, like it was nothing. Like what he did to her life was nothing. What he did to her.

She lifted her head and glared at him. "You did that."

His eyes widened. "Roslyn. I didn't touch you."

"You didn't need to."

"What are you on about?"

"You were lurking," she said, voice rising with every word. She enforced her point with the tip of the knife, waving it directly below his nose. Anger didn't begin to cover it. Fury coursed through her, making her tremble and shake. "You're always lurking."

Nick leant back, gaze glued to the blade. "Calm down."

"Calm down? I can't even get away from you for a minute and you're back again, hovering over my shoulder. Stalking me. Sticking your nose into everything I do. You're fucking insane! You're keeping me hostage! Who does that? Huh? What kind of fucked-up individual pulls this sort of shit?"

Her livid words bounced around the cabin, echoing off the walls. The air hummed with them like static electricity. She could see the exact moment he snapped, when her abuse released the demon in him. Someone had flicked a switch.

"So put us both out of our misery," he roared. His face morphed from calm to enraged, lips drawn back in a snarl. He snatched up her hand, gripping it tight, and pressed the shiny blade to his own throat. "Go on."

"Nick!" If he frightened her before, he scared the hell out of her now. Strong fingers clenched her hand, making her bruise sting. The apple fell, forgotten, as she tugged on her wrist, fighting him for possession of the blade. "Stop it."

"Do it."

"No!"

"You know you want to." His eyes were lit with anger or desperation or who the fuck knew what. They terrified her. "The key to your padlock's in my back pocket. Now's your chance, sweet."

"Let me go."

"That's what I'm trying to do, Ros. You gonna co-operate?"

"I mean let go of my hand." She pulled, but he pushed back. His skin compressed into a single tortured point then gave. The tip of the knife punctured his neck. It was a pin-prick, nothing more. But blood bloomed bright and horror tightened her throat. "Nick."

He bared his teeth at her in a wide, manic grin. "It's not so hard, killing people. You can do it. God knows I deserve it, keeping you locked up like this. I'm an animal. You're right."

It felt like fire speared up her arm, her muscles straining furiously. He was too strong. But if he did this ...

"No regrets. Nice and fast, Ros. Come on." His fingers tightened around her hand. Panic scattered her wits and her heart beat so hard it hurt. Her pulse roared in her ears. *No, no, no.*

"Don't you dare," she cried, her eyes hot. Her vision swam. She blinked back tears, desperately trying to see him. "Don't you fucking dare, Nick!"

The man stopped and stared, eyes fierce and mouth tight. Incredulous—that's how he looked, as if he'd woken startled from sleep. "Me?" The back of his hand stroked softly across her cheek. "How about you? Crying is cheating."

"I'm not crying," she yelled in his face.

"You're about to."

"Yeah, well, you're hurting my hand," she said, the first thing to come to mind. His grip was bruisingly tight, but who cared? Compared to him threatening to slit his own neck with the knife, it didn't really factor. It might distract him, though.

"Sorry." He frowned. One by one he peeled back his fingers. Her skin was striped pink from his grip. "Didn't mean to hurt you," he said.

"And you think I want to hurt you?"

"Why wouldn't you? Stop that," he tsked and put his hands to her face. Gently the pads of his thumbs brushed over her cheeks. "Do you forgive me?"

Did she? Something big and ugly and tangled sat within her, dying to get out. Something rib-bustingly, heart-burstingly horrible, and it was all his fault. Her insides hurt. He made it impossible to breathe. She couldn't stand it any longer.

"You're crazy." Roslyn dropped the knife and pushed aside his hands. "How could you do that to me?"

Big hands enclosed her shoulders and drew her in. Violently she shrugged him off and shoved at him. Her palms slapped against his chest so hard they stung. The man actually stumbled back a step, proof of his own obviously addled state. "The chain or the knife?"

"Both."

"Look at me," he said quietly. "Please?"

She didn't want to, but she did. The pull he had on her was horrible. "What?"

"Hey." He gave her a contrite look, forehead furrowed and eyes full of woe. A spot of blood slid down his neck from the small cut. "I'm sorry I hurt your hand."

She jerked a shoulder, as close to a shrug as she could manage. Every part of her ached.

"Is it alright?" he asked.

"It's fine," she said. "I just said that so you'd cut the crap with the knife."

"Did you?" The side of his mouth kicked up into a smile and small lines wrinkled beside his eyes. "Huh."

"You're an idiot, but I don't want to kill you."

"No?" His voice sounded deep and hoarse. It rumbled right through her. "What do you want to do with me?"

She threw her hands wide in exasperation and he grabbed at them. With a growl she stepped back, wrapped her arms tight around herself. "No. I don't know."

"But you don't hate me."

After everything he'd done to her, she ought to. It was inexcusable that she didn't hate him with an unholy passion. But she didn't. Not even a little, just like he'd said.

Shit.

Guilt smothered her. Her eyelids squeezed tight. She shook her head, scowling so hard she could feel a headache coming on. Pain crept up the side of her face and fuzzed up her mind. How perfect, feeling bad for not despising someone. How ridiculous. She'd always tried to be a good person, tried to do the right thing. Falling into a big black hole of negativity never helped anyone, only he drove her insane.

He made to touch her and she shifted back as far as she could, which wasn't far enough.

"Nick, stop it. You're giving me a headache."

His hands grabbed for her again. No way did she want him touching her, but he easily evaded her swats. Fingers curved over her hips and attempted to pull her in, managing to drag her one reluctant step forward.

"Say it," he demanded.

"Stop." She opened her eyes and hit out at him. Her bruised knuckles stung and her arms sagged weakly. "Let me go."

"No." Nick leant back, trying to evade her half-assed punches. Then he apparently gave up and got closer instead. He hid his face in her hair and wrapped his arms around her. His breath tickled her neck. She flailed and fussed but he was strong. Strong enough to keep her exactly where he wanted her, as he had shown time and again. His hard arms held her tight, no matter how she squirmed. The prod of his hard cock was blazingly obvious against her belly, pissing her off even worse.

Anger kept the adrenalin pumping. Her whole body felt alive with it, shaky, edgy and wired. Not even remotely under control. She could have spit and raged and cussed him a treat. Then come back for more.

Like with Neil back at the school, she wanted to do this man harm. He'd hurt her. He continued to hurt her. So she should hurt him back. Shouldn't she?

Nothing seemed clear anymore. She liked knowing her place in the world. How she fit. And she didn't fit with him, no matter what other parts of her tried to say otherwise. Those thoughts were illusory and artificial. She wouldn't listen to them.

Nick was totally wrong for her in every goddamn way.

"It's okay," he said with his mouth pressed against her ear. "It's okay, Roslyn. I'm here."

"I know," she cried. Everything in her world was so fucked up and wrong she didn't know where to start. She could have drowned in the self-pity. At least it would have brought it all to an end. "I know you're here. That's the problem."

She could feel him laughing before she heard him, the motion of his chest bumping lightly against hers.

The fucker.

She'd kill him. She'd pick the knife back up and this time she'd …

CHAPTER SIXTEEN

Nick thought he might be losing it. A brain cell at a time she'd done him in, broken him down. Maybe he should just pick up the knife and hand it back to her. She sure as hell wouldn't fight him over it a second time. The situation being so fucked, what else could he do but laugh? What a mess. Hysteria may have helped him along. He didn't feel much in control of himself just then. No one had ever gotten to him like Roslyn did.

Soft hands still pushed at this chest, trying to win free. All the squirming didn't help things. It felt far too fucking good. He needed to apologize properly. Talk some sense to her and cool the situation off. He'd had no business scaring her that way.

"Roslyn," he said, trying to calm down the idiotic chuckling. Not good. She'd gotten worked up enough for both of them.

No reaction from her apart from a muffled snarl against his shirt.

"Ros. Stop it."

Nope. Nothing. This needed to end.

He cupped her face in one hand and made her look at him. Jerkily, she tried to turn away and he fisted her hair at the back of her head, held her still that way.

Aw, shit. Her eyes were glossy with unshed tears and her expression tight and tense and awful. Pissed off at him like nothing he'd seen. Never had he made a woman so mad. Her mouth trembled, same as when she thought he'd abandoned her. When she'd thought she would die.

Nick bit back a sigh as true regret slid beneath his skin. He'd done this to her, again. Only he could fix it. Nothing he could say would do, so instead he used his mouth for kissing her. Silently, he apologized. From the tip of her ear to the side of her face, the smooth line of her jaw and the jut of her chin. He must have caught her by surprise because the fists drumming against her chest slowed, lost their steady rhythm.

Roslyn deserved to be kissed, all over and all the time. He didn't deserve to be the one doing it, but screw it.

"I'm sorry," he said.

A frown puckered her brow and she tried to twist away again. His hand tightened in her hair and his mouth followed her. He kissed the edge of her lips, so sweet. There'd never been anything like it. She stuttered out a breath and made a tiny noise. It sounded a bit like a distressed hiccup. If only he knew what it meant.

"I'm so fucking sorry," he said.

Nick canted his head and brushed his lips against hers. She stood rigid against him. The fingers tightened in his shirt, nails digging into him through the material. Mysteriously, she didn't try to stop him.

Impossible to say exactly when she stopped fighting and let him kiss her. When she arched her neck and raised her mouth to him, allowing him closer. Somehow suffering his attentions turned into kissing him back. Instead of denying him, her lips actually sought him out.

Oh, man, bloody amazing. He couldn't believe it for a moment, but her mouth moved beneath his and it felt fucking perfect. Roslyn kissed him.

He moaned because his tongue was in her mouth and her mouth was heaven. A hot, wet, delicious, hungry heaven he couldn't get enough of. The taste of her hit him harder than her hands ever could. Floored him first go. If he hadn't had her to hang onto he'd have been flat on his back.

Her kisses were hard and angry. She pushed back against him, fighting for control. Sharp teeth nipped at his bottom lip and his eyes shot open at the sting of pain. When had he closed them? He'd meant to watch her. He'd gotten so wrapped up in kissing her he'd lost touch with everything else. His bottom lip throbbed almost as hard as his cock.

The woman had bitten him good. But then, she rarely did things halfway. He had a scar on his forehead to prove it.

Ros stood gulping in air, stunned. Her mouth hung open and her eyes were wide. Of course, he wasn't faring any better. They just stood there staring at each other, panting. The sound of their heavy breathing filled the place. It easily drowned out the noise of the rain drumming on the roof.

She'd actually kissed him back. The fact bounced round and round inside his head. God, her lips looked tasty. Swollen and pink and waiting right there for him.

Fuck it. He covered her velvet-soft mouth with his own and kissed her some more. Lost himself in her, never wanting it to end.

Her elbows bumped him as she wound her arms around his neck. The woman clung to him. Left no doubt in his mind she wanted him every bit as much as he wanted her. That she accepted him, thank God. The burning in him made it hard to think, though. The lack of blood to his brain as his dick tried to push a path straight through his jeans to her.

Action stations. He had to have her, right now.

His hands stroked over her back and kneaded her ass cheeks. She in turn rubbed herself against him in the best way, stirring him up even further. Acting like she couldn't get close enough. It was time for her to lose the jeans. His fingers dealt with the button and tore down the zip. Not breaking the kiss for a fucking moment. Mouths remained pressed tight together. He pushed the jeans over her hips, taking her panties along with them. Hurry, hurry, hurry. Down her thighs and past her knees.

Smooth, warm skin met his hands. The odd goosebump, too, but he got that. Their mouths finally separated as he ducked to go lower and her eyelids fluttered open. Her pupils were huge.

"Quick," she said and he nodded, understanding completely.

Her hands gripped his shoulders. He stripped her jeans down her legs and off her one free foot. Good enough. No more waiting.

"Nick," she whispered.

"I know." He stood and undid his jeans, shoved them down past his cock. "Come on."

She stepped into him and he took her hands, wound them back around his neck before she could go for his dick. Later she could play to her heart's content, but right now he had plans.

Actually, just the one.

He slipped his hand between her legs while kissing her once more, because the thought of not having her mouth on him was out of the question. She widened her stance and let him feel her. Soft, wet and fantastically hot flesh met his fingers. Bloody hell.

He cupped her pussy with his hand and she writhed against his fingers. Sexiest fucking thing ever.

Without a doubt she was ready for him. Her hot, wet cunt and the way she tugged on his neck like she wanted him to pick her up. And she could have anything she wanted. He would live and die to make her happy. Do absolutely anything.

"Now," she groaned.

Nick put his hands beneath the curve of her ass and lifted. Roslyn's legs went around his waist. He turned so he could set her back against the smooth wooden pantry door. The feel of his hard cock sliding against her pussy had him seeing stars and discovering God or something. She felt divine.

Her breath hit his ear in warm little puffs and her arms wrapped tighter around him. Cut off his airflow a little, but who cared. He lifted her high enough to guide the head of his cock to her and she took him. Sank down on him slowly, engulfing him in the tight clasp of her body.

A long, breathy moan left her and his legs shook.

Yes. Fuck yes.

He withdrew and thrust back into her. And again. And then they were off, with the hard and fast drive of his body into hers and the sound of flesh slapping. He couldn't seem to slow, to go easy, when he knew he should. Knew without a doubt he should, but his hands were filled with her gorgeous rear and her body trembled against him. He fucked her like a man possessed and she took it. Spurred him on by panting and moaning in his ear. Sweat slicked their skin and the scent of sex hung heavy in the air.

Nothing had ever felt this right. This necessary.

Fast, hard and perfect, with the cupboard door knocking out a protest every time he thrust into her and the chain jangling.

Her heels dug into his ass and her fingernails sunk into his skin. She said his name like it was a curse. He loved it. Her head lolled back against the cupboard door. She was close. She was whimpering and he couldn't hold out much longer the way his balls were climbing up into his body. He shifted the angle slightly. Enough to ensure he was raking over her clit on each withdrawal. A strangled noise filled his ear and her pussy clamped down on him. *There we go.* No chance of holding out. No control, but then there never had been.

Not with her. Not possible.

He came and came. Fingers clutching at her, half scared he'd drop her or something. He growled through gritted teeth and clung onto her like she was the only thing left.

Like she was everything.

CHAPTER SEVENTEEN

Roslyn lay wide awake, staring into space and watching the flickering light of the candles on the wall.

She'd had sex with Nick.

Rough, raw, animal sex.

It had shaken her tiny world apart, blown it to smithereens.

Thank God she was still on birth control. Neither of them had stopped to think of donning a condom. She was never so careless. Never. But then, she'd never had sex like that. Mind-blowing sex. Fucking.

No excuse.

She'd come so hard. Her body still hummed, satiated and pumped full of happy hormones. They weren't doing their job, though, not even a little. She was miserable. Her chest felt hot and hard, her eyes itchy, ready to explode into tears at a moment's notice.

How could she?

She'd had sex with Nick and there was no excuse. There were no gray areas. You didn't fuck the man who kept you captive. What kind of woman did that? Fell for her abductor. No, damn it, it was so wrong she couldn't comprehend it. It filled her with disgust and covered her in self-loathing.

Sure as hell, it couldn't happen again.

He was asleep against her back with an arm thrown over her waist. For a long time he'd toyed with her fingers, stroked her arm. Neither of them had said a word. Complete silence, apart from the occasional pop and sizzle of the wood in the pot-belly stove. Even the rain had stopped a while back.

It was mid-afternoon. Hard to tell exactly with the cabin all closed up. The scent of him seemed to be reaching out to her, trying to tantalize or comfort or something. The want to close her eyes and breathe him in deep horrified her. She hated herself for how she wanted him. For giving in to him. He'd never let her go now. She'd never be free to make her own choices ever again and it was all her own weak-willed fault. Somehow, he'd disarmed her, which meant her armor was made of flimsy stuff indeed.

She shifted and the chain clinked, reminding her of its presence. He'd said the key was in his back pocket. His jeans were on the kitchen floor. He'd stripped off fully after sex and undressed her as much as possible without taking off the chain. If only he'd taken it off her. Maybe then she'd have felt differently.

She sucked in a deep breath and held it as her mind reeled. The key. She could escape. She had to. To stay locked up like this was out of the question. She had to get out.

And if he woke she'd say she was going to the toilet or something.

Yeah. Great. All set. Bloody hell.

She could do this. First she eased a little way across the mattress and rolled gradually onto her back. No rush. Nice and easy. Now she could see him. Eyes closed, and his breathing deep and even. Some strange frisson went through her at the sight of him: fine, firm lips and straight nose, the hollows in his cheeks. It hurt to look at him. This situation wasn't tenable. Nobody could live like this.

He looked different fast asleep. Unguarded. She'd never seen him like this before. Her anger evaporated. It had fortified her for so long that its absence left a gaping hole. He looked so alone in the bed without her. The sight of him hurt her heart. People always talked about sex making them feel closer to someone. In all honesty, she'd never felt that before today. The connection had never seemed especially profound, not until Nick. How fucking unfair.

But she couldn't stay.

Roslyn shut her eyes and gathered her reserves. Slowly she extricated herself. Every rustle of the sheets and clank of the chain seemed magnified tenfold. He didn't stir. First one foot touched the ground, then the second. Her body slid out from beneath his hand and she sat up, then stood.

Her knickers and jeans were caught on the chain. She pulled them back over her foot and up her leg. Inserted her other leg and drew them over her hips. Between her thighs was wet and swollen. Sore from what they'd done and how hard they'd done it. It had to have been eight or nine months since anyone had touched her there, and he wasn't small. There'd been few preliminaries—not that she'd wanted any. She'd been insane with need for him. She'd been insane, full stop.

Now wasn't the time to think about it.

She crept toward the kitchen. If he woke she was getting a bottle of water, nothing more. The chain sounded so damn loud. Her fingers curled into fists. The metal links clattered and crashed but he slept on. It would be okay. She'd steal the Golden Goose and get gone.

His jeans lay forgotten on the floor. She slipped her hand into one of the back pockets. Nothing. Had he been lying? But the other pocket ... yes, success. Cool metal met her fingers. Excitement beat through her. This was it.

Please don't wake up.

The key slid into the lock and it *snicked* open. She slid the links of chain free and set them down quietly. Almost didn't recognize her ankle without its restraint. There were a couple of red marks on her skin and a small gray bruise above her heel.

Roslyn scrambled into her T-shirt then rose slowly to her feet. Her bra was AWOL and she would have to go barefoot. She didn't dare open the cupboard to search for shoes. But she tucked his Swiss Army Knife into her pocket, just in case.

Fast asleep, Nick looked almost sweet and innocent. Candlelight softened his features. The blankets were bunched up at his waist, leaving his top half exposed. Such a beautiful body; it was awe-inspiring. And she didn't know if she loved him or hated him, but she knew she had to go. The ache inside her expanded and pushed at her ribs. So much pressure that she might implode. This whole situation was so wrong it warped her little mind.

Out the door she slipped. Out onto the landing and down the wooden walkway. She laid down the plank to bridge the gap and cautiously darted across. There was a noise behind her. Maybe the wind in the trees. Maybe Nick rising and looking for her.

She ran.

Gravel cut into her feet. Everything was wet from the rain, the scent of damp earth strong. She threw open the pickup's door. No keys. Where were the fucking keys? Not above the sun visor. She climbed in and reached for the glovebox. Maps and rubbish spilled out onto the floor, but no keys.

She'd run out of time. Her heartbeat was drumming in her ears, deafeningly loud.

The sun was lower than she'd anticipated. The cabin door remained closed ... but for how long?

Roslyn jumped out of the pickup and headed for the highway on foot. There'd be something. A car she could start or another house she could hide in for the night. She'd return to the school tomorrow and make them see sense, work something out.

Her thin T-shirt was useless against the ice-cold wind blowing through her. She jogged past the other cabins. Stones kept cutting into her feet, but she'd manage. There'd be no stopping now. Yes, she'd head back to the school. Neil wasn't selling her twice. She'd beat the wanker with a wine bottle if she had to. Bash some sense into him. Her days of playing victim were over.

The muscles in her legs burned. Nick would follow, but she'd deal with that later. She wasn't going back to the chain without a fight.

It was better when she hit the highway. The asphalt was kinder to the soles of her feet. There wasn't anything visible in either direction except trees. Lots and lots of trees with the evening's shadows growing beneath. Town was to the left.

Back up the driveway there were no signs of life. He wasn't coming. Probably wasn't even awake yet, because when he woke—shit. He'd be furious.

Except a part of her strongly disagreed. Nick wouldn't be stomping and yelling because he'd be too scared for her. He'd be beside himself. No matter the time of day, he'd follow her. She knew it. He would come after her to find her and protect her. No matter the danger to himself he would follow her out into the night.

A chill spilled through her.

Nick.

She stood by the roadside, frozen in place. Terrified at what might happen next. Disaster waited around every corner and one wrong step could cost lives. Her life, and maybe Nick's life too.

What if she did go back to the school? Because if she was brutally honest she had to admit that she'd be sitting there waiting for him. Waiting for them to sort this out and come to some sort of agreement where she wouldn't be torn in two.

Shit.

She needed to talk to him. They needed to sit down and work this out. What she was doing standing by the roadside as dusk closed in? She didn't even know anymore. Running away wasn't the answer. As her father had said more than once, cowards and pussies left things unresolved. Go Dad. Double shit. She had to talk to Nick.

"Fuck it."

Roslyn about-faced and headed back up the drive, swearing constantly. Badmouthing him and herself and the whole fucked up world. Not to forget this bitch of a situation. Of all the times to have unresolved feelings for a guy. How fucking old was she? Fifteen? God the drama, it sucked. The first star winked into existence on the horizon. It peeked out from behind the limbs of swaying gum trees, taunting her. The storm clouds were moving north. Her lips felt chapped from the cold, or maybe that had more to do with beard rash. Her poor pained feet were frozen.

The first moan came from a green tin shed, tucked back from the driveway. A second answered it from a nearby cabin. The door stood open. Something was inside there—an infected.

What the fuck had she done?

She pushed herself faster and something dug into her foot. A piercing pain shot up her leg. Hopping in place, she tried to keep her balance. A shard of rock had punctured the sole of her foot. Blood dripped from between her toes. With a tug and a wince she pulled it out. Damn, it hurt.

The next moan sounded closer. It came from a straggle of bushes beside the drive. The driveway hadn't seemed this far when she'd been running away. Like an optical illusion, the distance seemed to have lengthened and warped. She ignored the pain in her foot and pressed onward. Movement from the darkened doorway of the first cabin caught her eye. A monster shuffled out into the early night. Its white sundress had been stained in patches. Dirty, crusty scratches covered its arms and legs. Sickly, bloodshot eyes took up half its face above a gaping mouth.

Roslyn's stomach felt weighted, heavy with dread.

Another groaned behind her. A thick and heavy man. Or it once had been. Its bald head shone in the low light and its bloody mouth hung open, blackened tongue wiggling.

Roslyn sprinted, toes slick with blood and sore muscles straining. Climbing trees and aggressively fucking within a twenty-four hour period wasn't good for her. Not when she wasn't used to it.

Another infected stepped in front of her. It stumbled out from beside a parked car, a fancy new sedan. They were cutting her off. Closing in on her.

The knife—she still had the Swiss Army knife in her back pocket. Her hands trembled, slipping over the metal. It slid from her hands, useless anyway. Who was she kidding? She needed something that packed a punch. There weren't a hell of a lot of choices.

In the garden bed to her right a steel picket was tied to the remains of a long-dead plant. Perfect.

She limped over and grabbed the rusted metal with damp hands, wrestling with it. The dirt had softened from the rain; it had to give. The stupid thing was her only chance. She could hear them coming, the constant moaning and wheezy, overexcited breathing. Her arms strained, tugging at the rusted length of metal. Shoulders ached from the stupid fucking tree climbing. But there wasn't any giving up. They weren't getting her. She threw her weight against it, once, twice, and it gave, wobbling in its widened hole.

Yes.

She pulled it free and swung wild, spinning around and gunning for whatever was nearest. And screaming at the top of her lungs while she did it. "NICK!"

Thunk.

The long piece of metal knocked the bitch in the white dress down. Caught it at head height and sent it reeling. The infected stumbled back and lost its balance, landing on its back. Its ear seemed to be hanging off and there was sort of gunk on the end of Roslyn's weapon. Flesh and skin and whatever.

"Nick!"

Next came the big fat guy with the combover gone wrong. It snarled and spit dangled off its chin. This one probably wouldn't fall as easily as the white-dress bitch. And that one was stirring, slowly trying to climb back up onto its feet. Its head remained at a funny angle, like it was nursed by her shoulder. Like her neck had been snapped. Why wasn't it dead if it was that badly damaged?

"Nick!" she screamed again for the fun of it. Her throat felt stripped raw. "Nick!"

Nothing. No sign of him. Oh man, she was going to die, messily and alone. What the hell had she been thinking, coming out so late in the day?

The third one encroached, sneaking up on her side. More were emerging, coming out of the woods to join in the fun. Dark figures stumbled out of the shadows. In front of her the big bastard's teeth chomped.

Snap. Snap. Snap.

She needed Nick.

A sweater hung in tatters from its chubby arms. Its filthy claw-like hands were outstretched and grasping for her. The tips of its fingers were just centimeters away.

She'd been on the girls' softball team one lone semester, aged fourteen. Sports had never been her thing. But she'd stayed just long enough to pick up the basics. Steady your feet. Draw back. Eye on the target. Line it up. Put your all into it and step into the swing.

It turned its head at the last moment, catching the length of metal in its mouth. The sound of teeth shattering and its jawbone breaking ... she'd never heard anything like it. Gray eyes rolled back into its head and it dropped at her feet.

Roslyn skipped back a few steps, straight into a prickly bush. The big bastard was down for the moment, but the white-dress woman reached for her. Three more infected gathered close.

She swung again with the steel picket, catching the bitch in the shoulder and sending it sprawling over the bastard at her feet. But Roslyn's hands were too sweaty. The metal bar flew out of her grasp and landed on the driveway a couple of meters away. Past the big bastard, who was slowly coming to. Beyond the bitch in the dirty white dress. Prickly bushes at her back and infected at her front.

A gathering crowd of mindless killing machines staggered toward her. Five now, she could see five. One was a child still clutching a toy truck.

Oh, God.

The bitch clutched at her bare foot and Roslyn shook it off. She was out of time.

"Oh, I'm so fucked," she sobbed, took a deep breath and hollered his name one more time. Really put everything into it. "NICK!"

Then she fell to her knees and scrabbled beneath the bushes. Bare branches caught at her clothes and sticks and pebbles scored her hands. Tore at her skin and stung like shit. And tears of fear and pain fell from her face in a constant stream, which didn't help at all.

Growling came from close behind. So fucking close that it sounded almost on top of her. Something grabbed at her ankle and she kicked back, trying to dislodge it.

Boom. A gunshot. Could only be a gunshot. The noise echoed down the valley. *Boom.*

"Roslyn!" Nick yelled. "Where are you?"

Boom.

"In here!" she yelled back.

Boom.

The infected tugged on the leg of her jeans, trying to drag her back. It was surprisingly strong and very determined. One bite to one of her bare feet and she was dead. She kicked back and it pulled again at the same time. Her balance went to shit and she landed on her belly, winded, coughing and choking. Fingers dug into her legs through the denim and a long hungry growl crept over her. She'd have screamed, but her lungs had shrunk, making it hard to breathe.

"Ros."

Oh, his voice. He'd come for her.

Suddenly the bitch grabbing at her vanished. *Boom.*

Nick carefully pulled Roslyn back, extricating her from the tangle of bushes. His face was set and his rifle hung from one shoulder. Hurriedly, he looked her over, checking her for injuries.

"I'm okay," she said.

With a nod he took her hand, holding on tight. Her grip was tighter. The scrapes from crawling through the garden stung in protest, but no way would she ease up. She clung onto him, wiping away tears with the back of her free hand.

"Come on, there's more coming," he said.

Together they jogged back up the drive toward the cabin. She limped, mostly, due to her foot. Moaning came from behind them and the buildings to their left. A couple of sheds and what must have once been the office and caretaker's house. Where the hell had they all come from? She hadn't seen a single one when they'd gone jogging. All the noise from the gun and her yelling must have drawn them out of hiding.

Ahead, the cabin came into view, light flickering within. Much more light then there should have been.

"No. No!" Nick dropped her hand and shot forward.

From within the cabin an infected shambled out, backlit by the fire raging within. The zombie must have gotten in across the boards and knocked over the candles. Its clothes were alight.

Nick stood ahead of her, fists clenching and unclenching in the dwindling light. The set of his shoulders made it clear he was furious. Absolutely livid. He tore the rifle off his shoulder and aimed. *Boom.* The infected toppled onto the walkway, gone for good.

The wooden cabin was ablaze with light, well beyond hope of saving. She had to shield her eyes from the heat and the light. Nick gave her one quick, filthy look, nostrils flaring angrily.

No. Not her fault. There had been extenuating circumstances.

"Get in the truck," he said. He didn't look back at her.

Nick strode to the driver's side door, wrenched it open and threw himself in. She hobbled to the passenger side and climbed in as he gunned the engine, revving the life out of it. Tension lined his face, clearly visible thanks to the fire blazing in front of them.

She felt that she should say something, but she couldn't think of a single word.

"Put your seatbelt on," he said.

She did so.

He threw the car into reverse and she jolted forward against the restraint. They tore out of there.

CHAPTER EIGHTEEN

Nick had been hoping Roslyn would keep quiet. All night would be nice.

She'd been silent on the half-hour drive, had made only the barest of comments as he broke into a large shed suitable for holing up in. An uncomfortable night lay ahead, but they were shit out of luck when it came to options. He needed to get her somewhere safe and dark had settled in. Staying on the road would only get more dangerous. More infected would be coming out and the noise of the engine and the lights attracted them. The roads were covered with all sorts of debris. One blown tyre and it would be all over. They'd be sitting ducks.

He drove the pickup into the shed and left the parking lights on. Got out and locked up the big double bay doors. The inside of the place was cluttered with crap but secure. He'd given it a going through while she waited in the vehicle holding her tongue. But there were lots of sidelong glances. She was working her way up to saying something. He could feel it. Goddamn, he wished she wouldn't.

Everything in him felt wound tight, making him keep his mouth shut solely because his fear of losing his temper was huge. Their home was gone. Just ... fucking gone. Their security and almost all of their supplies were up in smoke. The big metal box on the back of the truck had some weapons and a basic first-aid kit, but nothing fancy. He thought he'd thought of everything. What a joke. One fucking candle knocked over and the place was tinder. Hadn't thought of that, had he?

"We could go back to the school," she said, disturbing his peace.

"No." Not even remotely an option, but she didn't know that. Hell, it had probably been where she'd been headed.

An old single mattress sat in the corner. He dragged it out and dusted it off a bit. It would do. He carried it over to the back of the pickup and slid it onto the bed. Better than her being on the floor. There were probably mice and cockroaches scuttling about. Now for a blanket or something to keep her warm.

Shit. They literally had nothing but a selection of guns, a few knives and some ammunition. Plus the good old basic first-aid box. She wasn't wearing shoes or a jacket and he wasn't much better.

"Nick, we need to talk about this."

"Not now."

"Yes, now." She positioned herself in his path, hands on hips and her mouth a determined line. "I need to explain."

Every last bit of him rejected the idea. He had so much anger churning him up inside that he didn't know what to do with it. He needed to hit something. A wall or the side of the truck would do. Just drive his fist into something solid that wouldn't give a fuck for the abuse. He sure as hell did not want to open his mouth and say shit he couldn't take back. And that was what would happen if she kept pushing it.

"Ros ..."

"I was coming back," she said.

"No." He stepped back and shook his head, shoved a hand through his hair. Not wanting to hear a fucking thing she had to say. At least, not right then. But ... "What? You were what?"

"Nick—"

"Did you say you were coming back?"

She wrung her hands in front of her. "I changed my mind. I got down to the road and I realized I couldn't leave like that. I realized we needed to talk things out."

His mind reeled. "You did?"

"Yes."

He barked out a laugh. It was funny, but it wasn't. Mostly it wasn't. "You were coming back. Bloody hell, that's great."

Her features sharpened. Brows descended. And that was fine. Let her be pissed. Let her share the fun. "What did you expect, Nick? You've been keeping me chained. Of course my first instinct was to escape."

"And you did. And now we're fucked."

"Which is *not* all my fault."

"Did I say it was?" Of course he hadn't. He'd been doing his best to keep his mouth shut to prevent exactly this sort of shit coming out. "Did I?"

"Close enough," she said, voice rising. Because she never bloody learned.

"Keep. Your. Voice. Down."

Her nostrils flared. "You put me in an impossible situation, Nick."

"Was it worth it?"

"What?"

"Nearly getting killed," he said. "You were about to be eaten alive by a pack of infected when I found you. So was it worth it, Ros? Do you feel better now? Work out whatever you needed to?"

"Oh, you *asshole*."

"That was our home that just burned down. Our home. Do you get that? Is it sinking in?"

"Hard to think of it as home when you were keeping me prisoner."

"I treated you so badly?" he asked. He took a step closer, forcing her to back up or have him right up in her face. She was right, he was an asshole. But he was so damn angry he didn't care. She'd left him without a word. "Well? Is there anything I didn't give you?"

"A gilded cage is still a cage, Nick."

"You betrayed me."

"You never trusted me, Nick, so how exactly did I betray you?" Roslyn looked away and sucked in a breath, shoulders hitching. "Look, let's just stop. Let's go back to the school and regroup."

"They're dead, Ros. Everyone at the school is dead."

She stopped, stared. "You're lying," she whispered.

"Why would I?"

"To t-try and keep me."

"No. It's the truth. Your friends screwed up and let in an infected. Apparently your old friend Neil didn't secure the gates well enough after we left. I should have told you earlier. Maybe you would have thought twice about bolting.

"How do you know?" she asked.

"Janie was infected. I stayed with her ..."

"Why didn't you tell me?"

Probably because he was an idiot, just like she'd told him many, many times. An idiot to think it could work out between them. He rubbed the back of his neck. "I didn't want to upset you. Stupid, huh? Me worrying about your delicate feelings. You have no fucking clue when it comes to life these days. Sheltering you was wrong."

"But ..." She just kept blinking at him. "They're dead? All of them."

"Yes."

Silence. Her face blanked.

Oh, shit. Second thoughts filled him, along with third and fourth. Maybe he shouldn't have told her like that, just blurted it out.

All he could think of was the infected clawing at her, about to bite her foot. She didn't have a fucking clue how close she'd come to death. He wanted to howl every time he thought about it. The woman needed a dose of reality. Needed to know how serious things were, so hopefully she'd think before she acted. This couldn't happen again; it would fucking kill him.

"Roslyn."

She shook her head, turned and walked away.

Fine. They both needed time. They also needed blankets or they were going to freeze their asses off. He set about searching the rows of shelving lining the walls. No comment from her. Not a peep.

He was not the bad guy here. He wasn't. He'd done every-fucking-thing he could to please her.

Some crappy old camping gear stood in a corner. A moth-eaten canvas tent and a sleeping bag that had seen better days. A ratty-looking tarp with a couple of burn marks. A moth took flight when he nudged the tarp. He shook the sleeping bag out and clouds of dust filled the air. Quickly, he turned his face away before he copped a lungful of it. Roslyn stood by the pickup with her arms wrapped around herself.

The infected's mouth had been bare centimeters off sinking its teeth into her toes. Its filthy fingers had been clawing at her legs. If she hadn't been wearing jeans, if he hadn't woken when he did and heard her screaming. If he'd been a second later, just one second, it would have been too late. He couldn't think about it. Couldn't stand it, but it wouldn't stop repeating inside his head.

If he'd lost her ... No.

Nick cracked his jaw and bundled up the tarp, took it and the sleeping bag over to the vehicle. It should be enough to keep them warm at least. He doubled the tarp over the ratty old mattress and placed the sleeping bag between the layers. "We'll sleep up here. Come on."

She gave him a blank look.

"You've got no shoes on. No jacket. It's cold."

She nodded dully and moved to the end of the bed, climbed up. The tarp crackled as she slipped beneath it, into the sleeping bag. Nick switched off the pickup's parking lights then followed, pulling off his boots. He hadn't stopped to put on socks. She'd be dead now if he had.

Having both of them in the sleeping bag made it cozy. He put an arm beneath her neck and the other over her waist. Her feet felt freezing so he pressed them between his, trying to warm her. She didn't fight him, but she didn't exactly help either.

"You should have told me," she said.

"You were upset enough that day." His stomach growled, loudly. Sex always made him hungry. It had been hours since they'd eaten and it would be hours before they stood a chance of finding food—tomorrow morning at the earliest.

A mattress spring stuck into his hip. He'd slept on floors that were more comfortable. The air in the shed was frigid. They should have been in the cabin, curled up in bed with a roaring fire. They should have been fucking like bunnies. Everything else smelled like dust but she smelled like sex and feminine sweat. His dick gave signs of life and he angrily ignored it.

No matter how pissed he was at her, he still wanted her. Not a surprise.

There'd be no sleeping. He wouldn't risk leaving her unguarded. This place didn't feel that secure. Besides, every time he closed his eyes he saw that thing about to sink its teeth into her. One second later and she'd have been gone. Maybe he should take her to Blackstone. She'd be safe there, even if he wasn't welcome. The walled community was still probably a hundred people strong. They were organized. She could have a life there.

The thought of it made his guts burn. Maybe she'd given him a stomach ulcer. But maybe Blackstone was the only choice.

Had their cabin burnt to the ground yet? Probably. Place had gone up like someone had poured on kerosene. What a balls-up. All of his plans had turned to shit. How would he protect her now?

"Were you really coming back?" he asked in a hard voice. He needed to know for sure. Inside of him felt like a fucking mess. He couldn't make sense of the feelings.

"Yes," she said.

"Why? You finally got away from me."

"I told you. I realized we needed to talk things over."

"Like what?"

"Like everything." Her voice was so quiet that he had to strain to hear her.

"Because we fucked?" he asked, choosing his words with care.

She sighed. "Honestly, Nick, I don't know."

CHAPTER NINETEEN

Roslyn stood patiently on the curb and watched as Nick broke into a clothes shop. They'd already gone through the drugstore across the street. Or he had. She'd been instructed to stand outside within view and wait. Like a dog being trusted off its chain, barely.

He still wouldn't give her any more of the details of what had happened at the school. It had obviously been bad. The lost look in his eyes when she'd asked had stalled further questions, for now. It seemed surreal. Her brain wouldn't quite wrap around the information.

The last of the people she'd known were gone.

Grief crept over her in waves. Crashing down on her and then withdrawing again. She didn't know how to feel one second to the next. Her throat would tighten and her eyes tear up, and then, *poof!* Gone, as her mind busied itself once more in dealing with the here and now. Trying to figure a way out of the maze of this messed-up situation. A time or two she caught herself about to giggle hysterically. Maybe she was losing it.

She and Nick were half talking to each other. Sentences consisted of the smallest number of words possible and a meaningful flick of the hand. Sometimes he varied it, doing a grunt and a chin-tip instead, which was big of him.

The soles of her feet stung from the freezing cold concrete. She bounced her bag full of drugstore goodies off her legs, rattling the contents. Fidgeting always had helped distract her.

"Stop it," he said. "You'll break the reading glasses."

"Oh. Why don't you break the glass in the door?" she asked, then realized the answer. "Oh—the noise." He paused for a moment and his shoulders tensed. Then he resumed tinkering with the lock, apparently foregoing the opportunity for a snarky reply. A moment later the door swung inward and he rose to his feet. He jerked his stubbly chin in the direction of the shop's interior and gave her a meaningful look.

"Sorry?" she asked, maybe because contrariness was becoming her nature, at least when it came to him. And maybe because she was sick of the half-assed silent treatment.

He turned back to her with a pained expression, and looked at her from beneath dark brows. "Come inside. Please."

"No problem." Asshole. And to think she'd had sex with him. Never let your private parts dictate your choices. Therein lay the path to destruction.

Lay. Ha. Bad word choice.

Inside, the shop looked immaculate. Farm wear-type stuff, mostly, men and women's. A bit of kidswear and some school uniforms, as well as bathmats and towels. There was an impressive amount packed into the neat little space.

Nick shut and locked the door behind her, then strode past, obviously going to check out the back room. His rifle was slung over his shoulder and he'd tucked a pistol into the back of his belt. She'd asked him for the gun and he'd just given her a nasty look. She hadn't bothered to ask again. Couldn't be that hard to find her own and she knew how to shoot. Her dad had insisted she knew enough not to shoot herself in the foot.

There was a counter topped with glass, displaying purses and scarves beneath. But more importantly there was a water cooler standing at the end and it was three-quarters full. Oh, yes.

When Nick strode back in she was covered only in goose bumps, busy washing herself as fast as humanly possible with soap from the drugstore and a hand-cloth fresh off the shelf. He stopped dead and stared at her breasts. Suddenly being cold didn't seem to matter so much.

"What are you doing?" he said, sounding like something choked him.

"Washing. You?"

He said nothing, just continued to stare.

"Give it a rest, Nick. You've seen it all before."

His gaze jumped to hers and his face heated. He could blush. Who knew? She'd have laughed, but her teeth were chattering and it wasn't really a laughing kind of day. Besides, laughing would probably lead to crying and she needed to keep her shit together.

His jaw did some strange side-to-side thing. Suddenly he got busy on the other side of the room with his back to her. But she hadn't missed the bulge in his pants.

She'd quickly brushed her teeth and hair while he'd been looking out back, but this bathing felt like a whole new level of lovely. She'd cleaned her scratched-up hands, gotten the worst of the dirt and sweat from her body. The bruises on her knuckles from punching Neil had faded. Impossible to believe he'd died, busted nose and all. He'd been a wanker, but he hadn't deserved that.

Nick stood over by the neatly folded stack of jeans. He selected and discarded, then he moved onto men's shirts. His back remained to her at all times. The man was dedicated.

She'd started rubbing herself down with a towel when he dumped a selection of clothes on the counter beside her.

"Those should fit," he said.

A pair of jeans, a long-sleeved shirt, and some matching underwear in plain black cotton. Funny, he'd always been about the silk and lace before. And there were some racier alternatives available. She'd seen them. "Thank you, but I can choose my own clothes."

Another grunt. His eyes stayed elsewhere at all times. Screw him. He wasn't making her feel awkward in her own skin. A skin that, until yesterday, he'd been all too keen to jump.

She yawned so hard her jaw cracked. "Excuse me."

"You didn't sleep well last night."

"I didn't?" It had been a bit cold and uncomfortable, but still.

"No, you woke up a couple of times crying about your friends at the school."

"I did?" Huh. She had no memory of it.

"Yeah, I talked to you and you went back to sleep." He shrugged.

For a moment she just studied the unattractive industrial carpet and searched for something to say. He'd chased away her bad dreams and she didn't even remember it. Mad at her or not, he cared for her and held her when she cried.

And yet, the chain ... there was always the damn chain to remember. "Thank you," she said.

"Your friends died. You had reason." He wandered off toward the range of sturdy-looking work boots, grabbing a backpack or two on his way. "Besides, you're a pretty restless sleeper. I'm used to it."

How long had it been? Five nights? And he was used to it. Used to her waking and used to soothing her back to sleep. Used to doing for her. When was the last time someone had shown the least predilection for caring for her? She couldn't remember. Whatever weirdness lay between them needed sorting, now.

"Nick?"

He turned and his gaze dropped to her boobs before shooting back to her face. She could have covered herself with an arm but she didn't. Rattling Nick made her feel good.

"Mm?"

"Aren't you going to wash up too?" First thing to come to mind. Hygiene was the best she had. How sad.

His mouth opened but he didn't speak straight away. "Later."

He about-faced and strode back toward the selection of boots. There was a whole wall full of them.

He was still mad at her, obviously. The thing was, while she'd started off angry, she got it. He hadn't told her about her friends out of compassion. She didn't like it, but she understood. Him choosing her clothes, however, amply displayed he needed to learn how to let her make her own decisions. But he cared and she couldn't deny it. She also couldn't deny she'd chosen to be with him. It would have been nice to have ignored the facts, but grown-ups didn't do that. Or they shouldn't.

Sex-wise in the kitchen, and then again when she made the decision to turn back on the driveway, she'd chosen him. Then, when she'd needed him, when it was life or death, he'd come through for her.

"It wasn't because we had sex," she said.

His whole body flinched and his hand stopped mid-motion, stretched toward a set of black work boots. "Let's just ... let's just get sorted. Alright?"

"That's what I'm trying to do. I turned back because I chose you."

"I don't want to talk about it."

"Yeah, I know. But we're going to."

He turned to look at her, his eyes stark. He strode toward her and if she'd had a whit of sense she would have been scared. But she wasn't. No way would he hurt her. Nick didn't stop until they were toe-to-toe and he loomed over her like a storm waiting to break. The hollows of his cheeks and the tense lines beside his fine lips. The look in his eyes. No one looked at her like he did, whether he was angry or happy or anything in between. It scared her and seduced her equally.

"We're not talking about it," he said in a quiet voice. "We're going to stock up and hit the road."

"But—"

"Don't."

As if. "Because you're still mad about the cabin."

He shook his head slowly, eyes never leaving hers. "No. Because your stubbornness and stupidity nearly got you killed yesterday."

She didn't even bother fighting him over the stubborn part. "It's not stupidity to reject living as a captive, Nick." Odd, he'd seemed so worked up about his home the night before. "How many ways can I explain that to you?"

"It wasn't going to be forever," he said. "Just until ..."

She waited for him to finish but he didn't.

"Until what?" she asked.

He shook off the question. "You acted without thinking yesterday and you nearly died. And I dunno how to make sure that never happens again." He crowded her, but her days of backing down were done. "So I can't keep you safe. Can I?"

"Chaining me isn't an option," she said.

"I guess not." He looked away. "Get moving. We shouldn't stay here too long."

There were bruises beneath his eyes, dark circles. How hadn't she noticed that before? "You look tired. Didn't you sleep at all?"

"I had a lot on my mind."

"Like what?"

"I'm fine, alright? Enough talk, Ros. Get dressed. Standing there arguing with me in nothing but a towel isn't smart."

"Am I rattling your cage, Nicky?" she asked, deliberately being painful. The slit-eyed look he dealt her only spurred her on. "Deal with it, big boy."

His gaze dropped down her, doubtless taking in the state of her hard nipples on the way. Damn obvious despite the towel. "You're getting cold."

True, but she was also a lot turned on, oddly enough. Because having him stand so close with his eyes taking her in so matter-of-factly worked for her. Or maybe it was the argument, all those heated words. Whatever it was he did to her, he did it with ease, just by being his own sweet self.

Which meant she didn't know whether to kick him or kiss him, but she wouldn't be rushing anything. Truthfully, she wanted his mouth on her. She wanted the heat of his kisses and the comfort of his touch. After what they'd been through, she needed it.

"Ask me," he said.

"W-what?"

He came closer. "Whatever you want. Just ask me and I'll give it to you."

There were a lot of things she wanted. Half of them were vague, unformed ideas, but they all involved him. But there were priorities to consider. "Promise me we're equal partners from here on in."

"Ros."

"No more denying of liberty or any of that crap. Promise me."

He took a deep breath. "And you'll just believe me. After everything?"

"Yes."

He hesitated where she hadn't. It hurt.

"Nick?"

"You're getting cold." His hand reached for the bra on the counter, the sensible black one. He threaded it over first one of her hands, then the other. The straps were drawn up her arms and positioned on her shoulders. "Turn around."

She did so, part bemused and part bitter. "You can't do it, can you? You can't give me your word."

Warm fingers eased the bra cups over her breasts, fastened the hooks at the back. "You nearly died."

Next came the flannel shirt. A good choice on his part, because he'd been right, she was getting cold now. Standing there in next to nothing, waiting for him to do something he couldn't. But also wanting him to take the choice out of her hands so she wouldn't have to feel torn and frustrated and stupid. Wanting to grab onto him and yet unable to, so uncertain what the price would be. What part of her pride and self-respect would she have to sacrifice this time?

"I can do this," she said, gesturing to the pile of clothes.

"I know. Arms."

She put her hands into the sleeves and he dressed her. Reached around from behind and started doing up the buttons from bottom to top. He paused halfway and she almost held her breath.

"Promise me, Nick."

He was hard against her back and he didn't bother to hide it. His pelvis rubbed against her rear. Not gratuitously, exactly, but more than enough to let her know the state of affairs. Nice to know she wasn't the only idiot being led astray by her hormones.

What was he going to do? So many possibilities. She waited.

When he hesitated, she raised her hand to move her boob. It didn't feel right.

"Let me." One of his hands held open a bra cup while the other slid down inside it. His palm brushed against her aching, tight nipple. Fingers cupped and lifted her breast, positioned it.

"Thank you," she said.

"Hmm."

"What would you do if I tried to leave again, Nick?"

"Why would you?" His hands did the same with her other breast, plumping it up within the confines of the cup. She let him. Hell, she liked it. The warmth of him at her back and the touch of his hands made blood rush to all her best bits. He made her feel alive. Her body responded amply, but her mind held back. Her heart was wary.

"You won't survive out there on your own," he said. "Didn't you get that last night?"

He did up the last of her shirt buttons and reached for the simple black cotton underwear beside her. His hands skimmed down her sides as he dropped to his knees. The feel of him touching her was electric. Still, this wasn't getting them anywhere.

"Here," she said. "Give them to me."

"No." Fresh knickers were held before her and she stepped into them, a hand on the counter for balance. He drew them up her legs, onto her hips.

"Nick, I'm not a child."

"I know. Hand me the jeans," he said, his voice low.

"I can dress myself."

He looked up and caught her gaze. His voice dropped to somewhere below ground level. "The jeans, Ros."

Whoa.

The deep, no-nonsense tone really did something to her. Something she probably could have done without. Life was complicated enough. She swallowed hard and steadied her legs. Deliberated for about a second, then passed him the denim. Doing as she was told, for some reason. Because you had to pick your fights. And also, because some part of her wanted to give into him. Something about it worked for her.

Maybe he was right. Maybe she did like him telling her to do sex things. But she sure as hell didn't need him making all of her choices for her. Which was exactly what they'd been discussing before he started putting his hands on her and scrambling her wits.

"I need to know what you're going to do," she said.

"Lift your foot."

She lifted first one foot, then the other. Slowly he pulled the jeans up her legs, stopping shy of her torso. The muscles in her thighs were taut and she had the worst feeling her new knickers were already damp. How bloody embarrassing. Having a serious conversation under these conditions was unfeasible.

"Ask me for something else," he said. His breath heated her belly and his hands curved over her hips. He rubbed his face against her, beneath the hem of her shirt. She could feel the soft of his cheek bone then the scratch of his stubble. His facial hair was longer today. Not so sharp on her skin. "I know you want to."

"Alright." Her hands trembled as she gripped the counter behind her. "I want a gun. I want to be able to defend myself."

"Why couldn't you just ask me to give you head, hmm? It's obvious you want me to." He pressed his face against her covered mound, making her stomach dance. "You smell so good. You make my mouth water." His hands slid beneath the cotton of her underwear, cupping her ass cheeks. He shredded her will, decimated it. "Ask me, Roslyn."

"No." Oh God, yes please. Her sex throbbed, needy and desperate. Her fingers itched to get grabby with his hair and make him deliver. But it was a battle of wills she couldn't afford to lose. Let him off the hook now and he'd never take her seriously. "Give me the gun."

"No." He lifted his face and his eyes met hers. "You go off on your own, you'll die. I won't let that happen. I can't."

She could have kicked him, the stubborn bastard. "I need to know the choice to be with you is mine."

"Bullshit," he growled. "You want to be with me. You said so."

"I need to know I'm with you of my own free will."

He grunted and kept his eyes on her as he kneaded her butt cheeks, dug his fingers in and spread them just a little, enough to wake every last nerve in the area. God help her. Her toes curled into the scratchy carpet.

"Stop it," she whispered.

"Let's see who gives in first. Better hold onto the counter."

Her fingers clutched at the smooth glass edges, hanging on for all she was worth. "Nick, this is not a game."

"You said you chose me," he said.

"We still have things to work out."

"No. We don't." His tongue traced circles around her belly button then blew over the damp skin. Her breath hitched.

"You're complicating something simple," he said.

"Nothing is simple about this."

He bit at the waist of her underwear and her stomach muscles quivered. The man bordered on feral. It was wildly exciting.

"Yesterday afternoon ...?" he started.

"What about it?" she asked, her voice uneven. His lips were so damn close to where she needed them, and yet not there. It took all of her willpower not to just shove herself in his face.

"When I woke up and you were gone ..."

"Mm?"

"Then seeing that thing about to bite you. Shit, Ros."

"So give me the pistol. I know how to use it."

He growled and kissed her mound, drew a deep breath. "Ask me. Put us both out of our misery."

"Give me the gun."

"I bet you taste perfect." The heat in his eyes almost undid her.

"I-I'll pick one up somewhere. You know I will."

He nipped at her inner thigh. "Don't you want to come on my face? Wouldn't you like that?"

"Stop it, Nick." Oh no, not a visual like that. Not fair. "This isn't a game."

He did something; something involving his tongue and the seam where her sex met her thigh and holy hell. Her whole body trembled.

"G-give it to me," she said.

"I'd love to."

Smug bastard. The fingers massaging her butt moved to soft strokes along the lower curve of her ass instead. Damn, he was good at this. She'd stick him next to *The Joy of Sex*. 613 or 618? She couldn't remember. Shit, her mind was failing her.

"The gun, Nick. Give me the gun." She squirmed in his hold.

With a snarly noise he got to his feet. His hands pulled her in against him and she grabbed hold of his shoulders for balance. "I can protect you if you'd stop fighting me for one bloody minute."

"I need to be able to protect myself. You're always saying I need to get a clue and adjust to how things are now, so let me. Help me."

Slowly he withdrew his hands from her knickers. His face was lined with tension. Then he pulled his pistol from the back of his jeans and set it on the counter beside her. "Alright. You win."

"I do?"

"Yes," he said.

"Ah, thanks."

"No problem. You fire that thing and you send every infected in the vicinity an invitation to come kill us. Keep that in mind." Nick stepped back and her hands fell from his shoulders. "I'll get cleaned up and we'll hit the road. Grab whatever you're going to need—a couple of changes of clothes at least."

"Sure." Her pulse pumped away in her privates. She could barely hear him. Her hand reached for him of its own volition, all yearning-like. "Nick?"

"No." He turned his back on her and stripped off his shirt.

No?

Oh. No.

Alright. Fine. She didn't need the jerk. She'd take care of it her-self.

"Your hand goes any lower and you're not going to like what happens." He toed off his boots. Bare feet could be surprisingly sexy. All the plains and angles of his body were being gradually revealed for her viewing pleasure. She should put her tongue back in her mouth. Soon. He dealt with the button and the fly of his jeans and shoved them down his legs with sharp movements. Her tongue nearly disappeared down her throat that time. There was nothing beneath but very aroused Nick. Damn him. The thick length of his cock rose from a tangle of dark hair and his sack hung heavy below.

Her hand, meanwhile, sat poised at her waistband, ready and willing, awaiting further orders. What would he do, really? He wasn't even watching her. Instead, he wet a fresh cloth and rubbed it over himself. First his shoulders and neck, then his chest and beneath his arms. More water and he efficiently dealt with between his legs. Next he picked up the soap and got busy. The air was chill enough to deflate any man, but it made no noticeable difference. He had a beautiful body, with an athlete's grace and a very hard cock.

And she wanted him bad, damn it.

Had she ever been quite so pathetically cock-struck? Doubtful.

After all of the horrible, something good had to come out of today.

He dealt her a sidelong glance dark enough to give her pause, her and her hand both. Probably best not to find out what he might do. Things were edgy enough between them as it was.

Roslyn ignored her aching breasts and groin and hitched up her jeans, fastened them resolutely. She picked up the gun and weighed it in her hand.

"You going to shoot me?" he asked. His didn't even sound all that curious.

"No." Though it was tempting. "Maybe later."

The side of his mouth twitched and he returned to his washing with his big cock bouncing in front of him.

CHAPTER TWENTY

Nick concentrated on the road and not the woman crossing and uncrossing her legs beside him. She kept twisting about on the cracked leather seating like she couldn't get comfortable. Good. He sure as hell wasn't comfortable with stomach cramps. But better that than blue balls. Maybe he shouldn't have been so stubborn.

But why couldn't she have picked him instead of the gun? Why couldn't she trust him to protect her? Damn it.

He'd steered them vaguely toward Blackstone, and what the hell it meant he didn't know.

Roslyn frowned again behind the big black drugstore sunglasses taking up half her face. He could see her through the side. She stared out the window at the passing scenery, what little of it there was. Plains full of blade grass and barbed-wire fences. They'd driven for four to five hours, but they hadn't gotten far. What with finding routes around road blocks and having to stop to siphon petrol, the pace was slow. Now it was getting late. In another hour the sun would set.

A crappy-looking motel sat on the outskirts of another small country town. It was a long, low white brick building with eight or nine rooms and an office with a restaurant attached. Sad-looking palm trees swayed above the murky green pool. A beat-up brown Holden sat beside a sporty coupé in the parking lot. Next came a big boss of a black pickup with a covered tray. Lots of trim, top of the line. It probably had some real horsepower under the hood. Probably chewed up petrol like crazy. Funny, he could have almost whatever he wanted these days. None of it much mattered now that money was gone. It was all just lying around, waiting. But older and simpler made more sense. He could have decked Ros out in diamonds and it wouldn't mean a thing. It still wouldn't have been enough.

"You look like you're in love," she said with a smile.

"Maybe." The boss pickup would stay where it was. He grabbed his rifle and bowie knife. "I'll check out inside. See if we've got any company. Wait here."

"No." She threw off her seatbelt and jumped out of the vehicle before he could grab her. "We do this sort of thing together from now on."

"Ros, wait in the truck."

"You're not taking all the risks on your own, Nick." She flicked off the safety on the gun and strode toward the nearest room like she was Clint Eastwood. "That's not a partnership. Are you coming?"

"Roslyn," he hissed.

Up onto the pavement and tugging on the door handle with a gun in her hand but no clue. The door didn't open. He took a deep breath. It was locked, thank fuck. She'd give him a heart attack before she was through.

He fell in line beside her at the next room along, number three. "Alright. But we stick together."

"Sure, Nick." Her ready smile didn't soothe.

"And you stay behind me. That's the rule."

She flashed him a frown, but moved back a step. Exactly how the hell he would keep her in one piece he did not know. That was what kept him up at night. Not her bad dreams and talking in her sleep, but his concerns for her safety, plus his fear of losing her. Combined, they were more than enough to give him cold sweats.

The next room's door opened. Inside everything sat shadowy cool. On the far side of the room the curtains were open and dust particles filled the sunlit air. Nothing else moved. He lifted his rifle, just in case. Ros came up so close behind him she jostled his arm.

"It looks okay," she said.

"Shh." He held up a hand, motioned for her to stay put as he took a few steps inside. It was your standard motel room. Small table and chairs with a big bed and a built-in cupboard. He threw that door open, but there was only a few wire hangers and a neatly folded blanket inside. The bathroom waited down the end with its door ajar.

"Stay here," he said.

White tiles and mold. He pushed back the gray shower curtain with the end of his rifle, half expecting trouble but happy to be let down.

"We're clear," he said.

"Okay. So, we do the next room?"

"No. We only ever look where we need to."

Roslyn sat on the edge of the lime bedspread. "Well, we need food."

A mini-bar sat beneath a side table. Inside were neat little bottles of alcohol, lined up. Tiny cups of long-life milk and a couple of individually packed chocolate chip cookies. In the drawer above were sachets of nuts and some small boxes of breakfast cereals. Fortunate, seeing as the couple of petrol stations and one small supermarket they'd passed had been picked over already.

He tossed her a cookie. "Here."

It flew past her and she scrambled after it.

"We're going to be living rough for a while," he said. "Get used to it."

"We could look in the restaurant."

Yeah, they could. He probably should. But the chances of her agreeing to stay behind were shit. "We've got energy bars from the drugstore. That'll do."

She sat back on the edge of the bed and tore into the cookie.

"I've been thinking about what we should do next," he said.

She nodded and munched away. A crumb sat at the corner of her mouth, messing with his thinking. The urge to lick it away was distractingly strong. She swallowed and cleared her throat. "As your former captive, I just wanted to say how much I like this use of the word *we*. Especially when you actually mean it. Go team."

The pistol sat beside her on the bed, silently accusing him. "Ros …"

The smile she gave him turned him inside out and upside down. She'd clearly been a happy person before everything had gone to shit, you could tell. He'd never imagined ending up with a chirpy chatterbox. Nothing had worked out how he'd imagined. But to see her smiling despite everything and no matter the state of the world did something to him.

"So what are our choices?" she asked.

"There is somewhere to go." Not a place he could go, but for her Blackstone would be perfect. The alternative would be to have her running amok in a world she couldn't handle. A world likely to kill her if he didn't watch her every second of every day. He didn't trust himself that far, not now. What if he fucked up? What then? She died.

Nick stretched out his hand, splaying his fingers. All of his choices sucked. He hated each and every one of them. Her safety came first, but he didn't know if he could do it. He didn't know if he could give her up and he didn't know if he could give her what she needed.

Whatever the fuck that might be.

"Where can we go?" she asked, trust burning bright in her eyes.

Thought he'd had it all figured out, but he didn't know shit. There was the truth. He had no business demanding she believe in him and rely on him. Not with the way he treated her.

"There are no bullets in the gun," he said softly.

She paused. "What did you say?"

"The gun I gave you. It's empty."

Her words, when they came, were slow, careful. "Why would you do that, Nick?"

"I don't know."

"Yes, you do. Was it some kind of test?"

"I don't know. Maybe."

She nodded and looked away, face carefully set. No surprise, though. That's what was wrong with this picture. Shit.

"You knew?" he asked, voice incredulous.

She gave him a grim smile. "I told you I knew about guns. You emptied the clip when I was gathering clothes in the shop, didn't you?"

"Yes."

"This is never going to work, is it?" Her lips looked pinched and she stared at her hands for a long moment. "Of course it isn't. I was so angry at you but now ... I'm, um, I'm tired."

"Roslyn."

"You know, I wondered how long it would take you to admit it. How much guilt I'd have to heap on you till you cracked," she said. "If you'd crack ..."

"I'm sorry."

"I know." She slipped the half-eaten cookie back into its plastic bag. "You always are, Nick. But things stay the same." Her face turned away from him and she crawled onto the bed, placing the remains of the cookie on the bedside table. "You can't possibly guarantee you'll always be there for me, because accidents happen. You don't know what the future will bring. But you won't help me to protect myself. You say you want me, but what you really want is some pathetic doll, completely dependent on you and available to fuck at your convenience. That's the truth."

The quiet in the room was complete when she stopped speaking. She lay down on her side, facing away from him. A pretty obvious message that he chose to ignore.

"I don't want a doll," he said. "I just don't want you to die."

Silence.

"Roslyn—"

"I have made some bad decisions, I'm not denying it. Thing is, those situations will keep occurring if we don't change what we're doing. The way we're behaving toward each other has to shift. Either that, or we need to part ways." Her voice sounded scarily matter-of-fact. "I don't see any other choices."

Panic stirred inside him. Without thought, he moved to her side, lying down behind her. She stiffened, but didn't otherwise object to the arm he put around her waist. The sunlight had started to fade, the room dulling down to shadows. There'd been a torch out the back of the shop they'd raided and some girly scented candles in the drugstore. All of them sat in their packs in the back of the pickup. He should go get them. But for the moment, he needed to stay with her more. He needed to fix this.

Problem was, in the past he'd always bailed at times like these. Chances were he'd say the wrong thing now for sure. His mind scrambled to come up with something he could use. Something to soothe her.

"Thank you for trying to come back yesterday," he said, getting close enough to press up against as much of her as possible, his front to her back. "It does matter."

"It didn't work out so well."

"No. But you tried."

She made a humming noise. "I am sorry about the cabin."

"I know," he said, fingers daring to toy with hers. "We'll find somewhere else."

A small nod.

"Here's what I'm going to do," he said. "I'm going to go out to the truck and bring in our stuff. Then I'm going to put the bullets back in your clip. Tomorrow, we're going to start talking over scenarios. Situations you might face and how you'd deal with them. Stuff like that. I'll teach you some skills. Okay?"

She didn't answer for a moment. "Do you mean that?"

"Yes. We might even work our way to looking at clearing a room together. Maybe. When I judge you're ready, and not before."

Ros wriggled about, rolling over to face him. Cautious eyes studied his face. "I can't tell if you're serious or not."

"I'm serious."

"Be warned. If you're lying to me, I may actually shoot you this time."

He sighed. "Yeah, I know."

"Good."

Slowly, he laid the palm of his hand against the soft skin of her cheek. That she didn't turn away or try to stop him was humbling. But then, Ros could be far too kind and forgiving for her own good.

"Honestly," he said, "I only want you available at my convenience. Not a doll. Not anyone else."

The corner of her mouth curled just a little. "Wildly romantic, Nick."

"Not everything you accused me of was bad. I kind of liked that idea."

"Did you?"

"Mm."

"Great." She smiled but then her gaze dipped, avoiding his. "Don't lie to me again, Nick. Please. I don't think I could take it."

CHAPTER TWENTY-ONE

"You just shot me again," Nick griped at her. Honestly, the man could be such a big baby.

Roslyn sighed somewhat dramatically. "I did not shoot you."

"Yeah, you did. You flinched and your finger squeezed the trigger. If it had been loaded, I'd be dead."

"Oh, please." She rolled her eyes and slumped against the motel room wall. It had to be close to midnight. They'd been doing the same damn clearing-a-room exercise for hours, with him picking on every little last thing she did. She'd nagged him into starting immediately. "Nag" being his word choice, not hers. But she forgave him for being short-tempered. Amazing how benevolent she could be when she got her way for once. Nick, however, had brought highly strung and crabby to a whole new level.

"It was an accident," she said, not really bothering to keep the smile off her face.

The eyebrow went up. "That makes me feel a lot better. I mean, I'll be dead, but still, an accident."

"You surprised me!"

"I'm meant to surprise you," the man growled. Nicky had quite the temper once he got going but, fortunately, he didn't scare her. Not in that way. If anything, his getting all riled up could be rather thrilling in the right circumstances. Blood warmed his face and his eyes were narrowed on her in irritation. Her body heated in response and she bit back a grin. Really, right then, life wasn't so bad. In fact, it could be pretty nice with the right company, apocalypse or no.

"Zombies will surprise you coming out of hiding," he said, much in the manner of one handing down a sermon. "But I'm going to be around, too, and you might not always know exactly where I am. It'd be great if you didn't just react but thought about who you're aiming at and what you're doing. You clear your immediate right, then work your way across the rest of the room. You do not shoot until you're certain of your target. Is that understood?"

"Yes, Nick." She tried for contrite but he kept right on scowling.

"Why are you smiling?"

He definitely thrilled her. Maybe it was the lecturing. There'd been a professor back in her university days who'd filled her fantasies for months. The "thou shalt do as I say" attitude had a powerful pull on her, apparently. Maybe he was right and she had daddy issues or something. Or maybe it was the way he worked with her for once, instead of against her.

"Why are you smiling, Ros?" he repeated.

"No reason," she said airily.

He just looked at her. Candlelight didn't soften the harsh lines of his face, accentuated by his present pissy mood. Nick wasn't handsome, exactly, but he had presence. Which by no means meant she'd roll over and take his bossiness like a good girl.

"And why are we even using guns?" she asked. "I mean, if they're so loud and dangerous, then why not replace them with something more suitable for the job?"

"What, you want a sword now?" he asked, voice heavy with disbelief.

"Maybe, or a machete or an axe ... a crowbar would work, right?"

"It would." He strolled toward her. "But, Roslyn, what do you think would happen if you got splattered with infected blood? What if your mouth was open and some got in, hmm?"

"It would be bad. I know that. But to kill them effectively with something other than a gun we're going to need to get within a reasonable distance."

"Exactly."

"And? They move slower than we do. What is your point here, Nick?"

"Close-quarters combat is dangerous. Didn't you learn that yesterday?"

"Everything is dangerous!" She threw her arms wide and he caught her hands, held onto them. He swung them back and forth by their sides as if they were children. Then he stepped closer.

There was a distinct gleam in his eyes, something other than anger but every bit as heated.

"Did I please you?" he asked in a low voice.

"What?" The sudden change in topic threw her, that and his nearness. His scent enveloped her, warm, male, and familiar. It lured her libido right in. And the way he'd phrased the question—his words circled inside her head and held her in thrall. His eyes had also darkened. So ... everything. Everything about him threw her. "What do you mean?"

"You wanted to start training immediately, so we started. I kept my promise."

"Ah. Yes," she said. "You did. And you pleased me. I am officially pleased."

Nick slowly nodded. "Okay."

"Okay," she repeated, because she was apparently a brain-dead, sex-hungry parrot with damp panties. Lust filled the air with the promise of hot times ahead. She couldn't be imagining it.

"Alright." He swallowed and stepped back, dropping her hands. "We'd better get some sleep."

Then the man turned and walked away from her, snuffing out the extra candles as he went, leaving only the one on the bedside table alight. He didn't look back.

What the fuck?

Slapping her couldn't have been more effective. For the second time that day, he'd said no to sex.

"Nick?"

"Yeah?" He sat on the end of the bed and tugged off his boots and the socks beneath, too.

"What's going on?"

"Hmm?"

"I don't understand what's going on here."

He shoved a hand through his hair. "It's late. We should get some sleep."

Clearly, they'd entered a different dimension, one where Nick didn't want her. Except that couldn't be right. He'd been plenty hard in the shop earlier, and his jeans sported an impressive bulge now. So, whatever his issues were, her sexual attractiveness to him didn't seem to be a part of it.

Men were such complicated creatures. Women were so much more straightforward.

He grabbed the back of his shirt and dragged it off over his head. The revelation of his hard body made her swoon. The bands of muscle and the way they flexed as he rolled his shoulders. He had a certain grace to him, an efficiency of movement. She could watch him for hours.

"You want to sleep?" she asked.

"Yeah."

"Okay."

She sat on a chair and removed her own brand new boots and comfy socks. Pulled her shirt off and dumped it on the small table. His gaze jumped to her, taking in the sensible cotton bra, but was hastily diverted. He scurried into the bathroom and she heard the sounds of him brushing his teeth. When he emerged he got straight into bed, climbing beneath the blankets. With eyes shut, he gave every appearance of settling in for the night.

So he missed the removal of the rest of her clothes.

"I guess you're really tired," she said, throwing back the blankets on her side of the bed. She climbed onto the mattress, clad in nothing but her own skin.

"A long day."

"Yeah, it was," she agreed.

His eyes shot open when her hand slid over his chest. The heat of his skin and hard flesh beneath felt sublime.

"I think I know what's going on here," she said.

"That so?"

"Male nipples are so nice." She rubbed the side of her thumb over one hard nub. "Useless, but nice."

"I can think of a use for them."

"Can you?" She leant forward and lapped at one, secured her lips around it and sucked. His sudden intake of breath and muttered 'yes' curled her toes. Her pussy was swollen and slick. Ready. But she'd been ready for the better part of the day, damn him. She tightened her fingers in his chest hair and tugged, just a little. Giving him a small serving of her ire seemed more than justified.

Nick's hand covered hers. "Ros."

She moved onto his collarbone, tracing it with her tongue. "I think your delicate male pride was wounded when I chose the gun over you earlier today."

He didn't reply.

"See, this is a precarious situation we're in, Nicky. Relationships don't generally evolve from one party holding the other party hostage. Not healthy ones, at least."

"You think we're in a relationship?" he asked. His voice held no malice, but still.

Ros lifted her head. His forehead was furrowed and his fine lips were sealed tight. If only they'd stayed that way. He stared back at her, dark eyes unreadable.

"If mentioning that you abducted me and held me hostage upsets you, we're not going to get very far." Which was the absolute truth. She swung a leg over him, straddling his long body and seating herself atop his jean-covered hips. Actually, not a comfortable position. The zipper dug into her, raised as it was by his hard-on. She shuffled forward onto his bare, flat stomach. Much better. Nothing to chafe her there.

Nick licked his lips and his gaze slid down her warily as if her naked state worried him. So it should. His hands held back, not touching her. Fine, she could do the touching for both of them. Her fingers stroked the soft skin of his face, the arch of his cheekbones and the dips of his temple. For a while the day before, when she'd been fighting off the infected, she'd thought she'd never see him again. Never get to be this close to him, ever again. It put things into perspective. He had issues, but then so did the rest of the world. Nothing was normal anymore. Man-wise, it seemed she'd been searching for perfection, but it didn't exist. Unicorns were more likely. People, on the other hand, were infinitely fallible.

"I also think that us leaving the cabin has got you feeling a bit discombobulated," she said. "All of your careful plans have fallen by the wayside. That can't be pleasing to your inner control freak."

"I'm feeling what?"

"Confused. Unsettled."

"And that's why you're sitting on me bare-ass naked?"

"No," she sighed. "I'm sitting on you bare-ass naked because I want to have sex with you. I want to connect with you and feel close to you. Because you're important to me beyond your ability to protect me."

"Because you still think you can go out there and do okay on your own."

She held back from rolling her eyes, just. "I'd manage."

He snorted.

"But that's not what we're talking about," she said.

"No? So what are we talking about? I'm confused, apparently."

In answer she kissed his firm lips, trying to tempt him, to show him. Thank God, it worked. He opened his mouth to her on a groan and she slipped him her tongue. God, he kissed well. But then, he did all the physical stuff well. His hot, wet mouth hungrily kissed her back. It made her feel so much better. She squirmed against his hard stomach, rubbing herself on him oh so surreptitiously. As if he didn't notice. Hands covered her thighs, fingers kneading her flesh. She kissed him until her head spun and she had to come up for air.

They both panted. But Nick took his hands off her and set them back on the bed at his sides. The look he gave her reeked of a challenge.

"Are you saying no to me?" she asked.

"No, I'm not saying no to you."

"So I can do what I want?"

He cocked his brow. "Do you even know what you want?"

"I don't think there's a lot of doubt about that right now." But she ground her wet pussy against him in case there was. "Talk to me, Nicky. You're giving me cause for concern here."

He hesitated, staring over her shoulder. "I think we went about this the wrong way. I think ... I rushed things between us."

Her world turned topsy-turvy. It spun and bounced and careened off the walls and made absolutely no sense at all. "And now you're trying to slow things down? Right now? After today?"

"I said I was sorry about the gun," he answered softly. "I meant it."

"Yeah, you did. I know."

"And I've been thinking since then ..."

She waited. He didn't elaborate.

"You've been thinking?" she asked.

He nodded. "About where we go from here."

The silence held for a long moment as she attempted to pull her thoughts together. Her heart beat somewhere between her legs and he wanted to discuss their future. Random didn't begin to cover it, given their not even a week-long history. She looked down and, good God, she was leaking bodily fluids over the man's six-pack. The trail of hair leading from his belly button beneath the waist of his jeans clung damp to his skin. The musky scent of her overeager sex surrounded them.

"No. No. This is unacceptable." She scooted backward and started in on the button and zipper of his jeans, tearing his pants open. "I am not doing this now."

"Ros. I'm serious. I'm trying to do the right thing here! For once," he finished bitterly.

"No."

"Ros. Wait." He waved his hands in the air and she ignored them.

"You picked the wrong time, buddy." Grabbing two handfuls of denim, she dragged them down his thighs, freeing up the essentials. And the essentials were unperturbed by his bullshit, serious-relationship, ill-timed nonsense. It was the first time she'd come this close to his cock. Well, face-to-cock, as opposed to having him inside her. He looked to be just the right size, long and thick with veins wending up his length. The man had a rather attractive appendage, actually. She wrapped her hands around his hard length, testing the feel of him. Taking her time to learn him.

"I like this," she said.

His mouth opened, so she stuffed hers full of his cock and sucked. No more excuses. No more talking. He tasted wonderful and felt even better, with silken smooth, salty-tasting skin over such solid flesh. Creamy pre-cum trickled onto her tongue. His hands cradled her head and fingers sunk into her hair. Nothing mattered but her hunger for him.

"Shit," he muttered. "Sweetheart."

She took him deeper then pulled back, drawing on him fiercely. The encouraging hands in her hair calmed her down some, signalling his capitulation to her. She massaged his sweet spot with the tip of her tongue and he groaned, stomach muscles clenching.

"You win," he said.

Which was really all she needed.

His cock slipped from her mouth with a wet pop and she crawled up his body, covering him with kisses as she went, from those hot muscles that delineated his hips to his neat belly button, his pecs and the flat discs of his nipples. The crook of his neck smelled divine; she could kiss and lick him there all night.

Amongst other things.

"What were you thinking?" she asked, tickling the rim of his right ear with her tongue.

"I don't have a fucking clue."

The heat of his cock filled her hand and she fit him to the wet lips of her sex. Slowly, gently she took him inside. He seemed to need gentle now. Giving in didn't really suit him.

The worried expression gave way to ecstasy as she worked herself onto him. His lips parted and teeth clenched.

"Are you wet enough?" he asked and she nodded.

Wet and determined. The push of him into her pussy felt wonderful. Hard and fast was fun, too, but they'd been a bit out-of-control crazy last time. This time she could savor the experience, the feel of him stretching her, filling her until finally her body rested against his pelvis. In this position, every time she rocked back against him her clit rubbed against his body in the best way. Pressure could be the most amazing thing.

"Oh, that's nice," she murmured.

She kissed the side of his face and the bristle of his short beard. Talk about an intriguing sensation. Having him go down on her sometime hit the top of her to-do list. Capable hands smoothed over her sides and slid around to cup her breasts. He teased her nipples, rolling them between his fingers—and damn, sensation shot straight through her spine. Her inner muscles grabbed at him and they both moaned. But she kept the pace lazy, indolent. A struggle, but well worth it. Fucking him like this had to be the most pleasant indulgence ever, shitty motel room and end of the world be damned.

"Does it feel like we're in a relationship now?"

He chuckled. "Yes. It does."

"Good. It does for me too."

She sat up higher, her hands braced on the mattress beside his head. Nice to give him room to maneuver, but even nicer to add a swivel to her hips and gauge his reaction. His eyes widened and his cock bumped against something awful good inside her. Holy hell. Pleasure flooded her until her eyes nearly rolled back into her head. They needed to do that again and again.

Oh, yeah. Everything in her tightened in anticipation. They were right where they needed to be. She was right where she need to be, with him.

She picked up the pace, taking him harder. Heavy breathing and the slap of flesh meeting flesh filled her ears. His hands seemed to be everywhere, all over her, working her into a fever. Fingers lightly pinched her nipples and stroked her thighs. Their bodies knew each other just fine, knew exactly how to get where they needed to go. Her movements grew frantic, faster and harder. He stared up at her and she stared right back, unwilling to break the spell.

Until she couldn't see any longer.

Gray blurred her vision and her cunt clenched at him, waves of the most astonishing sensation washing through her. Hard hands gripped her hips, kept her moving when she faltered.

Her heart stopped; she could feel it. Her head fell forward and her body jerked atop him. Nick pounded into her, again and again, fingers sunk into her flesh. His cock surged into her and she felt him explode. The heat of his come filling her. He groaned and held her tightly, keeping her in place until he finished.

She lay down on his chest, or maybe she fell. The sweat on her back chilled as her body cooled. Her front stayed toasty warm, heated by him, but her spine was another matter. Pity she couldn't bring herself to move.

Nick shifted a bit and drew up the covers. That was good. He reached over and pinched out the last candle on the bedside table.

His arms surrounded her.

Something moaned from out in the parking lot and she shivered.

CHAPTER TWENTY-TWO

"Fuck." Nick pulled the pickup to the side of the road out of habit more than anything. It wasn't like anyone would need to pass.

The front half of the huge plane sat embedded in a house, torn apart on impact. Bits of blackened metal were strewn across the road in front of them. Its ass was a burned-out husk in the garage across the road. Little remained of the actual brick and tile dwelling the Hercules had hit, the walls having caved in around the wreckage. The Humvee it had been carrying lay further down the street, smashed to smithereens. Bodies were scattered around, most of them too badly decomposed to be identifiable. But their equipment he recognized just fine. These boys had been Special Forces. The Minimis, M4s and other fancy toys confirmed it. All of it was the sort of stuff that would be useful for buying Roslyn's way into Blackstone.

"There's something you don't see every day," Roslyn said, gaping at the wreckage.

"This isn't going to be pretty. But I'll feel better if we have more weaponry." He'd also feel better if she kept her lovely self in the car, but small chance of that.

Right on cue, the woman threw off her seatbelt. "Yeah, me too."

Shit. He hated the idea of having her out in the open, but they needed those supplies. "Okay."

A cold wind sent ice down his spine. Everything seemed calm, still. There were no signs of life nearby. Another perfect blue-sky day in a typical suburban street, near the edge of yet another country town.

Ros pushed her sunglasses further up her nose and held her gun in a good grip. She seemed to know what she was doing. Fuck, he hoped she did. In the years to come, her knowing how to handle herself would mean everything. She'd been having entirely too much fun when they'd been meant to be training last night. Not taking it seriously enough.

He handed her an empty backpack, care of the country store yesterday, and shouldered one himself. "Collect anything of use."

"Got it."

He gave her a hand up over the decimated concrete garden wall, helped her skirt a rose bush. The stupid thing was covered in more than flowers. Thorns cut into his hand when he held back a branch. It stung like shit.

"Damn it." Blood dripped from a deep scratch on his palm and a slice across two fingers. It had gotten him good.

"Are you alright?" Ros leant over and tugged on his arm, trying to get a look.

"I'm fine. You concentrate on you."

"Hold still." She ignored him and pulled a clean tissue out of a pocket, pressed it into his hand. Her forehead furrowed. "We should put some antiseptic cream on that."

"Later. Come on."

He'd never admit it, but she'd been right about his being confused. Discombob-whatever. Things had changed too fast. Twice today she'd turned and caught him frowning at her. She'd given him hell when he refused to talk about it.

Women ... you didn't need to discuss everything. Besides, things would sort themselves out soon enough. Blackstone was now only three or four hours' drive away at most. He hadn't changed direction. Instead, he'd slowed them down, dragging out the time he had left with her. Tomorrow he'd give her up. One more day wouldn't hurt anything.

"Come here." He nudged the remains of a soldier, skin sunken and gray. "You check they're properly dead, then grab everything off their belts. Any packs strapped to their legs or chests."

"This is so craven."

"No, Ros. This is survival."

Her mouth pursed, but she nodded in understanding. "Yeah. We should bury them."

"You could spend the rest of your life burying the dead. Just concentrate on keeping yourself alive."

Her gaze moved between him and the dead soldier, a heavy frown on her face. He almost asked her what she was thinking. And then he spied it, tucked beneath the corpse's foot. "Here we go. This is a H&K Tactical. It's got all the bells and whistles." He dusted off the dirt and ejected the clip. It all looked to be intact and the cylinder didn't appear to be jammed. "I'll clean it tonight and then it'll be yours. Grab any ammunition."

Obviously curious, she stepped closer. "That's a silencer, right?"

"Right, and this is a flashlight. But it's the silencer that's crucial. Noise attracts infected. These boys came prepared."

The Hercules had been torn in half, leaving the internal floor sitting almost at ground level. It was easy enough to walk in. Several chairs were still intact. So were several passengers. The stink of rotting bodies messed with him, even after this long. Every time he thought he'd gotten used to it, a corpse came along that proved him wrong.

Wiring and other assorted shit hung down. The nose of the beast lay in semi-darkness ahead of them, cockpit door open.

"Stay back," he said.

Carefully he picked his way toward the front, watching his footing. Shit had been tossed everywhere, smashed laptops and other equipment, parts of the plane's interior. A decapitated body hung over the back of a chair. Interestingly enough, it wore a skirt and a suit jacket. Several of the other corpses still buckled into their seats wore ties.

"They were moving VIPs. Politicians, probably. Getting them west, away from everything."

"I thought they'd have a bunker or something," she said.

"This might have been the back-up plan."

Ros nodded and stopped beside the remains of a soldier sitting upright in a seat. She started stripping the equipment with her face screwed up. So long as she did it she could make as many funny looks as she liked. This was life now, scavenging for supplies amongst the dead. Doing what you had to, to survive. Dirty and horrible as it was, it wouldn't be changing anytime soon.

A mass of cases and boxes sat piled at the front. It looked like medical gear and rations packs, probably dislodged during the crash. Supplies would have been packed in the rear. He picked his way around the debris, heading for the cockpit. Time to make sure they were totally alone. Inside the wreckage felt even colder than the air outside. He kept his gun in one hand and a flashlight in the other.

It was dark in the cockpit. The pilot was missing, the empty seat patchy with dark stains. Opposite, the co-pilot's remains were still strapped into the seat. Its mouth stretched wide and teeth embedded in its shriveled forearm. Nothing much remained of its other arm. The white of bone gleamed in the light, almost intact with the exception of several fingers. Unable to escape, the infected had eaten its own flesh rather than starve.

It was a fucked-up thing, seriously disturbing. He turned away, his stomach pitching. His mouth tasted foul.

An infected lunged at him out of the shadows, catching him by surprise. He bounced off the metal hatch, jarring his shoulder and sending his gun flying.

"Fuck!"

The thing didn't make a sound. Dirty fingers clawed at him, trying to reach him.

"Nick!"

"Stay back." He stumbled back through the hatch, falling on his ass as he tried desperately to evade that hand. "Don't you come up here."

With a wheezing noise the zombie lunged for him, but got drawn up short. Something held it back. Its left arm stretched out behind it, tethered still to the belt. How the fuck had he not seen it? It had to have been crouched in the shadows. He'd been fucking careless. It growled at him silently, lips stretched wide showing shattered teeth and a gaping hole. The thing had eaten its own tongue.

"Nick, turn away," shouted Ros.

"Shit. No! Don't."

She didn't listen. Her first bullet punched through the metal a scant half a meter above him, sending sparks flying. His eardrums pounded. The woman was going to fucking kill him. Quickly, he hit the ground, covered his head with his hands. Because the second bullet ... holy shit. The zombie dropped like a dead weight behind him. Everything fell quiet, all over. Nothing remained of where its heart had been. Nick's pants and shoes were splattered with gore.

"It's dead. You hit it," he said, stunned.

"Are you hurt?" Roslyn rushed to him, almost tripping over in the process. She was shaking with adrenalin. How she'd managed to hit anything he did not know. He was just thankful she hadn't hit him.

"No, I'm fine." He climbed back to his feet. "You did good."

"Thanks."

"You really got him with that second shot."

"The first was a warning shot," she said, taking a deep breath. "You needed to cover your face."

Huh. "That was on purpose?"

She nodded. "I was only five or six meters away. Unlikely I'd mess up and hit you at that range."

"Oh," he said. "Good job. But I could have handled it."

She cocked her head. "It was about to fall on top of you, Nick. I couldn't just do nothing."

"No," he said. "It couldn't reach me. Its arm had caught on something. It was stuck. Come on, let's gather this stuff and get out of here."

He did a more thorough search of the wreck while Roslyn carried some of the boxes to the pickup. Hanging around after firing the shots wasn't smart. But if they could just secure the food rations and medical supplies, round up the last of the weapons, they'd be doing well. She would be welcomed into Blackstone with open arms. No way could they say no with all this in the offering.

"Nick." She stood staring at the cockpit hatch, eyes so wide he could only see white.

"What?"

"It moved." She pointed at the dead infected, hand trembling.

"Ros, you killed it."

"Yeah." She stared at the thing, face deathly white in the low lighting. "I know, but it moved."

She'd had a long day. Hell, he'd had a long day. They had enough supplies.

He cupped her face in his hands. Her wide eyes didn't meet his, still trying to watch the infected.

"Let's find some place safe for the night," he suggested. "I'll pick a fight with you and then we can have make-up sex. You'd like that, wouldn't you?"

She gave him a pissy look. "I'm serious. It moved."

"Probably just air escaping."

"No. I know what I saw."

Everything was quiet outside. There was nothing to disguise the noise of a fast-approaching vehicle. His heart punched hard. Shit, no. Getting caught in the wreckage wasn't good. Tires squealed as someone slammed on the brakes. Car doors were thrown open.

"Get down. Stay behind me," he ordered. Ros pulled her gun from the back of her belt as he chambered a round in his own. They both knelt behind the rows of seats, cornered by the newcomers. Fuck no. This was bad. "I'm serious. Stay back."

"Hellooo!" a male voice called from outside. "Anybody there?"

Someone else spoke. There were at least two of them. Two people he could handle. And he wouldn't hesitate to kill them both if they were a threat.

"Hey! Anyone in there?" The voice sounded oddly familiar. But it was the next one that turned him stone cold.

"Pete, you see anything?"

No reply. Of course there was no reply. Pete would be working off signals, keeping silent because silent was smarter. If nothing else, Pete could be a clever bastard. Clever and fucking nasty. Not the sort of person he wanted around Ros. Nick could only hope the pricks were still wary enough of him to make no sudden moves on her. Amongst their group he'd been one of the fastest on the draw and he had never backed down when it mattered. Even Emmet had never directly challenged him.

One time a member of their party had taken exception to him. Not long after New Years, when the plague had well and truly set in and the dead lay rotting on the ground. The bastard had come up on him from behind and attempted to slit his throat. Nick had gutted him and left him to die, eaten alive by infected. The screams had gone on and on. He wasn't proud of it, but he'd done it. And if it kept Roslyn safe he'd do it again in an instant.

"I need you to trust me," Nick said, his mouth close to her ear. "No matter what, you trust me. Okay?"

"But ..."

"Trust me, Ros. Please."

Her pretty face scrunched up, but she nodded. "Alright."

"Pete, that you?" he called out, his voice echoing through the space. "It's Nick."

"Nick?"

"Yeah, mate."

"Fuck me. We thought you were dead." Pete chuckled and they heard the sounds of heavy footsteps approaching. "Man, this is great."

Either they'd shoot him straight up, or he was in with a chance. Hard to tell which, with old friends like these. Justin and Pete had been thrown out of Blackstone at the same time as him, but they'd parted company straight away. More accurately, he'd taken off on them. They were trouble. They'd been in tight with Emmet, their former sergeant. Emmet had been a vicious prick. He'd been the one to decide that they'd do surveillance on Blackstone and attack it when the time was right. Round up the women and dispose of the rest. Emmet had been a fucking psychopath, and that was putting it lightly.

Nick rose to his feet, gun still in hand. If it came to a showdown, he couldn't beat them both. Plus, Ros might get hurt in the cross-fire. There had to be a better way to get out of this.

"Thought you guys were heading north," Nick said for something to say. He should have known they'd be hanging around Blackstone, still plotting revenge. Not as if they'd have anything else to live for. But he had Ros, and he should have been a fuckload more careful.

"We got bored." Pete looked the same as always, big and mean. His smile didn't set Nick at ease in the least. Justin was smaller, but definitely more dangerous. He watched Nick warily, gaze all over his weapon. Let them be careful. That would give Nick more time.

"Who you got with you?" Justin asked. Of course he did. There was no getting out of it.

Slowly, Ros rose to her feet. "Hi."

"You got yourself a girl? Fuck me." Pete grinned, gaze glued to the curves of Ros's breasts. Nick wanted to gouge the fucker's eyeballs out with his bare hands. Holding back was hard. Thank God she wore a few layers. Eventually, Pete shook his head and laughed. "I mean ... sorry. It's been a while since we've seen a woman. I'm Pete, this is Justin."

"Roslyn," she said with a brave smile.

Justin just stared at her, setting off every fucking alarm inside Nick's head. He should have taken her straight to Blackstone. He shouldn't have fucked around and delayed. She'd have been safe then. The chances of these two letting her get away without blood being shed were non-existent. But that was okay. He was more than happy to kill them for her. Shits like this didn't deserve to breathe the same air as her. He just had to pick the time right, give her the best chance possible.

"Nice to meet you both," she said chirpily. Her smile didn't slip till the end.

Nick slung an arm around her shoulders, pulled her closer. Thankfully, she came, tucking herself in against him. "There's a stack of food and stuff here."

"Excellent," said Pete. "We've got a case of rum."

Nick smiled. "Let's party."

CHAPTER TWENTY-THREE

Roslyn concentrated on the flames dancing in the fireplace. Let them lull her, distract her from the conversation and the moaning outside. Both were bad. Both sickened her and scared her witless.

They'd picked a squat brick building to hole up in for the night, on account of the tall wire fence that surrounded the property. A collection of broken-down cars filled the front yard. Bodies had been found in a back bedroom. Justin had dragged them outside, poured petrol over them and lit them up, then asked her if she wanted to toast some marshmallows. The creep wasn't half as funny as he thought he was. He watched her constantly. Her skin felt ready to crawl right off her and slink away somewhere safe.

Pete, on the other hand, took dickhead depravity to new heights. Every second word out of his mouth was a smutty pun. The one saving grace was that he seemed to think she wasn't bright enough to realize. She tried not to jump every time one of the idiots accidentally brushed up against her in passing.

Meanwhile, Nick did nothing but dart her glances.

Nothing but throw back rum and laugh at their sordid jokes. Swap stories of the good old days. Tricks they'd played. Lies they'd told. Women they'd screwed. Even people they'd killed. She didn't know him as well as she thought she did. But how well could you get to know someone in the space of a week, special circumstances or no? Every time he opened his mouth it got worse. He kept stealing looks at her and she couldn't bring herself to meet his eyes any longer. They bitched about some place called Blackstone. The name came up time and again. That and someone called Emmet. Apparently his death was much lamented by good old Justin and Pete.

He'd said to trust him. She wasn't sure she could do that without putting her hands over her ears and going la-la-la for the rest of the night. Maybe if she tried really hard she could block them out. Yes, she could ignore them. And she could keep doing it right up until someone said his name. Right up until she heard his voice. Then she couldn't help but take in every last horrible, sordid detail.

"What about that chick in Perth." Pete's voice was a slimy sound that slid right through her and out the other side. He bounced a bone handled knife in his hand, waving the tip in her general direction. "The one you and Jonesy did."

Nick gave a broad smile. "Good times."

Fuck him and his ever-ready cock.

"Yeah. And there were those two in Darwin who took a liking to you." Pete snuck her a dark look while Nick chuckled and sipped his drink. He never did it when Nick was looking. It gave her hope. At least they were still cautious of him, for now.

A half smile curled Pete's lips as he threw the knife up in the air and caught it, over and over. Light from the fire flickered on the sharp edge of the blade. He sure was handy with the weapon. Justin asked Nick a question. She didn't hear what it was. The blade kept moving, mesmerizing her. It never stopped. She could almost feel the promise of the blade against her skin. Holding back the urge to bolt was hard. Her legs tensed, her back and shoulders, her everything. God, she wanted out of there so damn bad.

Pete gave her another look, promising all sorts of violence and pain. Not just her imagination. Her lungs were working hard, but she could hardly breathe.

"Nick, how about when you shot that bloody whingeing corporal?" Pete put down his knife and started rolling the biggest joint she'd ever seen in her life. The smell of mull outdid the combined smell of their unwashed bodies. Pete and Justin weren't big on deodorant, apparently. "You remember, just before they leveled the hospital. Can't say that didn't feel good."

"That bastard," said the man she might have been in love with but sure as hell didn't want to be anywhere near just then. "Nah, that felt fan-fucking-tastic."

Cue much guffawing and description of brain splatter. Ah, but they were witty tools. She kept her face calm, slack and made a list in her head of her favorite books, in alphabetical order by author surname. When Nick shot her a look she ignored him. Atwood, Austen, Bronte, Byatt ... who else?

Justin smirked. "If I had to hear about his poor wife and kids back home one more time I was going to do it myself."

Nick was just playing a part. She had to trust him. He didn't mean it. They were going to get out of this and all would be awesome. It would.

She sat beside him on a battered old yellow lounge, his big hand curved over her knee. The army rations from dinner churned in her belly. If she could make it through the night without puking, she'd be doing well. Everything about this nauseated her. Evil emanated off these two as badly as their BO. Only Nick's presence held them back for now, but that wouldn't last. Pete and Justin had taken him aside for a word earlier. She didn't even want to know what had been said. Well, she did, but she didn't. Lecherous Neil from school looked like child's play compared to these two. The air of menace in the dingy little lounge room was as palpable as the heat from the blazing fire, singeing the ceiling.

Her gun stayed tucked in her belt. Her back ached where it dug into her spine, but no way would she remove it.

"Time for bed, hey?" Nick gave her knee a squeeze and stood.

"What, already?" Pete said, then leered at her with a grin a hundred dentists couldn't have helped. "Can't say I blame ya."

"See you in the morning, boys." Nick winked and led her toward one of the bedrooms. The one furthest from where the bodies had been found.

"Don't do anything I wouldn't do," Justin croaked around a cloud of smoke and passed the joint back his friend.

Nick chuckled.

Her shoulders crept higher and higher.

The door clicked shut behind them and he set the torch on the floor. There was a dingy old double bed and a motorbike, laid out in parts on a layer of newspapers to protect the carpet. Considering it had been worn bare, she couldn't see the point. Nick grabbed the chair from in front of a desk and jammed it under the door handle, checking it twice.

"They've given me tonight to talk you around. I've got a plan." He touched her arm and she skipped back a step.

"Ros."

"Just ... give me a minute here."

"No. Listen to me." He reached for her and she reacted without thought. The flat of her palm smacked into his cheek. Her hand stung. Nick just stared at her.

"Shit," she whispered.

He looked every bit as stunned as she felt. He blinked at her again and again. His cheek was dark in the low light. Fuck, she'd actually hit him.

"I'm sorry," she said.

Then he really grabbed her. His hands wrapped around her upper arms and he pulled her in tight against him. Her breasts were mashed up against his chest and his mouth covered hers in a brutally hard kiss. One hand squeezed her ass while the other held the back of her neck. He wasn't gentle. But neither was she. Fear and anger fueled them both.

He fucked her mouth with his tongue. There was no other word for it. Fingers dug into her, holding her against him. She bit at him, or tried to. So mad, nothing made sense. The things he'd said, the words were a jumble in her head. She just wanted to hurt him. The way he'd talked about other women made her bloodthirsty. If she could have, she'd have crawled beneath his skin and done him damage from the inside out.

She tore at the button on his jeans, the zip, shoved the denim down over his hips. Her fingernails scratched at his hips and flat stomach. Beneath his hot skin, his muscles flinched. He groaned into her mouth.

Fuck yes, she wanted to mark him. Needed to.

When she slid her hand into his boxers and pressed her fingernails into the shaft of his cock, however, he stopped her quick smart. He grunted, grabbed her wrist and spun her, pushing her onto her stomach, onto the mattress. The air rushed out of her with an *oomph*. Her feet barely touched the ground. The spare reading glasses in her shirt pocket pressed into her. His hands dug beneath her, undoing her jeans and tearing them down her legs. They shackled her knees. He threw her gun onto the mattress beside her, but she didn't want to shoot him. Beat at him with her hands though, yes. She tried to get up and fight back, but she couldn't. Strong hands pulled her back until she was half standing, bent over the bed with her legs spread.

Without a word he shoved his cock into her, driving her forward onto the mattress.

Oh, shit. She wasn't ready. Pain tripped through her and a high, hurt noise escaped her.

Suddenly his arms were around her, drawing her back against him. His breath warmed her neck. She kept her hands flat on the mattress as her sex ached around the hard length of him.

"I'm sorry," he said. "Fuck, Ros. I'm so sorry."

One of his big hands joined hers on the bed. Fingers stroked her where they were joined. Teasing and appeasing her. Soft touches over the lips of her sex, her thighs and her belly. He moved restlessly over her body while his lips pressed kisses to her neck. He licked at her earlobe and rubbed his nose against the soft skin beneath. The warmth of his bare pelvis and thighs pressed against her. His cock throbbed inside her, feeling so much bigger than he ever had before on account of her barely being wet.

"Roslyn. Please, talk to me." His fingers brushed over her sex, sliding around her clit, making her soften for him. "Tell me to get out of you. If you tell me I will. I swear."

"No, wait."

"Sweetheart." He sounded tortured. A lot like how she felt, mentally, physically, everything. Catching her breath seemed impossible. Her lungs were fried. Her body bruised.

"Keep touching me, Nick. Just ..."

"Yes."

He kissed and nibbled the nape of her neck, mumbling nonsense. How perfect she was. How beautiful. How he'd never let anyone hurt her. But he was the one who'd done the damage.

She still couldn't resist him. His fingers felt so good. Whatever they did, she wanted more. Her sex wept for him and his cock shifted inside her. Ever so carefully, slowly, he drew back and his cock slid almost all the way out of her. She hated it, the emptiness, the loss of him. Her hips pressed back.

"Nick. Please."

"Carefully," he said, pushing back into her.

The pain changed, morphed into something akin to pleasure. The ache shifted to reside wholly behind her clit. But it should hurt. She wanted it to. Everything about this situation wounded her.

He pressed into her, filling her to overflowing, then retreating. The heat of his body left her back as he straightened to stand behind her. His hands stroked over her sides, her back, before coming to rest on her hips. He fucked her so sweetly she could have cried, face buried in the sleeping bags atop the bed.

Maybe, just a little, she did.

Pressure built inside her and his movements grew more ragged. The thrust and retreat of his cock inside her melted her down, made her liquid. If it weren't for his grip on her she'd have fallen. Her knees would have given out. No matter how badly she wanted to stay with him.

His body bucked against hers and he came with a noise unlike anything she'd ever heard. A harsh exhale with gritted teeth, an agonized groan. Her body shook but she didn't come. So close but she couldn't. Her mind wouldn't let go. So much was wrong.

Nick held her to him as he emptied inside her. There were no noises outside the room. Gently he rolled her over, climbed onto the mattress and pulled further up onto the bed with her pants hanging above her ankles. He'd already done his back up.

"Kiss me," he said.

"W-we need to talk."

He didn't listen. His hand slid down over her stomach, slid in the wet mess between her legs. Firm lips covered hers, kissing over and over until she gave in. Of course she gave in. When it came to him she was hopeless.

Muscles low in her belly tensed as his finger teased her. Her hands fisted in his shirt and her legs opened wider, giving him access. So damn close. The aching pressure built to epic proportions. He kissed her till her head spun and her cunt clenched greedily at the finger he slid into her. He rubbed at some secret spot inside her and his thumb brushed over her clit, back and forth, and she came hard. His mouth covered hers, silencing her as it went on and on. Her body bowed beneath the pressure, every muscle drawn tight. Not a single thought remained in her head. The orgasm drained her completely. She lay lax on the bed as he pulled her pants up.

Nick dragged the sleeping bags out from beneath her, covered her.

Raucous laughter came from somewhere outside the door. It chilled the blood in her veins.

Nicked leant in closer. "Keep your shoes on. I want you ready to run."

"What's the plan?" she asked, not looking at him.

"We wait till they're passed out, then you go out the window. Get in the pickup and get the hell out of here." Nick stood up and motioned for her to do the same. He spread one of the waiting sleeping bags out across the mattress. "Take your shirt off. If they check in on us they're going to expect to see you undressed."

Her hands shook as she did so. Shook so bad he had to help her.

"The bra?" she asked.

"No. Leave that on," he said, his gaze hard. "I don't want them seeing any more of you than necessary. "

He pulled off his shirt and turned off the light. They both lay down, a sleeping bag covering them, especially the tell-tale boots. He put his arm around her, drawing her closer to keep her warm. The temperature was cooler in the bedroom, away from the heat of the fire. Now that her body was cooling she could feel the difference. But she'd never been happier to get away from people in her life.

"Talk to me, Ros."

"And say what?" she asked.

He sighed, rested the side of his nose against her forehead, getting closer than she knew how to take just then. Pity she couldn't bring herself to move away.

"I didn't kill anyone who wasn't bitten or a danger in some other way," he said. "Some people lost it, couldn't take the pressure. They put us all at risk. I don't enjoy killing, but I won't hesitate if it's necessary."

She swallowed hard. He was a soldier ... had been a soldier. She knew this was part of his job but hearing him say it so coldly, so definitely—her little world trembled.

"What's Blackstone? Who's Emmet?" she asked.

"Blackstone is where you're going to go. You get back on the Northern Highway and you'll hit it. Okay? That's where you go when you get out of here. Don't hesitate."

"Alright. And Emmet?"

He shifted slightly. "He was our leader. The highest-ranked asshole left after everything went to shit. He wanted women and he was prepared to kill to get them."

"Bet your friends out there loved him. What did you think of him?"

He didn't answer for a while. "I wanted him dead. I just didn't do it."

"Why?"

"He killed anyone who stood up to him. But I think ... I think I was so used to being told what to do, it was almost second nature. I like to think I would have shot him before he hurt an innocent, but honestly, I don't know. I didn't even know why the fuck I was still alive back then. What I was supposed to do with myself. And everyone seemed to agree with him." He made a noise, soft and bitter. "But they were just planning when to take him out. They didn't trust me to help. I wouldn't have trusted me either, if I was them. I was a fucking mess. Drinking much more than I should have. Taking all sorts of shit."

"And the women Pete talked about?"

"Were willing. Always."

"And did you treat them badly? Because that's how it sounded."

Another deep sigh and his chest brushed against her through the thin fabric layer of her bra. "I wasn't always as respectful as I should have been, no. But I've never raised my hand to a woman, I swear."

At least he didn't make excuses. That was something. He had no need, because apparently she was prepared to make them for him.

His fingers stroked her hair, the nape of her neck. "I wish I could tell you I've always tried to do the right thing. But I can't," he said, his voice so very soft. His lips brushed against her temple. "I did what was easy and I did what I wanted. Other people didn't factor into it for me. I'm sorry. I know you deserve better."

She said nothing.

"I'll get you out of here. I promise."

"I'm scared," she admitted.

"I know." He huffed out a breath, held her tighter.

They lay in silence for what felt like hours. Her mind wouldn't quiet. All the things he'd said rolled around and around.

At some stage she heard footsteps outside. Seemed Pete and Justin were doing some guard duty. Mostly likely focused on keeping her in rather than the zombies out. Nick rubbed her back, mumbled some nonsense. Everything wasn't going to be okay but she didn't see the point in contradicting him. She got as close to him as physically possible and hung onto his arm. Sometimes acting brave was overrated.

Terror wore her out. She must have fallen asleep eventually, because Nick shook her awake. It was silent outside, in the lounge and in the outside world. Tension lined his face. He looked so serious, somber. But the big tell was the way he avoided her eyes. She'd never seen Nick afraid before. Not like this. It terrified her.

Nick put a finger to his lips, motioned her off the bed. Carefully, quietly, she moved. The shushing noises of the sleeping bag were like shouts. The squeaking of the bedsprings sounded like screams. He handed over her shirt and pulled back the curtain. The window screeched like a wounded cat as he slid it open. Kookaburras laughed somewhere off in the bush. The fence-line was clear. The sun had only just started to rise; stars still flickered overhead. Her heart pounded.

He slipped the pickup keys into her jeans pocket, helped her onto the window ledge.

"You drive straight through the gate and you do it fast. The pickup will break the lock fine. Up the highway until Blackstone. The tank is full. Don't stop if you can help it," he said, his voice low and rough. "There's a gun and ammunition in the glovebox. More in the storage chest on the back. You use them to buy your way in if you have to."

"I've still got my gun." She'd slept with it wedged into her belt, safety most definitely on. "You'll follow, right?"

Instead of answering he kissed her, mashing his lips to hers, hard and fast.

"Nick, tell me you're coming too."

He helped her out the window and down onto the dewy grass. Her breath misted the air.

"I'm going to follow," he said. His eyes told her differently.

"You said you wouldn't lie to me. Why aren't you coming?"

"Someone needs to distract them." He grabbed the back of her head and pulled her in, kissed her one more time. Her top lip felt bruised. So did her heart. How the hell had it come to this?

"Go," he said.

"Come with me."

"Go. Now." He gave her a push and pulled the window closed, his face set. "Run."

And she ran.

Frost covered the pickup's windshield and windows. She threw the door open and dived in, fumbling in her pocket for the keys. The tip of the key wouldn't go into the damn ignition. Her hands were trembling. Her blood pounded behind her ears. She could do this. In went the key, finally, and she twisted it hard. The engine roared to life. She jammed her foot on the clutch and threw it into gear, flipped on the windshield wipers to clear the frost. Her foot hit the accelerator and the pickup's wheels spun on the slick surface. Then it took off, thundering toward the double gates, bound with chains and rope in the absence of a padlock. If Nick said the truck would take them out then it would. And it did. The front of the vehicle crashed into the metal frames and sent them flying. The bone-rattling shriek of metal scraping against metal came from beneath the vehicle, then half of the gate lay on the road in her rear-view mirror.

From behind her came the first gunshots. The popping of a pistol, followed by the boom of something bigger.

"Nick."

They'd kill him. No. She couldn't do this.

She slammed on the brakes and the car skidded to a halt, smoke rising from the abused front tires. Nope, she couldn't do it. She couldn't leave him again. Driving away and leaving him alone to deal with those two bastards just wasn't in her.

She'd tucked her gun in beside her. Seatbelt on. She spun the wheel hard, cracked plastic digging into her palms. Time to go. The pickup flew back down the road toward the ugly little house. More shots were fired and Justin ran out of the house, into the yard. Violence beat inside her. The least the bastard deserved was a bullet.

Driving and shooting at the same time always looked simple in movies. Her hand searched for the weapon she'd put beside her on the carseat. Bullets shattered the windshield not far from her head. The vehicle swerved wildly and she clutched at the wheel, trying to get it back under control. A headlight blew. Everything was out of control. She screamed and screamed.

Through the broken glass she could just make out the figure of Justin with his gun pointed at her. Her weapon rattled around on the floor now, beyond her reach. More bullets punched holes through the glass and she ducked. Justin had a grim smile on his ugly face.

He wanted to kill her.

That was fine. She wanted to kill him too.

Her foot pressed down on the pedal and the truck flew, actually going airborne for a moment when she misjudged the entrance to the driveway and jumped the gutter. The return to earth came with an almighty crash. Her teeth clattered, her brain rattled. With one hand on the wheel she sunk down in her seat and bore down on the bastard.

A bullet skimmed her ear. It was the noise of its passing that alerted her. She barely felt any pain.

Justin made no move to get out of her path. Still too drunk and stoned or whatever, she had no idea. And then he was out of time. She tried to brake too late. Nothing seemed to work right. The truck ploughed into him, punching him into the wall of the house. Inertia threw her forwards and pain filled her chest. Bricks and mortar flew.

CHAPTER TWENTY-FOUR

Pete was waiting for Nick when he opened the bedroom door. The man sat on the dodgy old single lounge chair smoking a cigarette, yawning and rubbing his eyes. A shotgun sat across his lap. Justin had passed out facedown on the floor, not too far from the front door. The air stank of smoke from the fire, the cigarette, and the weed. It suffocated him. It felt like his heart and lungs had shriveled up inside his chest. But he wasn't done yet. His pistol sat tucked into in the back of his belt, fully loaded.

"Hey," said Pete with a slow smirk, looking past him for signs of Ros, no doubt.

"Hey."

Letting her go had been the hardest thing he'd ever done. Cutting off his hand would have hurt less. She needed to get away clean. And someone needed to finish these bastards. Beneath all the pain he felt strangely calm, knowing this was finally it. He didn't kid himself. The likelihood of him walking away from this was next to non-existent.

With a dumb-ass grin Pete waved him forward. "How'd it go? Talking to her?"

He smiled back calmly.

Pete's fingers slid lovingly over the barrel of the shottie. He didn't doubt the threat. Sooner or later Pete and Justin would decide to get rid of him. Their playing nice was never really believable. That Pete hadn't yet tired of Justin and taken his bowie knife to him came as a bit of a surprise. Pete had a nasty temper, and the only person he'd ever really been afraid of was Emmet.

Outside, the truck engine turned over.

"Stop her!" Pete screamed, his lips drawn back, exposing yellowed clenched teeth. He looked like a fucking animal, letting loose a roar that should have shook the building. To his left, Justin jumped up, making a dive for the gun on the coffee table.

Nick drew his weapon and fired. The bullets punched into the wall behind Pete's head as the man threw himself aside, toppling the shoddy chair. Pete fell onto the carpet and rolled onto his back, unharmed.

Justin scrambled for the front door.

The front gates clanged and squealed as Roslyn crashed into them, tearing them apart. They were too late. She'd gotten out. The relief nearly staggered him.

With a snarl Pete pulled up the shotgun. *Boom.* Nick dived back through the bedroom door as the hallway erupted into smoke and noise. His ears rang. *Boom.* Again the shotgun discharged. The wide open bedroom door exploded into a mass of splinters, a big hole in its middle that continued into the wall behind it. Dust filled the air.

Nick rolled onto his back, pulling up his weapon, but too late. Screaming his heart out, Pete charged through the door and fell on top of him. The man straddled him and fists pounded into his ribs. Pete's furious, bright-red face was beyond recognition. Nick blocked as many of the punches as possible, clawing at the fucker's face, trying to push him back. A sledgehammer of a hit landed below his ribs. Pain cramped Nick's guts as he fought to get the leverage to throw Pete off him. His legs flailed uselessly.

Out of the corner of his eye he spied the silver of Pete's bowie knife flying at his face. He grabbed the man's wrist with both hands, muscles straining. Pete snapped and growled, spraying his face with hot, wet spit.

Fuck, he could hear gunshots outside. Justin shooting at Ros. Please let her be gone by now.

Pete put his weight behind the blade. The wickedly sharp point of the knife pressed down, only an inch or two from Nick's eye. He pushed back, moving the knife a bare hand's length from his face. He couldn't move him. Not enough to count. A lunatic's grin curled Pete's lips.

The house suddenly shuddered and there was an almighty smash. The noise was deafening. Towards the front of the place, beams of timber snapped and the whole structure groaned. Plaster flakes rained down. For just a moment it distracted Pete. His brows jumped as he looked to the ever-widening crack spreading across the ceiling. With the last of his strength, Nick surged up, rolling the man. He reversed the blade, pointing it at his middle. Pete broke his momentum by putting out an elbow, bringing the turnabout to a halt. But it was too late. The bowie knife sunk deep into the man's side. Blood flowed onto the dirty carpet and Pete's eyes went wide and white. A high wheezing noise escaped him.

Nick pulled out the blade, fingers slipping on the slick bloody bone handle. In and up. Beneath the ribs and high towards the heart. This time Pete's skin felt like old leather, impossible to cut through. But Nick was plenty fucking motivated. Blood swelled to the surface, spreading out across Pete's gray T-shirt and staining it dark red.

No more movement. No nothing. Everything was quiet apart from the occasional death rattle from the house.

Where was Ros? What the fuck had she done?

He wiped off his bloody hands and grabbed his gun. Looked out in the mess of what had been the lounge room. Sunlight streamed in, lighting the clouds of dust and debris floating through the air. Fucking amazing. Half the roof seemed to have caved in. He could just make out the front of the truck, buried in rubble.

"Shit."

He raced to the bedroom window and pushed it open. Climbed out and ran toward the front. Bricks and roof tiles and fuck knew what else covered the crumpled hood of the truck. Blood covered the shattered outside of the windscreen and one of Justin's hands was just visible, still clutching a pistol. The rest of his body lay buried beneath the rubble.

Oh, holy fucking hell. What she'd done.

At the first sight of her bushy red hair his heart nearly gave up. She was slumped in the driver's seat, almost out of view.

"Ros." He wrenched the door open. "Ros!"

Her eyelids opened and she blinked repetitively, giving him a stunned look. Slowly, she smiled. "Nick."

Above her left breast, her shirt was covered in blood. Justin had hit her in the shoulder. More blood dribbled down from a small wound on her ear.

"It's okay. I'm here," he said, trying not to lose it. He tore off his shirt and held it against her, putting pressure on the gunshot wound. There was a med kit in the glovebox. He remembered it now. The compartment had popped open during the crash and its contents were spread across the floor.

"Hey," she croaked, her eyes glazed. "You got your shirt off."

"I know. Don't move." He grabbed up the bright red kit and tore into it. Gauze and pads. Tweezers and cream. A bottle of antiseptic. With his teeth and one hand he ripped open a packet of pads. Lifting the shirt for a second, he placed the pads over the bloody little hole in her shoulder. Fuck. So much damn blood.

"I drove a car into a building. Cool, huh?"

"Yeah, I noticed. Don't. Move."

"I'm fine," she said with an awkward giggle. Pain suffused her face and she grimaced. "Though that hurt."

"You've been shot, Ros."

"Yeah, my ear." She frowned and stared at her left arm lying uselessly beside her. "What? Why won't my arm work?"

"It's okay," he lied, biting open a packet of gauze. There was a roll of tape too. Amongst all of it he should be able to put together a decent enough bandage to get her to Blackstone. He had to. "Stay still for me."

"I couldn't leave you."

Everything in him squeezed tight. "I know. How do you feel?"

"Okay. Are you okay?" she asked, her voice slurred.

"I'm not the one who's been shot. You're going to need to sit forward for me."

"Just a little," she said, breathing heavy.

She whimpered when he carefully pulled her forward and he almost fucking burst into tears. Her skin felt clammy and her face was too pale.

"More than a little. You've been hit in the shoulder. Fuck, sweetheart. What were you thinking?" He pressed his balled up T-shirt against her, hard, and started working the gauze around her. "I was trying to keep you safe."

She didn't answer.

"Ros?"

Her eyes were closed. She'd passed out.

***

Nick stared at the remodeled dump truck that now served as Blackstone's front entrance with grim acceptance. It they killed him, then so be it. Whatever happened next was out of his hands.

He turned off the ignition of Pete and Justin's shiny green Camaro.

Roslyn's breathing was shallow. She hadn't stirred since he'd bundled her into the vehicle. Blood stained the makeshift bandage he'd tied around her shoulder. He'd never been so fucking scared in his life.

If she died …

A couple of men slipped out from between the truck and wall, rifles in their hands. Everything possible made up the wall surrounding Blackstone. A tipped train, bulldozed buildings, cars and trucks. Almost a hundred people lived inside the barricade of rubble surrounding the town's main street and a block or two in either direction. The only haven he knew of for her. The only place that could help.

Nick threw open the car door and climbed out, hands held high.

"Shit," muttered one.

"It's that bastard," said the other.

"She's hurt. Please." Nick stood still, empty hands stretched above his head. "Help her."

"Get on your knees," said one of the men while the other started talking rapid-fire into a walkie-talkie. "Slowly."

Walkie-Talkie Man moved around to the passenger-side door and looked in at Ros through the open window. The other guy kept his rifle pointed at Nick's head as he sunk slowly to the ground. Beneath his knees the bitumen felt like ice, as if the whole world had frozen. It had rained here recently and the damp soaked into his jeans. He hadn't bothered to find a shirt. Every second counted.

"Was she bit?" Walkie-talkie asked.

"No," said Nick. "I swear. We're both clean. She was shot. A couple of hours ago now. Please help her."

The man spoke again into his walkie-talkie. "Tell Lila she's got a patient. Is Tom on the way?"

"I'm here." A bull of a man slipped through the gap and strode forward. Late twenties, maybe. "What is this?"

"The woman's injured, Tom. He says it's not a bite."

Tom squinted at him against the glare of the sun, lip curled back in distaste. "That's not a risk we can take. Kill them."

"Hold it." Another two men pushed through, and these two Nick recognized. The taller, older, blond bastard was Captain Sean Manning. He'd been behind the coup against Emmet. The younger blond man was the town sheriff, Finn. Last time they'd met, both had threatened to kill him. Fine, as long as they helped Roslyn. He didn't give a shit what happened to him anymore.

"You said yourself, Finn, that you'd shoot him if he showed his face here again," said Tom. "Going back on your word now?"

"Why don't we wait till we know what's going on before we start killing people?" suggested the sheriff.

"Let me through!" a woman shouted from inside Blackstone.

"Keep her back there," Tom ordered.

Apparently Tom didn't have quite as much authority as he thought, because a woman stalked out with a hefty first-aid kit in hand. Thank fuck. Nick couldn't care less who was in charge. The idiots could stand around all day comparing dick sizes, so long as Roslyn got help.

He could feel his former captain's eyes boring into him. The man's hand lingered near the gun at his side. Funny, they'd been friends once. Sort of.

"Damn it, Lila," said Tom. "You're our only medic. You can't expose yourself like this. What if there were snipers?"

The woman ignored him, pushing Walkie-Talkie Man aside to get to Roslyn. "She was shot?"

"About three hours ago," Nick said.

"She's lost a lot of blood," Lila said with a frown.

"I'm O-negative, compatible with everything," said Nick. "You can give her mine."

Lila nodded. "Right, let's get you both inside."

"There is no way ..." Tom began. No one seemed to be listening.

"I warned you about coming here," said the sheriff in a low voice, stepping closer. The guy with his rifle trained on Nick moved aside to make room.

"So kill me," said Nick. "Just let me help her first."

"She needs his blood, Finn," said Lila. The woman summoned Sean with a wave of her hand. "Carry her. Be careful."

Sean leant down and emerged with Roslyn in his arms. Her head fell back, limp. He could barely breathe; it felt as if his ribs grew tighter by the minute. She had to be okay.

"I don't trust you," said the sheriff. "And I did promise to kill you the next time you showed your face here."

Nick said nothing. He knew, but he'd come anyway. He'd had no choice. Blackstone was the only place where he knew for certain civilization still existed. The only place that could keep her alive.

"She might need your blood. But she doesn't need you conscious. And I don't trust you awake." The sheriff nodded. The man beside him raised his rifle and slammed the stock into Nick's face.

***

Nick came to as they were carrying him through town, Finn supporting his left arm and one of the other men his right. His feet dragged on the ground. Fuck, he'd thought the bottle of wine had hurt, but Roslyn was a pussy cat in comparison to their hitting power. His head felt like it was caught in a vice, slowly getting the shit squeezed out of it. Even sunlight hurt. Plus, Pete had managed to land some decent blows on him earlier, giving him a full-body ache.

Sean carried Roslyn in front of them. He could only see her arm hanging down, her boots swinging with each step. She had to be okay.

Up ahead, Lila, the woman with the big-ass first aid kit, hurried into a small wooden house, directing the rest to follow. Nick staggered, trying to get his feet beneath him. Fuck, his head hurt.

"Stop," Finn said. "Hold him up."

The other man did as asked while Nick tried to make his knees work. It took a few goes.

"Hands in front of you." Finn didn't wait for him. He grabbed his wrists and slapped on the cuffs with professional ease. "Right. Inside."

Someone yelled out from behind them. An angry torrent of words he couldn't make out. Something hit his back, stinging like shit. A stone. They'd thrown a fucking stone at him. A crowd of people were gathering back down the street, watching with open hatred.

"Back off." Finn's eyes were furious, his mouth tight. "Right now."

"Get that bastard out of our town!" someone yelled.

A chorus of idiots joined in, with "yeah" and "fuck yeah" and other genius statements. Another stone flew past his head. One hit Finn in the arm and he swore a blue streak. Things were definitely screwed in paradise if they were taking potshots at the sheriff. Nick had expected to be met with extreme dislike, maybe even a bullet, but people gathering to stone him came as a bit of a surprise.

"Take him inside, now," Finn directed the other man.

They hustled him into the house. A good thing—his head didn't hurt so bad out of the sun. Roslyn was stretched out on a double bed in what had probably once been a bedroom, though most of the contents were gone now in favor of medical equipment. Her beautiful face was too pale. Her red hair looked shockingly stark in contrast. Sean was helping Lila strip her out of her bloody shirt, carefully cutting through the bulk of the bandaging. The medic cut through the strap of Ros's bra and peeled the bloodstained material down a little, away from the wound, exposing the top curve of her breast.

"Don't look," he growled and Finn and Sean kept their eyes averted. Just as fucking well. He was losing what little remained of his mind seeing her lying there so still. "How is she?"

Lila, the medic, pointed to chair beside the bed. "Sit here."

Sean pulled a pair of shattered reading glasses from the pocket of Ros's bloody shirt.

Nick could only stare. "She's going to be mad. She's always losing her glasses."

"What do you need, Lila?" Sean asked, hovering by the woman's elbow. He couldn't remember the captain ever hanging onto a woman's skirts before, but there was a first time for everything.

"I just need to clean the wound first so I can see what's going on," she said, her hands constantly moving.

Nick fell into the chair beside Roslyn and Finn fiddled with the cuffs, producing another pair so that he was connected to the sturdy iron bed frame. Then Finn stood at the end of the mattress, pistol in hand. The sheriff's eyes never left him. Fuck them. Whatever. So long as they helped her. He slumped tiredly in his chair. The place smelled of cleaning fluids, antibacterial stuff. Roslyn obviously wasn't the first patient they'd ever seen.

"Finn?" Lila sighed at the cuffs on Nick's wrists. "Isn't this overkill?"

"They stay on," said the sheriff. "Work around them."

The medic grumbled but didn't raise the subject again. Nick leaned over, resting his elbow on the frame to make it easier on the medic. Lila wrapped a band around his upper arm, preparing to take his blood. Next she swabbed Roslyn's forearm then got busy filling a syringe with something.

"What are you giving her?" he asked.

"Morphine for the pain," said Lila, a little frown of concentration on her face. Her teeth were sunk into her bottom lip. "Something to make sure she doesn't wake up while I'm digging the bullet out of her."

The way the woman said it gave him pause. "You've got experience in this sort of thing, right?"

Lila didn't meet his eyes. "A little."

"What? What do you mean?" Fear flashed through him and he jolted upright in his seat.

"Easy," Sean warned.

"What's going on here?" Nick edged forward and Finn raised his gun, pointing it at his chest.

Lila took a deep breath. "I'm a dental nurse. But I'm the best chance you have for her."

A wave of dizziness came over him. He almost had to hang his head between his knees. "A dental nurse? Y-you're a fucking dental nurse?"

"I will do the best I can for her."

Nick hissed out a breath. "Shit. She doesn't need her teeth cleaned."

"Lila's the only chance you've got, Nick." Sean gave him a look not entirely without compassion. "Just sit back and let her work. This isn't the first bullet wound she's seen."

"Oh fuck." Seriously, he thought he might hyperventilate. Lila stuck the needle into Ros's arm and he nearly decorated the floor with his puke. He couldn't stand it. "Please don't kill her. Please."

Lila glanced at him but didn't answer.

"Who is she?" asked Sean.

"Her name is Roslyn Stewart. She used to be a librarian." Nick breathed deep, did his best to get his shit together. Ros needed him.

His former captain watched him through narrowed eyes. "I've never seen you get intense about a woman before."

Nick ignored him. What the fuck could he say?

"How did you meet her?" Finn asked, lowering his weapon.

The medic picked up some ages-old–looking instrument of torture. A small pump in the middle, with tubing topped with a needle either side. Nick couldn't watch. He'd never been scared of needles or blood, but this whole scene terrified the shit out of him. The sight of her blood wrecked him. His hands shook, rattling the cuffs. Best to stare at the pale green walls, the butt-ugly dog picture.

Ros would be alright. She would be. She was tougher than she looked.

He swallowed past the rock in his throat. "Down near Stanthorpe. She was holed up in a private school with some other people."

"You joined them?" asked Sean. They really had been friends once, sort of. But Nick hadn't trusted him enough to include him in the plot against Emmet. Of course, if he had, Nick wouldn't have been thrown out of town and set on his way to meet Roslyn.

Funny how things worked out.

"Join them?" Nick coughed out a laugh. "Not likely. They were pricks. She wasn't safe with them. I offered them a van full of supplies for her and they took it."

The two men exchanged looks. Fair enough. It didn't sound so fucking fantastic now that he came to think about it. But it was the truth. There was no point lying, not now. Maybe if she died they'd put him down, save him the trouble of doing it himself.

"I figured she needed to see those people for what they were," he said. "For what they'd do to her, how little she meant to them. One of the bastards was going to hurt her before too long. Now

... I don't know. They messed up not long after, got wiped out. At least she wasn't there when that happened."

"What did you do after you picked her up?" asked Finn, fingering the safety on his pistol. He was a good-looking bastard, late twenties, blond and pretty. Roslyn would probably like him. If Roslyn would wake up and be okay, Nick would live with it. He'd give her up. Whatever price he had to pay, so long as she lived.

"I had a cabin set up, took her there. She attacked me." He grinned at the memory. "Swung a bottle of wine at my head. She can be so fierce. I kept her chained to the bed."

Something popped in Finn's jaw. The sheriff looked at him with murder in his eyes. But he'd play by the rules. Finn wouldn't put a bullet in him here and now. The fucker believed in law and order and all that shit.

"You raped her?" Finn asked.

"Fuck no," he spat, then calmed his voice. "No, I talked to her. I looked after her. I tried to ... I tried to explain to her what life was like now. She'd never been out of the school. Not since the plague first hit. She didn't know shit. On her own she wouldn't have lasted five seconds."

Lila swabbed the crook of his elbow and stabbed him with a needle. It stung. He didn't really blame her for putting a bit of extra zest into the job, though. The little pump between the two lengths of tubing made a sickly sucking noise as she worked it.

"Take whatever she needs," he said.

Lila nodded, not arguing.

A dental nurse. Fuck.

"What happened next?" asked Finn.

"We were doing okay, but our cabin caught fire and we had to move. Then we ran into Pete and Justin just a few hours out from here. They had plans for causing you guys trouble. But also, they wanted her," he said. Damn, but he wished he could kill them both all over again. Only slower this time. "I said I'd talk her into it. That it would be better if she was on board then trying to keep an eye on her all the time. Told them she was a sexually liberated girl. Better yet, that she was in love with me, would do anything to please me. I promised them I could talk her around."

"So you were in a sexual relationship with her? But it wasn't rape?" Finn stared him down, disgust clear in his eyes.

"No. Never." Nick shook his head. The silence that ensued was accusation aplenty. Fuck them. Ros knew the truth.

"So, how did she get shot?" asked Finn.

Nick gritted his teeth. "I got her out a window, told her to get in the car and drive until she got here. I figured you'd take her in. So long as she wasn't with me, right?"

No one answered. Yet again, it was answer enough.

"She wouldn't leave me. Drove the pickup into Justin, killed him. He was the one that shot her." Nick stared at Roslyn, lying unmoving on the bed. Nothing else mattered. Everything in his world burned down to just this. This one woman, living or dying. "She should have left."

No one said anything. Lila picked up what looked like tweezers and carefully probed the hole that the bullet had made. He wished he believed in God. Maybe he should say a prayer, just in case. Sean took over pumping the blood transfer. Nick could feel it, drawing the blood from his veins, giving it to her. Please let it be enough.

"Back at the cabin, she got away from me after a while," he said. "Stole the key and escaped."

Sean stared at him, face blank. "What happened?"

"She came back." He didn't doubt it now. The last few days he'd been wondering, unsure, but no longer. Ros had made her choice and turned back. She'd chosen him.

"Why?" Sean asked.

"Honestly?" He gave the man a grim, unhappy smile, and told him the absolute truth. "I don't know."

CHAPTER TWENTY-FIVE

Roslyn woke slowly. Someone was talking nearby, a woman. A man answered her, his voice low and smooth. Neither voice was familiar. Her brain felt floaty-light and her mouth tasted weird. Above her sat a white ceiling and below a bed with clean cotton sheets. She had a drip in her arm.

"Wha—?" Her tongue didn't want to work. She swallowed and tried again. "Where am ..."

"You're awake." A woman appeared above her, blocking out some of the ceiling. She had long black hair and a kind smile. "How do you feel?"

The man wandered closer. He looked like a Viking. A big, blond, frowny-faced Viking. How funny.

Roslyn tried to grin. The most she could manage was a lazy smile. Her face wouldn't follow directions. "Hey."

"Let me get you a drink." The woman grabbed a glass from the bedside table. Roslyn heard water being poured. Beneath her the mattress moved as the woman sat down. "Slowly, alright?"

Water had never tasted so good.

The room was spartan, basic but clean, with a bed and a table, a couple of chairs. A butt-ugly picture of puppies hung on the wall opposite. Who could make puppies ugly? How did someone even do that?

"Roslyn?" The Viking hovered at the end of the bed, handsome face still very serious. "We need to talk to you about Nick."

"Nick?" She tried to sit up. It took a few goes with the woman assisting her before she made it upright. All of her strength seemed to have been sapped right out of her. "Where is he?"

"It's alright," said the man. "You're safe. He can't hurt you any-more."

Viking dude looked so concerned, eyes intense. It made no sense to her. "What?"

The pretty black-haired woman huffed. "Now is not the time for this, Sean. You're distressing her."

Ros opened her mouth to intervene, to explain she wasn't distressed, just clueless, but they were already off and arguing. It felt as though she wasn't even there.

"We need to know what happened," said the Viking. "I've explained this to you already."

Lila faced down the big man, hands on hips. "Sean."

"Lila."

"I've explained this to you already, too. It can wait."

"No it can't. It's important."

"What's important is giving her time to recover. You've got your priorities wrong, buster." Lila gave him the evil eye. Clearly Sean was used to this, since he stared back calmly. Neither of them made much sense. But then nothing about this did. Her head felt useless and her body little better. What the hell was going on with the world now?

"Can I have some more water, please?" she asked when she could get a word in.

"Sure. You've woken up a couple of times, but always drifted back off to sleep straight away." Lila held the glass once more to her lips. "Do you remember?"

"No." Everything in her head was a muddy haze.

"Don't worry. It'll come back to you."

"Where's Nick?" Ros repeated for like the tenth time. Tingles raced across her skin as she tested her limbs, rolling her feet and scrunching her toes, shrugging her shoulders. Pain rolled through her. "Oh!"

"Be careful," said Lila. "Don't you remember? You were shot. Two days ago now."

Someone had shot her? Seriously? Oh, yeah. She remembered it vaguely, distantly. There'd been a fight.

"Ri-i-i-ght. When I drove the car into the wall." She was dressed in a plain white tank top with soft gray flannel pyjama pants on her bottom half. A square white bandage sat taped onto her skin below her left collarbone. It all came back slowly, sinking into her foggy head and falling into place. There was a crinkly little bandaid on her left ear, too. Shot twice—right. "We were with Justin and Pete."

They both watched her, waiting.

Justin and Pete and that horrible little house she'd basically destroyed—now there was an unpleasant memory. Even buffered by the drugs, it turned her stomach. "They were ... nasty bastards. I killed one of them. I've never killed anyone before. There was a lot of blood."

She searched herself for a hint of remorse and came up short. The lack of guilt made her feel guilty, but she'd live with it.

Sean scowled. "I should have killed all three of them when I had the chance."

Huh?

Whatever. "Where's Nick?"

"You're safe. They locked him up," said Lila. "How's your pain? Do you need something more? Give me a number between one and ten."

It hurt, but it was more of a dull ache than anything. It had just caught her by surprise at first. Plus, something more would probably throttle her last coherent brain cell. Her inability to think in a straight line bugged her worse than the pain. "I'm okay. Someone took out the bullet?"

"I did," said Lila. "We gave you a blood transfusion and you stabilized. Fortunately the bullet came out pretty easily and there's no sign of infection."

"Wow. It's lucky that you're a doctor."

The woman grimaced. "Actually, I'm a dental nurse."

"You are?" Roslyn nodded slowly. "Well, good job. Hang on. Did you say Nick was locked up?"

"Yes," confirmed Sean. "He's in a holding cell at the police station."

"What!" she screeched, wide awake now.

The Viking's eyebrows headed high.

Lila frowned. "You don't want him locked up?"

"No, of course not," said Ros. "Why? Why would you do that?"

"Because he's dangerous," said Sean.

She scrunched up her nose at him in disbelief.

Sean in turn scrunched up his forehead, looking less sure of himself by the minute. "Because he hurt you?"

"Nick didn't hurt me. Justin shot me. Pete and him wanted to rape me. Nick risked his life to get me out of there." She shuffled up, wincing all the while. Fuck, it was uncomfortable. Getting shot was distinctly unpleasant. She would never do that again. Plus her chest hurt. She took a peek down the front of her tank top. A dark, nasty bruise crossed her chest where the seatbelt had been. "What a mess."

"Roslyn, you can't get up," said Lila.

"Yes, I can." It hurt. It would never be her idea of a good time. But she could definitely do it.

Lila jumped up and helped her with a hand beneath her good arm. "Hang on. Take it slowly. The pain meds are going to make you groggy."

"Damn." The room spun and she wobbled a step forward on weak legs. She clung onto the other woman. "I need to go to the bathroom. Then I need to go to Nick."

"Roslyn, you got shot two days ago," said Lila, her brown eyes full of concern. "What you need to do is rest."

"I'm fine." Her knees trembled, defying her words. Stupid knees. "Bathroom?"

"Wait." The woman fussed. "Let me get this sling on you. We need to keep the weight off your shoulder."

Lila helped her into the loopy length of padded material. It kept her left hand up high, taking the weight off that limb as promised. The woman frowned but helped her to the bedroom door. They were in a small wooden house, an old cottage by the look of it. Across the hallway sat a bathroom. God, it felt good to empty her bladder. It was awkward to rise again, but well worth the effort.

She worked one-handed while Lila hovered with her back turned. Roslyn splashed some water on her face and finger-combed her hair. Nothing would save that bird's nest. It'd grow back eventually. Nick could take her as she came. An eager need to see him built inside her as she started moving about, gathering her meager reserves of energy. She felt stronger already, less shaky. Sort of.

"Are my boots around?" she asked.

"You're serious about this?"

"Very."

Lila nodded and opened the door. "Sean, can you carry her to the police station, please?"

"I should be able to walk," she said. Though, on second thought: "Is it far?"

The big man frowned at her, too. Then he put an arm beneath her knees, another behind her back, and picked her up without comment. Also without the slightest show of strain. The Viking had to be made of solid muscle. She held herself rigid, trying to keep some distance between her and him on account of his being a complete stranger. A complete stranger who had locked up Nick, which made no fucking sense.

"You might as well relax," he said.

She wearily did as she was told. "Thank you for this."

"How well do you know him?"

"Well enough to know you shouldn't have locked him up."

Little lines appeared beside Sean's eyes as he gave her a worried look, but off they went. Sunlight dazzled her as they stepped outside. It took her a moment to adjust. There were people, quite a lot of them. Many stopped what they were doing and gave her curious looks. She smiled back uncertainly. Neat rows of houses lined the street, with vegetable gardens filling the front yards where grass would once have been. Further down the road some kids played footy. Somewhere nearby a baby cried. It was all so normal, so right. This place was everything they'd taken for granted before the plague hit. Her eyes felt hot, gritty. Suburbia had always sort of peeved her previously, but now it was like nirvana. Growing up in cities, she'd never seen the beauty in this sort of scene. People building their houses a couple of meters apart from each other, everyone getting into everyone else's business. Her father had moved them here there and everywhere, but there had always been tons of people around. Those days were gone. She'd never again expected to see a community. It'd only been half a year, but everything had changed so much.

"So this is Blackstone," she said.

"Yes."

"It's lovely."

He grunted.

She kept smiling, though few smiled back. In fact, no one did. Some people passed by with their faces downturned, but some stared openly, their eyes hard. What the fuck? It felt a long way from nice to be studied that way. Ros did her best to be calm. So not everything here was Pleasantville. There seemed to be a whole lot of tension in the air. Fear lined people's faces.

"What's wrong?" she asked. "Why are people so ..."

Sean didn't meet her eyes. "How much did he tell you about the night we came here?"

"Um, that you killed your leader, Emmet. That he was a psychopath," she said. "Nick wanted him dead too."

Sean snorted. "Did he? Guess we'll never really know, will we?"

"Nick is not a bad person."

"He's not a good person either."

They passed through what a street sign designated Main Street. Crops grew where asphalt would once have been. Big, graceful jacaranda trees stood along the median strip running down the middle of the road. Shop windows were covered in curtains, now homes for people to live in. But a huge hardware store stood open, packed to the rafters with various goods. The place looked to be a veritable Aladdin's Cave of survival treasures.

"You're wrong," she said.

Across the road a group of people stood gathered deep in conversation. Sean gave them a long, wary look. A sturdy, muscular young man turned and scowled at Roslyn and Sean. At Ros in particular. His face tensed and he looked at her like she'd personally massacred millions. Inspiring such hatred in someone she didn't even know felt bloody unnerving. Being in Blackstone seemed like a truly bad idea all of a sudden. This place didn't feel safe, no matter the wall keeping the infected out.

"What the hell is going on here?" she hissed.

"Quite a few people died that night. One of them was a man named Sam Cotter. He'd been holding the place together, but he got bit," said Sean. "There's been a lot of internal fighting since then. Seems like he was the only person that could get everyone to agree. Since then, the welcome mat hasn't exactly been laid out to new comers."

At the end of Main Street they turned left. The police station was surrounded by flowering bushes. A man with a sawn-off shotgun stood outside the front door on guard duty. Not so normal or pretty.

"Why do they need a guard?" she asked.

Sean shot her a look she couldn't read. The guard nodded to Sean and held the door open. Inside it looked like a typical country police station. A counter and some chairs, and beyond was an office area. Lots of white walls and filing cabinets, a collection of old wanted signs. Off to the side, she could just make out the bars of a cell. Sean carried her straight through. Behind a desk a handsome blond young man sat cleaning a gun. But more importantly, where was Nick?

"Put me down, please," she asked.

"Hey, Finn." Carefully Sean set her down on her feet, holding her elbow steady while she found her feet. Sean was nice. "She wants to see him."

"Why?" asked the cute, albeit serious, blond. His face was curious but not unfriendly. How refreshing.

Knees wobbling, she circumnavigated the Viking. Nick sat on the wide cot pushed up against one wall, his chin braced on his hands, staring off at nothing. Giddy delight filled her at seeing him.

"Nick?"

He blinked and turned his head. He didn't smile back at her. "Roslyn. What are you doing here?"

A new big black bruise took up half his temple, sitting out in a swollen lump. He made no move to come to her, just sat on the stupid mattress giving her closed looks.

Like she couldn't read him by now.

"What the hell happened to your face?" she yelled.

Nick sighed. He rose and strolled toward her, bracing a hand on the bars. "Calm down. It's not like you haven't done worse."

"That's not funny."

"Don't pout." His fingers stroked over hers, wrapped around a length of cold metal. This was ridiculous. Unacceptable. "How are you feeling?"

"Why are you in here?" she asked. "What's going on?"

"I wasn't supposed to come back," he said. "But, you know, this cell is better than being shot on sight. What are you doing out of bed, hmm? You still look really pale."

"I'm fine."

He frowned at her. Why not? People had been frowning at her all day. She'd started to get used to it. Hell, she frowned right back at him. "They threatened to shoot you on sight and you willingly chose to come here?"

He just looked at her.

"Ms Stewart." The pretty blond man who'd been cleaning the gun stood close by, his mouth a set in an unhappy line. "Nick informed us he kidnapped you and held you against your will."

"Nick!" She turned back to the idiot in the cell, moving too fast. Her head felt topsy-turvy. "That was personal. How could you tell them that?"

"It's the truth," he said calmly, like he was resigned to his dire circumstances. People heading to the chopping block probably had a similar joie de vivre. "What I did was wrong."

"What you did is between us. I can't believe you."

The pretty blond cleared his throat. "Ah, Ms Stewart—"

And honestly, she'd had enough of this shit. More than enough of it. "Open the door. Let him out. He didn't hurt me. Though I may hurt him."

"But, by his own admission, he did hurt you. He held you against your will, at the very least."

She growled. Men! They were all such fools. "Do not try to tell me you are punishing him for things he supposedly did to me. I decide how that works, not you. You are not involved in this. None of you."

The pretty blond just blinked.

"And I'm not pressing charges, so don't try to tell me it's about the law either. Let him out."

"I'm sorry, I can't," said the pretty blond.

"Roslyn, it's more complicated than that," Sean said, stepping forward to take the blame. "A lot of people in town don't trust Nick. Letting him walk out of here would not be in his best interests. You noticed people weren't happy. They're still coming to terms with what happened that night. They thought they were safe inside these walls and they found out the hard way that they're not."

"He's right," said the pretty blond. "For a lot of people it was a big shock on top of what they'd already suffered. Nick would make a good target to take their fears out on right about now."

"What?" Her brain hurt. They couldn't be serious. Blackstone was fast turning from a dream into a nightmare. "Are you telling me someone still might try to kill him? Are you fucking serious?"

"We won't let that happen," said the pretty blond, looking highly competent but not soothing her in the least. This was Nick's life they were talking about. If anyone would be killing him, it would be her. And she didn't want him dead, so there.

"I'm sorry, what was your name?" she asked.

"I'm Finn," the pretty blond said. "Town sheriff, basically. Sean's right. For now, Nick's safer in here. If what you're saying is true and he didn't hurt you, eventually it might be best if we move him out quietly once things calm down. Let him be on his way."

"Move him out quietly?" She shook her head in disbelief. "You'd send him back out there. Mind you, after what I've seen of this place that might not be a bad idea."

"You'd stay," the big idiot in the cage announced. "You're safer here."

She doubted that, but it was beside the point. The idiot was trying to separate them. Now, after everything. "Shut. Up. Nick. The adults are talking."

Nick gave her another less-than-impressed look. "Ros."

"I'm serious. You've said enough this year." The world went wonky and she swayed, hip banging into the bars. "Whoa."

"Get her a chair," said Nick.

"No," she said with vehemence. Because for all the supposed intelligent life forms surrounding her just then, not one of the three men were making a shitload of sense. "Open the door. If you won't let him out then I'm going in."

Nick paced in his cage. "Like hell. You just got shot."

"That was days ago. Keep up."

Finn offered her a hand. "Ms Stewart—"

"Roslyn," she corrected.

"Roslyn," said Finn. "Please, let me help you to a seat."

"No. I'm staying with him," she said. "Did I happen to mention I committed vehicular manslaughter the other day?"

"It was self-defense," said Nick.

"No," she said, waving her finger at one and all. "Justin shooting me might have been self-defense, but I chose to run him down. So actually it's not manslaughter, is it? How far in advance does one need to plan before you can say it was pre-meditated, exactly?"

No reply was forthcoming from the sheriff.

"Never mind," she said. "I am a vicious and unrepentant killer who should be locked up. With him, my idiot boyfriend."

Finn stared at her, blank-faced.

Nick just looked pained. Fuck him. Love hurt.

"Open the cell door please, Sheriff Finn."

"Don't," said Nick. "Get her out of here. She doesn't belong here."

She shot him a filthy look. What an asshole, working against her. "Seriously, Nick. I am so mad at you right now I can't even say."

Nick didn't back down. "Finn, she's wounded, for fuck's sake. Please."

The sheriff looked at them both like they needed the loony bin more than anything, their eyes full of confusion.

"Go on, Finn." Another woman stood beside Lila, leaning against a desk. Roslyn hadn't even noticed the two of them enter. Lila watched her with worried eyes, two pillows and a blanket clutched to her chest. What a wonderful woman.

"I figured you'd be staying down here," she said, earning a bright smile from Ros. At last, someone who made sense. Maybe this town wasn't a total waste.

"Thank you, Lila," said Ros.

"Hi. I'm Ali." The other woman raised a hand and gave her a smile. Her small, round belly pushed at the front of her shirt. "You probably don't remember me. I spent some time sitting by your bedside while Lila ran errands."

Finn crossed his arms. "Al, you're meant to be home resting."

"Pregnant, not broken," said the woman in a bored tone of voice. "Let her go in with him."

The sheriff didn't back down one iota. "This doesn't involve you."

"You heard what she said, Finn. She chose him." Ali rubbed her belly, unperturbed. "Every time she woke up she asked for him. Without fail."

"Stay out of it."

Ali cocked her head. "You of all people should know relation-ships are complicated. Go on. Let her be with him."

"Al. This is business."

"Why, so it is." Ali gave her a small smile. It seemed she had friends she didn't even know about. Blackstone was looking better by the minute. "Actually, I feel quite endangered by her presence. Don't you, Lila?"

"Absolutely," said Lila. "She terrifies me. Right, Sean?"

"Shit." Sean wiped a hand over his face. He gave the dark-haired Lila a similar pained expression to the one Nick kept gifting Ros. Not bad, but Nick's was cuter. Lila raised her eyebrows and the Viking groaned in defeat. "Never been so scared in my life. She's so small and … wounded."

Lila beamed at him and the big man smiled back reluctantly, the love he had for the woman clear on his face.

"Please, Finn," said Ali, her eyes full of warmth and good humor. "Save us. You're our last hope."

"Fucking ridiculous." Finn pulled a key a set of keys out of his pocket and shoved one into the lock. The door swung open and he stepped back. "Roslyn, if you change your mind just call out, okay?"

"Thank you."

"Yay!" quietly cheered Ali.

"That's enough out of you." The sheriff gave the pregnant woman a long look. "We're going to talk about this later."

"I am at your disposal, my love," Ali answered with a smile.

Roslyn stepped inside the jail cell. There really was a first time for everything. If she'd been feeling half-alive she might have strutted. Thrown in a little Elvis 'Jailhouse Rock' hip swivel, maybe just for fun. As it was, dragging her sorry carcass to the bed was about the most she could manage. Her legs were all wibbly-wobbly. Nick stood with his arms folded across his broad chest, doing his best to intimidate her or something. Yeah, right. She wished him all the best with that.

"Lucky I happen to like that scowly face on you," she said. "Move over."

He did so and she carefully lay down on the wide single bed. Oh yes indeed, that felt good. The cot was actually more comfortable than it looked. Life on the inside wasn't so bad. Someone had even done some etchings on the wall beside her. They most closely resembled a man fornicating with a woman whose breasts were wildly oversized. The poor stick figure couldn't hope to support such watermelon boobies, let alone handle the size of the guy's equipment. The artist had been a real overachiever.

Lila shoved the pillows and blanket at Nick. "Get some food into her. Keep her comfortable. Send for me if she needs anything. Otherwise, I'll be back later with her meds."

The cell door clanged shut and Finn locked it. She was officially incarcerated. Huh. The places life could take you.

"Ah, life on the inside," she said. "How did the theme from *Prisoner* go again?"

"This isn't funny." Nick knelt down beside her, dumping the linens on the floor. "What are you doing?"

"Spending time with my beau," she said. "You?"

He breathed out a heavy sigh, poor boy. "I'm no good for you, Ros."

"You're awful cute when you trying to be self-sacrificing, Nicky. Less so when you've blurting out our personal affairs, but still."

"I'm being serious."

"Yes, so I see. I think you better hop down off the cross, honey. Someone else might need the wood." She stroked his cheek with her good hand, teased the bristle of his beard. The hair on his jaw was a darker shade of brown than his head. He had the hottest mouth. The things that mouth could do. Hmm. Happy thoughts flooded her and her body came sluggishly awake, despite the pain meds and the ache in her shoulder. "What am I going to do with you?"

Nick wrapped his hand around her wrist, his thumb stroking over her pulse point. "You're going to let me go. You're safer away from me."

"Perhaps. But I doubt it. I know for certain I wouldn't be happier. Funnily enough, these days, that really matters to me."

He said nothing.

"Nick," she sighed. "It will never belong in a Hallmark card, but I drove a car into a house and killed a man for you. You chained me up for days and I still wanted to come back and talk over our darkly sordid, slightly kinky, and a lot warped relationship. Face it, you're stuck with me."

His brows drew tight. "You're high as a kite right now, aren't you?"

"Maybe." She grinned. Actually, she felt pretty fucking fantastic now that she'd gotten her way. "Did you miss me? Admit it, you did, didn't you."

He gave her his exasperated face. The edges of his lips tucked down, brows drew in. Her poor, pretty boy. She couldn't help but wonder if he'd take his shirt off for her if she asked. What an awesome idea. Maybe after she'd had a nap. Yeah, she'd be sure to ask him then.

"638," she said.

"What?"

"638. You're my honey. That's where I'd shelve you." Her eyelids drifted closed. "You won't go anywhere, will you?"

"I can't. We're both in jail. You just saw to that."

"Excellent," she mumbled, settling back into the mattress. So damn tired, she could have slept for a year. "Good job."

"Get some rest, sweetheart." He pressed his lips to the palm of her hand. "I have a feeling you're going to need it."

CHAPTER TWENTY-SIX

Nick sat idle as Roslyn slept. He'd been staring at her, staring at the wall, feeling like shit. Getting her out had to be his first priority. But until she started working with him he didn't like his chances. The woman could be bloody stubborn.

"You really care about her," said ex-captain Sean, sounding mildly surprised.

Nick sat on the ground, his backs to the bars. "Noticed the medic has you wrapped around her little finger."

Finn had taken off a while back and Sean sat in the office, reading a book by the light of a lantern. The sun had set about an hour back. Sean and Nick had always gotten on okay. They'd had a decent working relationship. While the big man could be rigid, he played fair. Military through and through. Nick had never been part of Sean's inner circle, but he'd thought they'd understood each other. Being accused of the sort of shit Emmet was capable of had disgusted him. And worse, it made him feel vaguely ashamed. Because if he hadn't been standing against Emmet, what the fuck had he been doing?

Good question. One he was finding increasingly hard to answer.

He kept catching himself grinding his teeth, cracking the joints in his fingers. Nothing about this situation was okay.

Sean smiled. "Roslyn seems pretty convinced that you're trustworthy. That you wanted Emmet dead and we misjudged you."

"Everyone wanted Emmet dead."

"Not everyone."

True. Justin and Pete had thought the lunatic was packed full of good ideas. Ideas about raping and murdering and all sorts of shit most people couldn't stomach. Nick had wanted him dead. But he hadn't stood up to him. He'd followed orders, just like he'd been trained to do. When he finally stopped to think for himself everything had long since gone to shit and he'd been hiding in a bottle for over a month. Something he'd have to live with for the rest of his life.

So many regrets. So much guessing about what was right and what was wrong. It all fucked with his head.

"You ever think about the airport? The quarantine?" he asked.

Sean's nostrils flared. "I try not to."

"All those people." Nick shook his head, hating the memory. Those first days of the plague were the stuff of nightmares. He could still remember the stink of fear filling the air, and the terror on people's faces. Every five minutes a new command would be handed down with the latest contradicting the last. No one knew what was really going on, because no one knew how to stop it. They'd been screwed from the start. "They were terrified, didn't know what to do. Who could blame them, faced with a field full of tents and people in masks, men shoving machine guns in their faces. I would have panicked too. Man, I would have gone ballistic."

"Yeah."

"Was it worth it? Us killing innocent civilians?" he asked. "They were just people on holidays. Wankers in business suits. They weren't terrorists or anything and we had to shoot them in the back if they made a run for it. What the fuck does that make us? Not the good guys, that's for certain."

The captain didn't answer straight away. He stared at his book with a heavy brow. "If we'd been able to stop the bug at that point, we'd have saved millions of lives."

"Hmm." It sounded nice, but the chances of it ever happening were nil. As many seaports and international airports as there were in the country and the amount of travel people did, keeping out a microscopic germ wasn't possible. Maybe birds had bought it in. No one had figured out if animals could carry it too. There hadn't been time.

"We had to try," said Sean, his voice low. "We couldn't just sit by and do nothing."

"Yeah, you keep telling yourself that." Nick snorted, hung his head. The prison bars pressed into his back. "We've done some dirty jobs over the years. Things that needed doing, but nothing like that. When did you start questioning orders, huh? When did it get too much for you?"

Sean just stared at him.

"Ever have trouble sleeping at night, captain? Or is your conscience perfectly clean?"

No answer.

Fuck him.

Nick turned back to Roslyn, watched the easy rise and fall of her chest. Her breathing calmed him. Her very existence gave him hope. Always had done, from the first time he saw her. He had no idea what life was for, couldn't answer a single one of the big questions. But if he could keep her safe, make things better for her, then that would satisfy him. Make up for some of the blood on his hands. Funny, he could barely remember any woman that came before, but there wasn't an inch of her he could forget.

"To answer your question," Nick said, "yeah, I care about her."

Sean set his book down and walked toward the jail cell. "Problem is, Nick, you can be a dickhead on occasion. You like acting up. Makes you less than dependable."

Nick just waited.

"Maybe you were angry over the way we sent you packing," said Sean. "You could have been using her to get back into Blackstone. Could have had something planned with Pete and Justin, for all we knew."

When he didn't answer, the captain went on.

"The truth is even more insane. How could you have brought that girl, chained her up and yet still have managed to persuade her to give you a chance?" Sean said with a harsh laugh. "I mean, how the fuck did you pull that off? Explain it to me, please."

"Well, what you have to understand," said Ros, her voice husky from sleep, "is that I base my decisions on how people behave toward me. And while there might have been some initial early hiccups, there are still far more marks in the win column."

Nick shuffled over to her bedside, forgetting all about Sean and his bullshit. "How you feeling?"

"Hey." Big blue eyes watched him steadily. She held out her hand and he went to her. "He earned my trust, Sean. Yes he made some mistakes. But you have to keep them in context. Every time it mattered, he came through for me without hesitation. Actions do speak louder than words and he risked his life for me more than once. So I'd appreciate it if you didn't speak to him that way."

"You in pain?" Nick asked, wanting the topic changed. Frankly, it was a little embarrassing having her stick up for him. He didn't need Sean's good opinion. The man could go fuck himself. "Lila dropped some antibiotics and painkillers off before."

"I'm fine."

"You're not fine. There's still little bruises beneath your eyes."

"Nonsense. Come here." Ros's hand snaked up around his neck and drew him down until his lips touched hers. He gave her what she wanted, kissing her soft and slow. She made this noise, this low, needy, intensely horny noise. Fuck, the things it did to him. But he didn't want Sean hearing it. That noise was personal.

"Are you hungry?" he asked.

"You have no idea. Sean, can you give us some privacy, please?" asked Ros.

The captain's brows arched. "I'm not sure ..."

She clucked her tongue impatiently. "Wait outside please, Sean. The visit just turned conjugal and we do not require an audience."

Nick tried not to smile and failed. Her ability to mix prim librarian with sex kitten had to be the best thing ever. But still.

"You're hurt," he said.

"Yes, she is. But I'll let you two have a moment," said Sean, heading for the door with his face on fire. "I'll just be outside."

Ros grinned. "Half an hour would be great. Thanks, Sean."

The captain mumbled something along the lines of "for fuck's sake" and fled the room.

"I'm serious. You need to take it easy," Nick said.

"Thank you. Your flimsy protest has been duly registered." A little line appeared between her brows. "Why do I keep having to coerce you into having sex with me lately? What's with that?"

He rubbed at the line with the pad of his thumb. "Pain meds still working, huh?"

"Hey." She slapped at his hand. "I'm being serious. Is this some sort of payback, Nick? You're all gung-ho for a while but now it's my turn to run around after you? Do I need to prove myself? Is that it?"

"Of course not," he sighed. "Come on, Ros. Don't get upset."

"Don't tell me what to feel."

"Ros."

"Answer me."

Fuck it. He shut her up by kissing her. Truthfully, it all confused him. Her loyalty unnerved him. He'd done nothing to deserve it. Again, he'd meant to do the right thing and let her go, but it hadn't worked. No way did he trust himself to offer it one more time. He wasn't that nice and he wanted her too much.

She opened her mouth and he slid his tongue inside. Some things never got old. Kissing this woman topped the list. Her hand fisted in the T-shirt Finn had given him to wear, dragging him closer, trying to pull him on top of her. From low in her throat came the noise again. Every drop of blood in him rushed straight to his dick. His brain keeled over dead, gave up entirely. Well, mostly.

"Ros, you're hurt," he moaned, resisting the urge to get a leg up and join her on the pissy little bed.

"So be gentle. Just be inside me."

Shit.

What could he say?

His balls felt fucking tortured. The dreamy, needy expression on her face killed him. Her lovely wet lips and sharp little teeth kissed and bit him equally. A hungry woman and he had to hold back. His hungry woman. How fucking unfair.

"Nicky. Life is too short to hesitate. I think we've both seen this by now."

Getting enough of her mouth was out of the question. But when he stopped to think about it, there was something he hadn't gotten around to giving her yet. And life could be over in an instant. Pete had come damn close to putting a bullet in him.

"You have to keep perfectly still," he said. "I don't want you jarring your shoulder and re-opening that wound."

"I'll be on my best behavior."

God help him.

Nick re-checked the room, making sure they were alone. Then he drew her pyjama pants down her long legs. Roslyn bare took his breath away. The curls on her mound and the curves of her soft thighs blew his mind. He could smell her, hot and rich and ready. Nothing smelled as good as this woman's sex. He'd never been nuts over a woman's vagina before, but Ros's stayed on his mind day and night. Everything about her did.

No part of her didn't deserve to be worshipped.

"What are you going to do?" she asked, ever curious.

"Spread your legs for me, then stay still," he repeated, climbing up onto the bed. It wouldn't be the most comfortable of positions, but never mind. He had his priorities right. He crouched at the end of the mattress and slipped his hands beneath the cheeks of her ass. First he kissed her belly, her hips and thighs. She had the softest, most satiny skin.

Fingers slid into his hair, rubbing at his scalp. He stopped.

"What did I say?" he asked.

"Hmm?" Her eyes blinked lazily open.

"What did I tell you to do, Ros?"

The hand stilled. "To stay still?"

He raised a brow.

"Seriously? I'm not even allowed to touch you?"

"Can you do what I asked or not? Your choice."

She pinned her lips shut and her hand returned to her side.

"Good girl."

"Am I allowed to speak?" she asked in a cranky voice.

"Sure."

The woman opened her mouth, doubtless to serve him some smartass reply, but wisely shut it.

"That's a good girl." Nick nuzzled her belly button, brushed his beard lightly across her mound. The muscles in her stomach jumped.

"I don't know why I put up with your shit," she mumbled. Clearly hating everything he did to her. As if. He couldn't keep the smile off his face.

"Because you know I'll make it worth your while." He spread her open with his thumbs and blew air across her wet folds. So fucking gorgeous and pink. "And because you want to."

She huffed and he licked up through her pussy with the flat of his tongue, a nice broad swipe to coat his tongue with her taste. No point in half measures. He was a glutton for her. Her butt cheeks tightened and her hips shifted, trying to get closer.

"You're going to be damn upset if I stop because you can't behave," he said.

"I'm trying," she whined.

"Try harder. That was your last warning."

"But—"

He buried his face in her sex, lapping and loving her every way he knew how. Getting mindless on the touch and taste of her. So many times he thought he'd lost her, and yet here he was, eating her hot little cunt like the end was nigh. Fuck, he hoped it wasn't. He wanted decades with her, doing just this.

Her legs trembled and her breath stuttered as he drove her hard toward climax. No time for niceties—who knew how long they'd be left alone. He used his teeth to carefully tease her. He suckled at the lips of her sex and tickled her clit, before going back to swiping at her with the tip of his tongue. Her moans grew louder and louder but her hands stayed put, one by her side and the other in the sling lying across her body. Fuck, he hoped this wouldn't hurt her shoulder, but he couldn't stop himself. The scent of her sweat and the heat of her sex made him drunk. Her pussy fluttered against his tongue as he fucked her with it. Groans echoed through the concrete cell.

"Nick, please," she whimpered.

He rubbed at her clit with his tongue, sucked hard at her spread-open sex. Never had he seen a woman so fucking wet and ready. Perfect was Roslyn with her legs spread wide and his mouth on her as she stuttered his name. Heaven had nothing on this. His fingers dug into her, holding her to him as she shuddered and came, her pussy convulsing against his lips. He almost came himself.

She huffed and puffed and got her breath back as he sat up on his knees, tore open his jeans and shoved them down his thighs. They had no time to waste.

"Stay still," he said. "Remember?"

Dazed eyes blinked open. Her cheeks were damp with tears.

"Shit. Are you in pain?" he asked.

She shook her head. "No. Please, Nick."

He lay down over her, keeping his weight to himself with an arm beside her head. Without delay he fit the head of his cock to her and pushed in. No one else felt like this, impossibly slick and incredibly hot. How the fuck he'd kept out of her all day he had no idea. And she thought she had to seduce him. Roslyn breathing made him hard. Roslyn wide open and so wet he could drown in her pretty much owned him. Amazingly, he found he could live with that just fine.

He fucked into her sweet and slow, keeping the pace nice and easy, kissing away her tears.

"That was good," she said with wide eyes, looking at him in awe. The things she did for his ego.

"This'll be better," he promised.

Why hadn't he thought to take his shirt off? Then they could have been skin to skin. Damn it. He couldn't bring himself to stop. Her pussy made the best wet noises as he thrust into her. All he wanted was to be inside her for as long as possible. But distantly, he could hear voices outside. The thought of anyone else seeing her this way made him want to tear something apart. His fingers curled into the mattress and he could feel the material stretching, giving. Everything in him tensed. Something about her turned him into a caveman with an unending hard-on.

Roslyn had subtly drawn up her legs at some stage and pushed back against him, urging him on. Her sex clenched at him on every withdrawal. It felt impossibly good. Fire spread through him and his balls had crept up into his body, never to be seen again. He tried to slow down, but his pelvis only took orders from his cock and his cock answered solely to her.

"Faster," she said. Faster he went.

The corner of her lip curled up in a snarl and her hips bumped against him, seconding the demand. Sweat dripped off his face onto her. The tricky girl had him by the balls and he loved it. But it was time to even out the game.

She stared up at him, eyes huge. The first touch of his fingers to her clit had her neck arching. He slipped about in the wet mess between them, strumming the small, hard bead, getting her there. Her thighs clutched at him. That was what he wanted, the feel of her inner muscles trembling around him. She shivered and her mouth fell open in a silent cry. The grip of her pussy undid him. Once, twice more he thrust into her and then lost it completely. Grinding against her with a hand wrapped hard around her hip. He emptied every last bit of himself into her and she took it all.

He only just stopped himself from collapsing on top of her, remembering at the last minute to hold himself up and not crush her beneath his remains. Because for certain she'd killed him this time. She should bury him and call it a day. It was the best fucking feeling. Blood roared behind his ears. His poor lungs labored to keep up. His heart had burst a while back.

"You're a bad girl," he said, after a while.

She still panted, her breasts moving beneath him. "What? What did I do?"

"You didn't stay still." He leant his forehead against hers.

"I only moved a little," she said, trying her best to look down her nose at him. It couldn't have been easy to do, flat on her back with his softening dick still stuffed inside her. "I thought I was quite controlled, actually."

His cock twitched, valiantly trying to reanimate. It was a monster, out of control.

"Nick," she said. "You can't be serious."

"It's the uptight librarian thing. I have no defense against it." He sighed and pulled out of her. "Stay there. Let me clean you up."

She gave a low chuckle. "Is this Nurse Nick with a sponge bath? Because this librarian could totally handle that."

Fuck. So could he.

A bucket of water and some washcloths had been left care of her friend Lila. There wouldn't be any dallying over the task today, however. He could still hear voices outside.

He wet the cloth and smoothed it over her face and neck. Lifted up her tank top and tried not to linger over her breasts. God, he hated seeing that bandage on her. It didn't look like there'd been any fresh bleeding, thankfully. He kissed the bruising better and washed her gorgeous tits and stomach, the sticky mess they'd made between her legs. Going gently there, since her pussy was still swollen. In an ideal world, Roslyn would always look exactly like this, wet and well loved. But definitely without the bandages.

"You're covered in my come," he said, just because he liked the sound of it. The view was distinctly good. If only he had a camera.

She stared at the ceiling, her teeth sunk into her bottom lip.

"Am I embarrassing you?" he asked.

"Not at all," she said with an amused smile. "Please, Nick. Do go on about our combined bodily fluids currently coating my nether regions."

"Well, my sperm is all through the cute little tuft of hair just above your pussy. I'm really going to have to give that another wash. It's a bit sticky." He did so, diligently, while she grinned. Never mind, he took the task seriously enough for both of them. What an excellent job description. He'd be the caretaker of Roslyn's vagina. The guardian of her sweet cunt. "That's better. See, now your pubic hair is all beautiful and clean. Not a curl out of place."

"You're sure about that?"

He made a show of combing the little tufts of hair with his fingers before placing a gentle kiss on her mound. "Yes. Perfect."

Her body shook with laughter, lips trembling trying to hold back a smile. "I hate you."

He paused, the wet washcloth still covering her sex. So many times he'd heard those words come out of her mouth. This time, she didn't mean it. No doubt about it. He knew that. It still stopped him.

"Shit," she said.

"It's okay."

"No, it's not. Nick. Look at me."

After a moment he did. Her hand beckoned him closer and she started to sit up. Which was dangerous. She could easily hurt herself.

"Hey. Be careful." Quickly he put an arm behind her, helping her up. Her arms wrapped around his neck and hung on tight. He took as much of her weight as he could, letting her catch her breath.

"Oh," she said with a wince. "That's a bit sore, actually."

"Do you want to lie back down?"

"No."

"Hang on. I've got your pain meds and antibiotics." He picked up the neatly labeled pills and the bottle of water, popped the tablets into the palm of her hand. No way would she be getting an infection or something and getting sick. "Here."

She put the pills in her mouth and drank half the bottle of water in one go. Her face was still pale. Bruises lingered beneath her eyes. "I'm okay."

"You should lie back down," he said. "You need to rest."

"Shh." Gently she kissed him, over and over, until she'd covered his lips entirely. He held still and let her go on for as long as she liked. Forever would be fine. That would work for him. Her lips were so soft. But eventually she sighed and rubbed her nose against his. "I don't hate you. I don't. I never should have said that. I promise I will never say it to you again. I—"

"Nick," Sean bellowed, his timing fucking horrible. He ran into the room with a set of keys jangling in one hand and a rifle in the other. "Time to move. We've got a situation."

"What?"

Sean shoved a key into the lock, swung the door open. Nick had seen that tight-lipped look on the captain before. It never meant anything good. Dread sunk his stomach.

"Locals have put together a lynching party," said the captain. "Guess who they want to hang from a tree on Main Street?"

CHAPTER TWENTY-SEVEN

"Where are the guns we came in with?" Roslyn asked, letting Nick help her to her feet. This wasn't so bad. Her head spun a wee bit, but she'd manage. These yokels had left her with no other option. Over her dead body they'd hurt him. "They're not touching you."

Nick just looked at her.

"I'm serious," she said. "Pull any more of that self-sacrificing bullshit and I'll shoot you myself."

The man looked to Sean, eyes trying to communicate something. Did he think she was a complete idiot? Honestly? Without further ado she thumped him in the belly with her good hand. Nick gave a startled *oomph*. Truly, in her current mood, violence suited her.

"You think I don't know what it means when you make eyes at him?" She pushed past him.

The idiot winked at her. "Don't be jealous, Ros. I still like you best."

"You're not even mildly amusing." She stalked up to Sean the Viking. "Our weapons. Where are they?"

"They boys and I have agreed to help get you out of here, but that's it. You're on your own. I don't want this getting out of control," said Sean, his forehead bunched up.

"Then don't let it. They are not taking him. So you need to get us *both* out of here safely," she said, not-so-quietly fuming. "We're going to need our guns for outside your fence line."

Sean stared at her for a moment then nodded and crossed to a large locked cabinet on the wall. The keys were produced once again and an impressive cache of firearms revealed. "If either of you break the peace out there I will use whatever force necessary to stop you. Is that understood?"

"Perfectly," she said.

Nick came up behind her. "Ros—"

"No, Nick. I'm not staying, and you're not getting killed by these inbred, redneck imbeciles. It's not even up for discussion." Anger boiled up inside her. That these people would attempt to do such a thing blew her ever-loving mind. She grabbed her fancy gun with the silencer and torch combo then nabbed a second pistol, just in case. Looked like the bulk of what they'd arrived with had been confiscated and moved to the cop shop. Handy. Managing the weapon with her left arm in the sling would be annoying, but removing it would sic Nick onto her instantly. It stayed put for now. "Neither idea is acceptable. You feeling me?"

He was quiet for a moment. "That wasn't what I was going to say."

"Then what?" she snapped.

With a grim face he took in the gun. "Calm down. Concentrate on what you're doing. Are they both loaded?"

"Yes."

He nodded and cupped her face in his hands. His poor, beautiful head had taken such a beating. She hated the scar she'd put on him. Not that he hadn't deserved it at the time. The second one these people had added, however, made her furious.

"Alright," he said after a moment. "We get out of here nice and quietly. You stay behind me, okay?"

"Okay." She'd see how it went. Maybe for the moment he'd forgotten this was a partnership, but she hadn't. Till death do them part and all that stuff.

"I'm serious."

So was she. "Yes, okay. I heard you. Let's get moving."

His eyes narrowed but he let it go. "Sean, are there any shoes here for Ros?"

"Lila dropped off her boots earlier." Sean grabbed her footwear from a bag in the corner.

"Thanks." Putting boots on one-handed was harder than it looked. Nick knelt and wrestled them onto her bare feet. At least she wouldn't be adding to the cuts and bruises from the gravel back at the cabin.

"She's going to get cold," he said. "Is there a jacket or something?"

"I'm fine."

"Here." Sean stripped out of his own smart leather jacket and handed it to Nick. Her man seemed less than impressed at the thought of her wearing it. He rolled the righthand sleeve up just the same and proceeded to put it on her. The thing was size huge, falling off her left shoulder without her arm in the sleeve to keep it in place. He did up a couple of buttons and stuffed her pills into a pocket. She added her spare pistol to another.

"You're all sorted," he said.

"We need to move," Sean said. He grabbed an extra pistol and relocked the cabinet. "Come on."

Out front the night seemed still, at first. Shouting could be heard from Main Street, the rumbling hum of lots of voices. Though there didn't seem to be much light coming from any direction. Windows were sealed and the streets were dark. Without the aid of the moon she'd have been stumbling in the dark. However hyped up the people of Blackstone were, they weren't inviting infected to the party if they could help it.

No, they just wanted to hang an unarmed man. Nick would have been a sitting duck, stuck in that jail cell.

She shivered inside Sean's coat. The air was crisp to the point of brutal, everyone's breaths steaming in front of them. She felt chilled, inside and out.

Several more people waited outside. Sean didn't stop to introduce anyone, but Nick nodded to the two other men. They all seemed to know one another, though the looks ranged from frosty to friendly. Frosty wore an army jacket, while Friendly dripped with guns. So at least the right people were on their side. Friendly looked like a walking paramilitary team rolled into one thoroughly oversized fellow. But when you were that big, you could probably pull it off. He didn't quite reach Sean the Viking's height, but he was built.

"This way," said Sean, heading away from Main Street at a brisk trot. "Erin and Finn are trying to calm down the crowd."

Frosty snorted. "Good luck with that. Tom's been stirring shit for the last two days, since you arrived."

"Who?" she asked.

"Never mind." Nick kept an arm wrapped around her, helping her along. The meds were slowly sinking in, making her mind turn to mush. Things dwindled, the anger and fear fading, seeming not as sharp as they had been just moments before. Not good—she had to keep her focus. Had to stay with it.

They moved quietly down the darkened street. A door slammed shut as they jogged past and light seeped out from the sides of curtains as strangers snuck a peek. People were obviously expecting something and had taken cover accordingly. The ones who hadn't had joined the mob on Main Street. Civilization had obviously fallen by the wayside while she'd been stuck in that school. Shit like this shouldn't have continued to surprise her, but it did. Humanity had fallen fast and far.

"I won't let anything happen to you," said Nick.

He barely breathed hard and she puffed away beside him. Past houses and across the remnants of a park they went. Like everywhere else, this area had been turned into farming land. Mulch and wood smoke scented the air. A children's swing set sat in the middle of a crop of zucchini. An old slippery slide was surrounded by neat rows of beans. A cow gave a low, plaintive cry not too far away. These people were so lucky, so fortunate, and yet they wanted to kill. There'd been so much death. How they couldn't have already have had their fill of it, she did not know.

Ahead of them a refrigerated van minus its tires sat on an angle. It was surrounded by rubble from destroyed houses. She could just make out the crushed forms of cars embedded further along. The people of Blackstone had used everything at their disposal to build the wall. Had she been in a better frame of mind she'd have respected them for their ingenuity.

"Come on," Sean said, calling them closer.

One of the other men fiddled with a chunk of metal and Frosty joined in, slowly pushing it aside. The thing had to weigh a ton. A lot of grunting and heaving was involved in the sloth-paced process. The interior of the van must act as a tunnel through the wall. This was how they'd get out.

"Guess you don't trust these people as much as you'd like them to think," said Nick.

"Always have an exit strategy," said Sean. "You know that. Directly across the train tracks there's a warehouse. Inside are some vehicles kitted out and ready to go. Take one and do not come back here, ever."

"Aye, aye, Cap'n," said Nick. "Don't worry, we won't be back. I don't think Blackstone suits us after all."

Her and Nick against the world. Fine. If this was what remained of humanity then they were better off alone. Sure as hell they were safer.

The chunk of metal seemed to be taking forever to move. No one spoke.

The sound of footsteps drew close and Nick suddenly shoved Roslyn behind him, between him and the wreckage. She clung onto the back of his shirt to keep upright.

"Lila. Damn it, I could have shot you." Sean swore profusely beneath his breath. "What are you doing here?"

"Take these for Roslyn," Lila said, pushing a backpack at Nick, her pretty face tight with concern. "There's some food and medicine in there. Keep the wound as clean as you can. Good luck."

Frosty growled. "You told her about moving them?"

"No," said Sean, sounding not the least bit apologetic. "But she knows about the exit. I trust her."

"Yeah?" said Frosty, stomping from foot to foot, looking all kinds of hostile. "Well, clearly they don't."

The surly prick was right. A shadowy group moved fast through the playground toward them. One of them turned on a flashlight and shone it in their faces. The light blinded her. Gray and white blobs danced across her vision. Fear had a throttle-hold on her chest. She wouldn't let them take him.

Frosty faced the pack with his rifle but Friendly kept working at pushing the metal aside. She couldn't see Sean, but she heard him just fine.

"Tom," he said.

"I warned them you were planning something," the other man answered. "All of you will go down for this."

"We're not going to let you lynch him, Tom," said Sean. "That's fucking insane and you know it. We haven't fallen that far. We're not savages."

Roslyn had her doubts, but it was nice to know some people retained a shred of decency. Meanwhile, her head reeled from the meds. She leant her face against the back of Nick's shirt and kept a tight grip on her gun. They were escaping, whatever she had to do. The scent of him soothed her, but she still flicked off the safety on her gun. Nick's hand reached around at the noise, pulling her closer against him. The thought of losing him was untenable. She'd only just found him; she wasn't giving him up. Not yet, not ever. These people were no better than Justin and she'd mowed him down.

"The town will decide what happens to all of you," the man Sean had identified as Tom said. He had a sneery know-it-all voice. She hated him and she hadn't even seen him yet. "Did you really think we'd let you take our only medic away?" Tom laughed. It was a distinctly brittle sound. "She's ours."

"You're out of order, Tom. What I do is none of your business," Lila answered in a tight voice. "I don't belong to anyone but myself."

"Get over here!" Tom ordered.

"Do not talk to me that way," Lila said, her voice climbing higher and higher.

"Lila—" Nick started.

Ros could hear guns being cocked. Angry murmurs. The men with Tom were backing up his sentiments. But how many men had he brought with him? Frosty faced the party opposite with absolute calm. Friendly slowly turned to face their foe. The way had been cleared. A dark hole almost the size of a man sat opened at ground level, leading into the back of the fridge compartment. They could get of here, now. Escape sat right there, waiting, a bare few footsteps away.

She heard voices, yelling, and a multitude of feet stomping this way. Many more flashlights shone in their direction. Oh, no. The cold slid beneath her skin and took up residence next to her heart.

The mob was coming.

CHAPTER TWENTY-EIGHT

Nick drew a deep breath and let it out slow. Fear and anger stank up the air. Mobs like this one had gathered outside the hospitals and police stations soon after the plague first broke out. Volatile, pissed off people without a clue. Just like the people at the airport. The situation was about to go five ways to hell. Ros could not be here when that happened.

"Go through the hole," he said. "I'll be right behind you."

"Liar." Her voice was slurred and he could feel her leaning against his back. "We stay together."

"Sweetheart, the hole can only fit one at a time and you know I won't go first."

"No. These people will kill you."

In all likelihood, yes, they would. The mob were well riled up and many were armed. One helpful soul at the front even held a noose, all ready for him. Hard to keep calm in the face of such open hatred.

Lila stood close by, facing down Tom, the muscle-headed dick with authority issues. Fuck, if she'd just appease the idiot a little. Captain Sean, meanwhile, looked about ready to lose it. A tic had started up in his jaw and his eyes were everywhere, taking in everything. Nick had never seen the man so wired. It didn't give him a good feeling. But then, nothing about this did.

Moaning started up on the other side of the fence and Nick's blood dropped about a million degrees. He couldn't send her through on her own. Not now. The situation was fucked.

"Everyone calm down. Please." A young woman with dark hair stood to the side. Two of Nick's old company were either side of her with weapons at the ready. Sheriff Finn stood nearby and appeared every bit as pissed as Nick felt.

"Shut up, Erin. Lila! You will get over here now," Tom yelled, waving his gun in the medic's direction.

At which point Sean snapped. "Do not point that at her."

"I am not going anywhere, Tom." The woman crossed her arms. "All of you should be ashamed of yourselves. This is disgusting."

The mob gathered around and the moaning picked up in volume. They were making plenty of noise to attract the zombies' attention. Either side of the fence was fast turning into a massacre waiting to happen. Time to get out before more infected gathered. Inside this town their deaths seemed more certain by the moment.

Nick grabbed Matty's arm, pulling him closer and pushing Roslyn behind the big man. He'd covered himself in every weapon, as usual. Matty nodded and held onto her elbow, keeping her in place. Ros stumbled against the man's back.

The yelling continued.

Tom's face turned beetroot in color and the gun trembled in his meaty hand. "Lila!"

Nick was getting Ros out of there right now. Getting her into a car, and getting gone.

Sean moved to cover Lila.

Tom screamed.

And *bang*! The first shot was fired.

Lila crumpled to the ground, blood pouring from her neck.

"No!" Sean's cry carried clear through the night.

Tom turned the gun toward them but a bullet hit his hand, his gun fell and the man cried out in pain. Behind him the crowd roared as panic took over. The bulk of people took flight, but not all. In front of them, Cooper dropped, his blood misting the air. It all happened so fast. The surly prick was dead before he hit the ground, his face and chest torn apart by a man holding a shotgun. Matty aimed his semi-automatic and took out two of the men that had stood beside the still crying Tom. A woman behind them, caught in the chaos, clutched at her arm as blood slipped from between her fingers. An unarmed elderly man slumped to the ground, the victim of friendly fire.

Nick grabbed Ros, taking her down and keeping her covered. Sean cradled the dead Lila not three meters away. He said her name over and over as if he thought he could wake her up. More shots and Matty's bulk crashed down on top of Nick, nearly flattening him before falling to the side. Nick pushed Ros toward the hole.

"Stop! Stop this!" the brunette yelled while her two guards did likewise. "No more shooting! Cease fire!"

Finn joined her, his face set. Fools. They were just as likely to be shot down where they stood. Blackstone was out of control.

"Leave," a man said, a rifle in his hands pointing at the ground at Finn's feet. "You take your people, and you leave. Now."

"Hang on—"

"You stood with them, Finn. You too, Erin. Go. None of you are welcome here any longer."

"This is my home," the brunette, Erin, bit out.

"No," said the man, his tone of voice absolute. "Not anymore. You made your choice."

"You can't be serious," said Erin.

The man with the rifle looked beyond reason. "Enough! If you'd let them do what they wanted then only one person would have died. Just one, instead of all this. He isn't even one of us. You're traitors, all of you. Leave now or you will die."

A dark-haired man as tall as the captain came forward, leading by the hand the pregnant woman who'd been at the cop shop earlier. "Let's go, Finn."

"Are you fucking insane?" the recently ex-sheriff said. "We can't take her out there."

"You can and you will. Right now." The man with the rifle took a menacing step forward and five men backed him up. If people started firing again they would all die.

Eight bodies lay littered about on the ground. Tom and a woman who'd been part of the mob were injured but alive. Outside, the infected grew louder.

"Sean, that includes you." The man with the rifle advanced.

The captain didn't seem to hear at first. He stayed huddled over the dead woman in silence. When he looked up his face was stark with loss, embedded with lines. He appeared to have aged a decade in a moment. His hands were covered in blood.

"Will you bury her?" he asked.

"Yes. She'll be given a proper burial."

Sean carefully laid Lila on the ground. He picked up the backpack she'd brought and, slinging it over his shoulder, rose to his feet and looked around him. "Cooper and Matt, too?"

"Yes," the man with the rifle said. "We'll see to them too if you go peacefully. Now."

Sean nodded and turned to Nick. "I'll go first."

"Right," said Nick. He stood, pulling Ros up with him and holding on tight. She didn't complain.

"We're going to be fine," he said, willing it to be true.

Anything less was unacceptable.

Terror toyed with him, fucked him up just a little. He needed to focus. Roslyn couldn't afford for him to be anything but on top of his game. They were going out there.

Oh God, please let them be fine. He wasn't even convinced he believed in God, but just in case.

The rest of their group gathered around. There were nine of them. Funny, the night he'd first entered Blackstone it had been as part of a group the same size. On the other side of the wall the moaning and growling went on. Impossible to tell how many zombies had gathered. Definitely more than a few. They were walking out into a killing field.

"Stay close together. Noise won't matter now. Shoot anything that moves." Without a backward glance Sean ducked his head and walked through.

The man was covered in Lila's blood.

"They'll tear him apart," said someone behind him.

"Yeah."

CHAPTER TWENTY-NINE

Roslyn fought the haze filling her mind from the pain meds, the lethargy slowing her limbs. She could do this. She would do this. There was no other choice.

Nick stayed close, keeping a hand on her back as she crawled through the hole and emerged into the back of the refrigerated van. Sean took one look at them, nodded and threw open one of the back doors.

A sea of infected waited beyond with mouths wide open and arms outstretched. The putrid stench of them was overpowering. It filled her nose. Bile rose in her throat. The rotting remnants of clothes hung from emaciated limbs. No trace of humanity lingered. Every instinct in her screamed to turn and run.

More people came through the hole behind her and the van filled up. But what was claustrophobia when confronted with what lay ahead?

Sean fired his weapon into the crowd. Her ears howled in protest at the ricochet. Infected fell and the man pressed forward, stepping down from the back of the vehicle and onto the ground. There were so many of them out there, a veritable sea of monsters.

Her legs shook, partly due to fear but also care of the drugs rocking and rolling through her system. She was all over the place. This wasn't going to work. She needed both hands to have a hope of aiming the gun. Quick as she could she unbuttoned the jacket, still holding onto her gun, and freed her arm from the sling. Her movements were slow, sloppy. She stuffed her left hand into the coat arm and pushed up the sleeve. Much better. The spare pistol still sat in a coat pocket along with her medicines. Truth was, they were probably going to die. But they'd go down fighting.

"Stay close to me," said Nick, and followed Sean out into the night.

Growling and gunfire filled the air. One foot after the other, she stayed close but not too close. Nick needed to be able to move.

Carefully she pointed her weapon out into the horde. She took aim at the nearest, a woman in a tattered dress, and fired. The semi-automatic only had a mild kick, but it set her wound to stinging.

It hadn't seemed quite so dark inside Blackstone but out here the world was murky gray. She could feel, more than hear, the people behind her. More gunfire and more moaning ahead. The rising stink of blood and guts and gore as they pressed forward. Beneath her feet was gravel. At least she was wearing shoes.

A man in overalls, his face caked in blood. She aimed and fired. Pain swamped her shoulder at the jolt to her body. A boy who couldn't have been more than ten or twelve. It looked like its face had been skinned. Thank God it was too dark to see properly. Her bullet hit it in the chest. For a moment he faltered, but then started reaching for her once again.

Shit. Impossible, but there it was. Just like the zombie in the downed plane. They weren't dying.

"Head shots! You have to shoot them in the head," yelled Sean.

"Fuck me," swore someone behind her.

"They're not going down," said another, a woman.

"Get 'em in the head, take out the brains."

The virus must be mutating, evolving to survive. Infected were running out of food so the plague made them hardier, harder to kill.

The boy stumbled toward her. Her first bullet flew past it but the second punched into the side of its forehead and it fell. Head shots worked. Blood soaked into the bandage on her shoulder. Felt like she'd ripped some stitches. She gritted her teeth as pain coursed through her. Without the meds she'd have been rolling on the ground in tears.

"Watch out for the train tracks," Nick said.

Someone called for ammunition and another answered. Something tugged on her foot. An infected lay on the ground, its mouth stretched around the toe of her boot. It had no legs below the knees. She could see one bloody stump, the white of bone. It was all so surreal. If only her hands would stop trembling. Her gun muzzle jittered all over the place. She bent and placed it against the thing's head and pulled the trigger. Brains splattered her arm and shoe. Disgusting didn't cover it. She straightened too fast and the world slid. Deep breaths. They had to make it. If she fell now she was screwed.

A big building loomed ahead, blocking out the stars. It might as well have been a world away. They'd come to a complete stop. There were too many infected. Ammunition was running low. Zombies surrounded them.

Sean reversed his rifle and slammed the stock into the face of an oncoming infected. Bone crunched and the thing dropped dead. Roslyn's head swum woozily. She shook it off and aimed at the next target, trying not to see too much. An old woman. A child. A man missing an arm, with his neck torn open. They were all monsters now.

Blood soaked her bandage. Her left arm felt numb and her hands were slick with sweat. Sure enough her boot caught on a train track and she lost her balance, almost falling on her face. Nick hauled her upright, not missing a beat. She almost sobbed in gratitude. Maybe she did. The noise of the guns was unending, and it was impossible to hear anything over it.

They were going to die here. If something didn't happen soon, they were not going to make it.

"We need a distraction," yelled Nick.

"Yeah, we do." Sean plucked the semi-automatic from her hands.

"Hey," she cried, startled.

"Get them out of here, Nick," he ordered. He flicked on the little flashlight and shone it in the faces of the oncoming infected, then he dove into the crowd. "Come on! Come on, you fuckers!"

"Captain!" one of the other men yelled. "Shit."

The lunatic Viking ran deep into the seething mass of the horde, flashlight waving madly. It didn't distract all of them, but it distracted enough of them. Heads turned in his direction. Feet shuffled away from them. Suddenly the group of survivors moved forward again toward the building. Nick tugged at her arm, leading her on. She could barely hear Sean yelling hoarsely somewhere, lost in the crowd. The bright beam of the flashlight cut into the night. She stared at it in horror, hand fumbling over the grip of her spare pistol. The grip was smaller and slid in her damp hands. She struggled to hold it, pins and needles filling her left arm and shoulder screaming bloody murder.

What Sean had done was suicide.

"Move," someone said behind her.

"Hurry," Nick kicked in a door on the side of the building, a pistol in hand.

Gravel gave way to concrete as she felt her way up a step.

Holy shit, they'd made it.

Inside was no darker than out. The other side of the building seemed to be missing, or maybe it had always been open, and part of the roof had fallen in. Several zombies shambled toward them. Her shoulder throbbed. Her finger jerked at the trigger until the gun clicked uselessly empty. Nick and another man pulled at a tarp and it slid free, revealing a black SUV.

"Come on, Ros," Nick said.

A man ran past, reaching for another tarp covering yet another vehicle. More infected stumbled into the warehouse. They started pouring in from every direction. Shadowy figures shambled towards them. Nick pushed her into the back seat of a vehicle, still firing at the oncoming horde. An engine roared to life and headlights flicked on, blinding her with their sudden brilliance.

"Move!" someone yelled. "Ali!"

The doors opposite her flew open, both front and back. People jumped in. A man gunned the engine. The brunette slid in beside her and slammed the door shut. Nick climbed in and shut his side. There was no sign of Sean. Of course there wasn't. He'd be dead by now, ripped apart. He'd sacrificed himself so they could make it. She barely even knew him. He'd given up his coat to keep her warm. Everything was numb inside her.

"Go," said Nick.

The SUV powered into the darkness, throwing her back against the seat and rattling her brain. It ploughed down the infected in front of them with barely a hiccup. Behind them the second vehicle followed.

"Do we even know where we're headed?" asked the brunette beside her.

The man in the passenger seat turned, bracing himself against the console. It was a hell of a rocky ride. "There's a place we scouted about two hours from here, an old convent. It's got good high walls and the gate is still intact."

"St Catherine's," said the brunette, her voice flat, defeated.

"Yeah."

The man turned back and the brunette stared out the window into the dark. Never had the world seemed so horribly unwelcoming.

Nick laid open her jacket and swore. "First-aid kit?"

"Here," The guy in the front produced one and the brunette flicked on the little interior light.

"S'okay," said Ros, her eyelids dragging downward. Keeping them open was too much hassle. She could sleep for years with the aid of her friends the pain pills. It felt so good just to give into the pull of them. "It's just bleeding a little."

"Fuck," hissed Nick. "She's torn it open."

Had she? Huh. It didn't even hurt. She was so damn tired.

Nick started to say something but sleep had already claimed her.

CHAPTER THIRTY

Nick stood on the frosted front lawn of St Catherine's as the sun came up. The once-immaculate gardens had run wild and the front door stood open. Without a doubt, there'd be zombies inside the walls of the big old mansion. But the stone walls stood a story tall and the modern steel gates worked just fine.

"We're going to have to clear it out," said Ros.

Her face still looked too damn pale but she seemed pretty steady on her feet. Not that he'd be removing his arm from around her waist to test that theory. It would be nice to tell her to get her butt back in the car, to go rest. Those days, however, were gone. He'd had three separate heart attacks through the night. Years had been taken off him. Fucking amazing that they were still alive at all, really.

Ros had kept her head. Turned out she wasn't a bad shot after all, even heavily sedated.

"I smell funny," she said.

He tightened his arm around her, needing her close. That was the truth. "Yeah. Me too."

She'd cleaned up with some wet wipes, but still. They could have all done with a bath. The front of her T-shirt was stained with dried blood. Her wound had been seen to, sealed with some super-glue and re-bandaged. An old army trick for emergencies. She'd have a bad scar, but she'd live.

The group all stared at the open door in silence. Everyone was worn thin. At least they were still alive. He'd had serious doubts they'd live to see the dawn.

"Let's see if we can draw them out," said Erin. "Better than spilling infected blood inside."

"There'll be noise either way." Ali shrugged, a hand rubbing over her belly.

"What if there are people in the area? Do we really want to announce we've arrived?" The big dark haired dude, Dan, stood beside her with an arm slung around her shoulder. Apparently she had Finn and him on a string. So long as no one made eyes at Roslyn, Nick couldn't much care.

"There's been no signs of life nearby," said Joe, one of his former workmates. He'd been watching the sleeping town below through binoculars for the last few hours. "We've been keeping an eye on the area for a while now. Just in case. The captain was diligent about that."

No one spoke much about Sean, or Matty and Cooper. And Lila, the woman who'd helped Roslyn, she went unmentioned too. Everyone looked fucked-up. Tired and worn out. Hope had dried up for the moment, disappeared into thin air.

Finn said little. Like Erin, he seemed to have taken the expulsion from Blackstone particularly hard. Either Joe or Duncan shadowed Erin at all times. For the most part she appeared to ignore them. Apparently it had been going on for some time. Clearly Erin was a far more reasonable woman than Ros. She'd have had a pink fit at being followed around. Tempting to try it though.

Joe gave him a look, eyes flicking to Erin for a moment. None of them wanted to get into close-quarters combat inside. Keeping the people they cared about safe was an ongoing battle as it was.

"Might as well meet any neighbors," said Dan, breaking the standoff.

"Do it," said Finn. "We've lost enough people. Let's keep this in the open as much as we can."

Joe raised a pistol in the air and pulled the trigger. The noise shredded the dawn quiet. A flock of birds squawked and took flight from out of one of the huge Norfolk Pines nearby. Moaning came from within the building.

There'd been a stash of weaponry in the car, first-aid packs and energy bars, plus some bottles of water. Finn held a machete. A brutal choice of weapon, but highly effective. When the first zombie stumbled out the front door he was more than ready for it. It looked like the former sheriff of Blackstone had some anger to release. The thing's head went flying. Another wandered out into the garden from somewhere out the back. The blade sunk into its skull and stayed there. Finn put a foot to its face and pulled the machete free with a slightly scary smile. A third and fourth came shambling out and fell just as fast. With a snarl the man strode into the grand old building and no one moved to stop him. No one was that damn crazy.

"He needs to get it out," said Ali, her mouth set.

Dan kissed her hair. "Yeah. I'll just make sure nothing sneaks up on him, okay?"

The woman nodded and Dan headed inside after the cop.

"You must blame us for this," said Ros, out of the fucking blue. Not the best timing, nor the right topic. He was half tempted to cover her mouth with his hand and hustle her back to the car. Get them the hell out of there before someone took offence. Everyone was armed to the teeth and she had to start talking about feelings.

Nick cleared his throat. "Sweetheart—"

"I mean, you've been kicked out of your home. People have died tonight because of us."

Ah, shit. There was no stopping her. The woman was a landslide once her lovely mouth got going. Damn it. Why couldn't she have kept her lips closed for a little longer? Digging at these people's fresh wounds couldn't be smart. Her and her need to know could be damn inconvenient at times.

Joe just looked at her, all contemplative-like. Everyone looked at her. And Ros looked calmly back, waiting.

Nick tensed. He still had his gun in his belt. One wrong move on anyone's part in Ros's direction and they were out of there.

"Dad would have been horrified at what happened tonight," said Erin, finally breaking the silence.

Ali nodded and sighed. "I still can't believe they did that. Just forced us out."

"No, we don't blame you," said Erin. "Your man brought you to us rather than see you die. And we stood up rather than see him get hanged based on nothing more than supposition and fear. People have been afraid for months. Newcomers were a conveni-ent target. I'd prefer not to fall into that trap."

Joe said nothing. But then, he always had been a tight-lipped bastard.

"My father had a way with people ..." Erin studied the ground at her feet. "He kept them calm and gave them hope. Gave them a purpose. Once he was gone they lost it. No one seemed to know what to do or who to listen to. And too many people wanted to be heard."

"Everyone wanted to be top dog," said Ali. "There was a lot of infighting. Dan, Finn and I copped a fair amount of suspicion for arriving so soon before it all went bad."

Ros watched everyone with an eerie calm. Or at least it seemed eerie to him. Though any time he couldn't read her it spooked him out. He just hoped she knew what she was doing. It felt a lot like skipping through a field of landmines to him.

"We'd even talked about the possibility of leaving a couple of times," said Ali. "But Finn was so certain things would calm down. I think they just wanted to feel safe. But the fear of other people and what they might do ate at them. "

Erin nodded.

Joe stepped forward. "You trust Nick?"

"I do," said Ros. "Implicitly."

"You're trusting him with our lives too," said Erin. "Do you understand that?"

"Yes," said Ros. "It you want us to leave, we will, and without malice. But I'm hoping you're not going to do that. Neither of us mean any of you harm. We never did."

And suddenly every eye in the place was on him, measuring his worth. None seemed openly hostile. Plenty, however, looked guarded.

"It's hard to know who to trust these days," said Ali, her hands smoothing over her baby bump. The woman had to be afraid. Delivering babies wasn't always as simple as nature intended. There were no doctors on standby here, no one who could really help if things went to shit.

He was just glad he and Roslyn weren't in that situation. Yet. Hell, they'd never even talked about kids. His mind emptied. It just blanked. The idea scared every last thought clear from his head. Talk of future plans was such a bizarre notion.

Roslyn as a mother. Okay, he could imagine that.

But him as a father? Fuck.

There went the fourth heart attack for the night. It was all he could do to keep to his feet.

Ros tucked her hand into his, a silent statement of solidarity. He held on tight.

"Alright," said Joe. "He's fine with me for now. We can talk more about it later."

Erin nodded jerkily. He had the worst feeling the woman was about to cry. But then, it had definitely been one of those nights.

Ali gave him and Roslyn a small, mysterious woman-type smile.

Duncan stared off into the distance. He'd been close to the late Captain Sean. The lack of ready acceptance wasn't really a surprise. Maybe this wouldn't work out, staying with these people. But if Roslyn wanted to try then it was fine with him. Safety in numbers and all that. It might be nice for her to be around people who wouldn't sell her out anytime soon. His faith in people had disappeared over the years, but the events of last night were making him think twice.

Cool little fingers squeezed his hand.

"It's going to be okay," said Ros.

"Yeah," he said, feeling pretty amazed actually. "I guess it is."

CHAPTER THIRTY-ONE

"I've been watching you," Nick announced, like it was something unique.

"That's nice. But you do tend to do that." Roslyn sat down on the end of their mattresses and tugged at her shoelaces, toed off her joggers. It had been a seriously long day. Her shoulder ached. "I have noticed."

They'd been at St Catherine's for a week. The rambling building had been converted into an Art Gallery/Cafe/Gift Shop some years back. Today they'd finished sorting the remaining foodstuffs in the cafe, taken the rotted and or otherwise useless goods out back to be burned or buried. Mattresses and sheets and so on had been gathered from nearby shops and houses to stuff inside the 'cells'. While far from roomy, at least these cells didn't have bars on the doors. They were comfortable enough, though the nights regularly dropped to zero degrees Celsius.

Apparently the good folk of Blackstone didn't tend to come this way on account of the climb up the mountains chewing up gas. Plus, St Catherine's sat on the edge of a tourist town. All the folky arts and crafts you could hope for, but farming supplies? Not so much.

"I've seen the way you look at Ali, Dan and Finn," he said, obviously going somewhere with all this. Probably nowhere good, knowing him.

"I know. Isn't it beautiful to see people so in love?" She lay back on the bed and grinned at the hot man currently glowering at her. "So refreshing after all the bloodshed and violence."

Nick grunted and knelt on the end of the bed. He reached back and tugged off his own boots. "That wasn't what you were thinking about when you looked at them."

"No? Wow," she drawled. "Can you really read minds now, Nicky? That is so cool. So what was I thinking?"

"You think you're clever, don't you?" The man gave her a hard little smile and her belly quivered. Her belly and her sex. And maybe her knees too, damn it. Fortunately she was lying down.

"Maybe."

"Maybe I can read your mind. Or maybe everything you think shows up on your face."

She scoffed. "It does not."

He just looked at her.

"Does it?"

"Without fail."

"So what was I thinking, then?" she asked.

He bent forward and undid the button on her jeans, followed by the zipper. "You were thinking about what it would be like to fuck two men at the same time."

"Such smutty thoughts have never entered my brain." Actually, she had been wondering. Wildly curious and then some. Her imagination had run overtime, he was right. Ali was a lucky, lucky girl having those two big hot men at her disposal. Not that Roslyn wasn't content with her one surly male, but still ... *two*. Some people were enjoying their apocalypse a little too much.

So, yes, there had been the odd covetous thought involved. She even had the common decency to experience a twinge of guilt over it.

Nick pulled her jeans and knickers down her legs and tossed them into a corner of the small room. "How's your shoulder?"

"It's fine, just a little stiff. I used the sling for most of the day. I didn't lift anything heavy."

"Good." He started in on the buttons on her shirt.

The brush of his hands over her bare skin gave her shivers as he pushed back the material. No bra, courtesy of the still-vivid bruise across her chest. Her perky nipples rose to the occasion, of course. Her body was a fool for him. Her heart and mind weren't far behind.

"I just don't want you feeling like you're missing out on something," he said.

"Nick, I'm not." She reached out for him and he came to her, pressing his mouth to hers in a distinctly hot kiss. Had she thought the air cool? Forget that. This man had her overheated in moments. Their tongues tangled and his hands slipped into her hair. But still he stayed on his knees, hovering high above her.

"But just in case ..." he said, pulling back from her.

"What?"

"I picked up a few things for you in town today." He reached for the backpack he'd come in with and pulled something out. When she tried to sit up to see what he pushed her back down with a hand to her good shoulder. "Don't strain your shoulder. Lie back. Relax."

"What is it?"

"You can either lie back and relax like a good girl, or I can go play cards with Duncan and Joe," he said. "Your choice."

Shit. She'd seen that look on his face often enough to know he meant it. Hard-on tenting the front of his jeans or no, the man would walk out on her. He loved letting his inner control freak out to play when it came to sex. Sadly, she enjoyed it just as much.

"I'm lying still," she said.

"Good. Though I need you on your stomach, so let me help you roll over." Big hands helped her to wriggle into position. He slipped a pillow beneath her shoulders, another beneath her hips. "There we go. Are you comfortable?"

"Yes." Comfortable, but dubious. "What are you up to, Nicky?"

"You'll see." His fingers trailed over the curves of her ass then slipped down between her legs, caressing her inner thighs. And pushing steadily outward. "Spread, sweetheart."

She did so. Of course she did. The man made her a shallow puddle of sex-starved ooze without even trying.

Shuffling noises behind her. Warm breath on the small of her back. Hot, damp kisses on a butt cheek. And the sound of ...

"What have you got? What is that?" she demanded, trying to turn her head far enough to see.

Nick's face came into view instead. "I think they're playing poker tonight. Should I go find out for sure?"

"No."

"I think you need a safe word," he said.

"Why? What are you going to do that's so bad?"

He stared back at her, face much too calm. "When your shoulder's healed, I'm going to tie you up and gag you so we can't have these discussions."

"I don't think that's the point of BDSM, if that's what you're attempting."

"You've read about it?" he asked.

"A book or two, here and there. Maybe. I've never done anything, but ..."

Another grunt. What did a grunt even mean, really? Lucky she trusted this Neanderthal.

"It interests you." He kissed the back of her neck, took a roll of skin beneath his teeth and toyed with it. It felt weird but nice, ticklish almost. His voice sounded husky against her ear. "Here's what we're going to do. You talk as much as you want and I'm going to go about my business, down here." Big, threatening hands smoothed over her buttocks. "Unless you say, 'I hate you'."

"What? No. I promised to never say that to you again."

"I know. Best safe word ever."

"Nick, that's cheating. And it's not funny."

"Okay," he chuckled. "Calm down. How about ... 'wattle'?"

"Wattle?"

"Yeah. It was the name of our cabin. And it's not a word you're going to say by accident."

"Oh," she said, relaxing a bit. "That's nice. 'Wattle' it is. But I still think you should leave my butt alone. You have enough holes at your disposal."

"I disagree." His trailed kisses down her spine, fingers massaging her ass. "You either trust me, and let me experiment a little to see if you like it, or you say 'wattle'."

Damn it, he was serious. Fear and excitement fought it out inside her. So of course, she talked. "You know, it sounds vaguely like 'waddle', like a duck. Don't you think?"

He ignored her.

His tongue slid through the divide between her cheeks and her hands fisted in the blanket. This too felt weird but nice, and unnerving. More shuffling noises. Capable hands opened her up, exposing her poor defenceless butthole to the pervert. How nerve-wracking. She hid her face in the pillow.

"Nick, I'm not sure about this."

Still no reply.

Kiss after kiss he laid around the area. The back of the top of her thighs were particularly sensitive. A thumb rubbed over her tightly puckered anus, massaging. God help her, then his tongue was there, flicking over it, teasing her open. All those little nerve endings fired to life, thoroughly weirded out at the new, if perhaps pleasurable, sensation.

"You can't kiss me there," she said, her words muffled.

"Why not?" His tongue dipped down, lapping over her pussy. That she knew and recognized and enjoyed just fine. She arched her hips, silently begging for more and he gave it, bless him. A hand slipped beneath her, putting pressure on her clit. His teeth tortured her in the best way possible, gently playing with the lips of her sex. Everything low in her lit up, her stomach tightening and blood rushing. She almost didn't notice the tip of his thumb pushing at her rear, slowly gaining entrance past the tight ring of muscle.

"Nick," she gasped.

"I think you're fucking gorgeous everywhere," he said, mouth moving against her sex in the very best way. His words sent tremors through her. "Stop fighting me, Ros. Relax."

"I'm trying."

"Good girl."

He tongued her sex while he played with her rear. Never going too far, just teasing the entrance. Then the thumb was gone and his mouth moved up. Noises. She could hear noises again. Her ears were on high alert. Something plasticky-sounding was being opened behind her.

"What are you doing now?" she asked. "What is that?"

"Ssshh."

Lube was squirted between her cheeks and she squealed. Damn it, what a godawful noise. But nothing was ladylike about this. A finger pushed at her hole, in a little, out a little. Steadily, slowly, it worked its way into her. Impossible not to grab at it with her muscles.

"Oh. That feels so odd."

His finger worked deeper into her until it was slipping in and out with ease. She could feel it, the pressure in that oddest of places. Her ass as an erogenous zone, who'd have guessed? Her empty sex wept and the pad of his hand rubbed at her mound and her clit. Happily, she pushed right back, seeking contact. His ministrations were getting her worked up. She was more than a little desperate for it. The edge of the pillow teased her hard nipples. Holy hell, she could come from this. She really could. A little more stimulation and everything would be superb.

Nick pulled his finger out then pressed back in, only this time stretching her wider, demanding more.

"What's that?"

"Easy," he said. "Two fingers now."

He kissed her back. Licked up her spine. She clenched on the two fingers. It still burned. No way could she take him there.

"Nick, I don't think I can—"

"I know. Not today," he said, reading her just fine. "We're just going to play a little. Try and relax."

"O-okay."

The two fingers did strange things inside her ass, twisting and turning, stroking her in odd ways. The burn eased and gave way to pleasure. Some inexplicably sweet sensation stole through her. She had the worst feeling she actually liked it. Worse still, that he knew.

"That's it," he said.

Then the fingers were gone. Just when she'd gotten used to their presence they slipped free of her body and her rear felt strangely empty. More noises. Packaging being undone by the sound of it.

"Stay put," he said.

More lube. She tried to tuck her butt in and escape it, but there was nowhere to go. He held her open, his big body situated between her spread legs. Something pressed against her anus again.

He hummed in satisfaction. "Press back against it, Ros. That's it."

"What is it?" she asked, her voice all breathy.

"It's only a little one."

"A little one what?"

A hand held her cheeks apart while the other fucked something into her. Not his fingers. Something else about the same size, at first. He pushed, then retreated, easing the foreign object inside her. It got bigger and her fingers dug into the mattress.

"Nick."

"Nearly there. You're doing really well."

He turned it around a little, played with it. Whatever 'it' was.

The burn returned. Not quite pain but not really pleasure. A gray area in between that she wasn't sure of. He stretched her opening wide, then in it went. The strain lessened. Her butt was not on fire. It was okay. But something was definitely inside her.

"Explain," she barked out.

Instead, he turned it on. The fucking thing vibrated. Her ass was buzzing. What it did to her pussy was dreadful and wonderful all at once. Her mind blanked as her body took over.

"You're so wet, sweetheart," he said.

She said the first thing that came into her poor, addled brain. "I'm going to kill you."

He clucked his tongue.

Big hands lifted her hips and his cock nudged at the entrance to her sex. The poor, desperate, throbbing, needy thing that it was. All she could do was dig her fingers deeper and hold on.

She moaned as his cock surged into her. God, yes, she needed it, needed him inside her. The width of his cock felt close to overwhelming with that thing filling her rear. Still vibrating. Her whole pelvic region seemed aglow with it.

"Fuck yes," he groaned.

She could feel the hairs on his thighs against the backs of her legs, the press of his pelvis against her butt. The slap of his balls when he thrust harder, picking up the pace. It seemed she was oversensitive to everything. Nothing escaped her but her mind reeled, unable to focus on any one thing. Again and again he thrust into her. Her traitorous body pushed back, takingly him joyfully, wanting everything he could give her.

Nick pounded into her. Together, they set a feverish pace. Nothing mattered but coming, climbing that peak as hard and fast as possible. She was mindless in her pursuit of it, so damn close that it was all she could feel. The heat and sensation built until it burst wide open inside her. She shook and shuddered and shouted into the pillow. Hands pulled her back onto him as he pushed as deep into her body as he could get and came too. Those hands and his cock were the only things holding her up. Then his cock slipped free of her. His hands lowered her back onto the mattress. He collapsed beside her.

Nothing but heavy breathing.

A hand fumbled over her ass and the thing stopped buzzing. Probably for the best. Carefully he pulled it out of her. Her body was too tired to react. Her mind had been defeated. Nick was master of them all. Damn him.

A wet cloth smoothed between her tender butt cheeks.

"You okay?" he asked.

She turned her head. It was easier to breathe without her face in the pillow. "No. I think you broke me."

He lay beside her, dark eyes searching her face.

"That would account for the fuck-drunk smile," he said.

She tried to frown at him. It didn't work. "You're a bad man."

He smirked.

"You're my bad man."

"Mm. I'm going to do that to you every time I catch you daydreaming about threesomes with other men," he informed her. "And the plugs will get bigger."

Like hell they would. Best not to tell him that, though. He'd only see it as a challenge.

She stretched lazily as gradually some semblance of life returned to her sated body. "To be fair, Nicky, you were one of the men in my imaginary threesome."

He gave her a skeptical look, his brow arched high. Of course, since she had bisected the other brow he could really only raise the one. Lucky it looked good on him.

"Hey, I don't want any other men."

"No?" he asked, shuffling over until they were close as they could be.

"Nope. I don't suppose you've got a twin, though?"

His hand clapped down on her butt cheek. It stung.

"Ow. Sorry. I'm sorry. Just joking."

"And you actually wonder why I abuse your ass," he said, ever the gentleman. One of his hands rifled around in the dreaded backpack once more. "I picked up some other things for you today."

"Do I even want to know?"

"I don't know. Do you?" he asked and carefully put a funky-looking pair of reading glasses on her. "There we go. How are they?"

She blinked experimentally, peered around the room. "Good, I think. Thank you."

"Wear them the next time we fuck. That would be thanking me."

"Aww. You say the sweetest things."

"Don't I? There was also this." He set a blue velvet jewelry case on his bare chest. A ring-sized one.

"Holy hell." Her heart lurched at the sight. It was the strangest thing. After everything they'd been through, she was going to lose it over a piece of jewelry?

"I saw it in a shop in town. Thought you might like it, so I grabbed it."

Carefully, she popped the case but left it sitting on top of him. Of all the things he could have picked up for her, right on out of any shop window now that alarms and money and all the rest were gone, he'd gotten her this. A circlet of seed pearls surrounded a small winking diamond in an antique rose gold setting. It was lovely. Heartbreakingly perfect.

"Okay. What does it mean?" she asked.

"Huh?" His face blanked.

"Nick, you can't just give a girl a ring without it meaning something. You do know that?"

His forehead furrowed up.

"I mean, it has to say something."

"What?" he asked. "Why?"

"Come on, Nick. The ring says something. Work with me here, please."

He looked at the ring like it had suddenly sprouted poisonous tentacles. "I dunno. I just thought you'd like it."

Honestly, he was such an idiot. He could probably spend an hour explaining the vibrating butt plug to her, but he couldn't even string together a sentence about the ring. Her mind was officially blown.

"Come on," she said, voice sounding more than a little aggravated. "Surely there was more thought behind this."

"So you don't like it?" His big hand closed around the case and he went to put it away. Like he wanted to die. "It doesn't matter."

"Don't you dare! That's mine." She clambered across him, straddling him and wrestling for custody of the ring. And not being gentle about it. "Give it."

"Ros." He wisely let go before her teeth could sink into his arm. "Shit. Calm down."

With the ring case in hand she sat triumphant atop him. One cranky-faced man with a world full of attitude. His lips were a tight, unhappy line. Poor baby. Bad luck, he'd chosen her. Now he'd just have to live with it. She wouldn't be letting him off the hook anytime soon.

"Alright, I will tell you what the beautiful ring says. Since you clearly find yourself incapable of manning up and dealing with the moment as you should." Carefully she pulled it front its case and slipped it onto her ring finger. Perfect fit. She gave quiet thanks to the universe at large. "It says that I love you and you love me."

Nick looked at her and sighed, his face relaxing. "Well, yeah."

She allowed herself a small, satisfied grin. The ring really did look splendid on her finger. "Exactly."

"That easy?" he asked.

"You thought that was easy? Hell, Nick. I'd hate to see your version of hard." She kissed the end of his nose.

"There was some news from Blackstone," he said, distracting her from pondering her ring's magnificence. "Duncan's been keeping an eye on the place."

"What?"

"Someone killed Tom. Slit his throat."

"Wow," she said. Her good mood started to slip through her fingers. "That's cold."

"He did kill Lila." Nick's eyes were thoughtful. Stuff was happening deep inside his brain. She could feel it. Lila's death had been so unnecessary, such a stupid waste. Ros hated thinking about it. Maybe if they'd moved faster she'd still be alive. Memories of that night had woken her panting and covered in sweat, more than once. The sounds of the zombies coming out of the dark, surrounding them, and the mindless hatred and fear from the people of Blackstone. Lila had been nothing more than an innocent bystander. The noise Sean had made when he'd lost her ... Ros couldn't forget it. Whoever had killed Tom, she couldn't bring herself to believe it was entirely a bad thing. If that made her a bad person, well ... the world wasn't what it used to be.

"Hang on," she said. "You think Sean did it? That he might be alive?"

The man shrugged and drew her down for a kiss. "With the captain, who knows?"

"Nicky. There were a lot of infected and he had her blood all over him." A shiver worked through her at the thought and she laid her head on his chest. Most sublime place in the world. "God, that was a horrible night."

"Never again."

"No," she seconded.

"I was talking to Dan and Finn today," he said.

"About?"

"Whether it'd be better to move on or stay here. It is only a few hours from Blackstone."

His heart beat away beneath her ear, good and strong. The arm of her reading glasses dug into her, but damned if she was moving anytime soon. "Erin and Ali seem to have settled in for the long term. Is Blackstone really a threat? I mean, if we stay out of their way they shouldn't be a problem, right?"

Nick shrugged, his body shifting beneath her. "They could get angry about Tom's murder. Who knows what they're thinking. Duncan and Joe are monitoring the radio, listening to their chatter, but it could still be a risk staying this close. So far as we know, they're unaware of our location."

"Other groups out there could be a risk too," she said, looking up at him. "We just don't know. But we've got walls and a defensible position here. Seems a shame to leave it."

His smile lit his eyes. "Yeah, we do. That seems to be how the others see it too. But do you want to stay here with these people? There's no reason we can't go find another place like the cabin. Set ourselves up comfortably on our own."

She sat up, staring down at him over the top of her glasses. "Is that what you want? Has someone been giving you a hard time?"

"No, sweetheart. Everyone's been fine. Surprisingly friendly, actually." He licked his lips. "But it's your choice whether we stay or go. Whatever you want is good with me."

Her heart hurt in the best way possible. "Really?"

"Yeah."

There was a big wide world out there at their disposal and Nick was doing his best to hand it to her on a platter. Some parts of it were terrifying, but still, whatever she wanted. It was a heady feeling. "You know, I think I'd like to stay here for now."

"Okay."

She took a deep breath and let it out slow.

"I love you," he said, his hands smoothing over her back.

She buried her nose in his neck and smiled. "You do?"

"Absolutely."

"Hmm." And that was really all she needed to know.

Acknowledgments

With thanks to ... Tracey O'Hara, Kylie Griffin, Mel Teshco, Jess Dee, Rosemary Courtney, Vassiliki Veros, S. E. Gilchrist and anyone else who read bits or answered random questions for me. Thanks to my family and friends who tolerate a phenomenal amount of shit and are always supportive. Thanks to Anne, Joel and Mark at Momentum for being the constant delights that they are. Thanks also to my lovely editor Sarah JH Fletcher. Special thanks to Romance Writers of Australia for simply existing. Thanks to Maryse, Katrina, the Twinsie Girls, Cath, and all the other book bloggers who pour their heart and soul into reading and reviewing. And extra-special thanks go to the people who read *Flesh* and wanted more.